Jo.

Thanks for being such a good friend

M. C. Lagrange

Enjoy!

© Copyright 2005 Michel Lagrange.
All rights reserved. No part of this publication may be reproduced, stored in a retrieval system, or transmitted, in any form or by any means, electronic, mechanical, photocopying, recording, or otherwise, without the written prior permission of the author.

Note for Librarians: a cataloguing record for this book that includes Dewey Decimal Classification and US Library of Congress numbers is available from the Library and Archives of Canada. The complete cataloguing record can be obtained from their online database at:
www.collectionscanada.ca/amicus/index-e.html
ISBN 1-4120-3711-5
Printed in Victoria, BC, Canada

TRAFFORD

Offices in Canada, USA, Ireland, UK and Spain
This book was published *on-demand* in cooperation with Trafford Publishing. On-demand publishing is a unique process and service of making a book available for retail sale to the public taking advantage of on-demand manufacturing and Internet marketing. On-demand publishing includes promotions, retail sales, manufacturing, order fulfilment, accounting and collecting royalties on behalf of the author.

Book sales for North America and international:
Trafford Publishing, 6E–2333 Government St.,
Victoria, BC v8t 4p4 CANADA
phone 250 383 6864 (toll-free 1 888 232 4444)
fax 250 383 6804; email to orders@trafford.com

Book sales in Europe:
Trafford Publishing (uk) Ltd., Enterprise House, Wistaston Road Business Centre, Wistaston Road, Crewe, Cheshire cw2 7rp UNITED KINGDOM
phone 01270 251 396 (local rate 0845 230 9601)
facsimile 01270 254 983; orders.uk@trafford.com

Order online at:
www.trafford.com/robots/04-1539.html

10 9 8 7 6 5 4

Author's Notes

This story has been coming for quite some time now. It all started in 1981; I was sitting my back against an old Oak tree in one of the parks a Saturday afternoon with my head in the clouds as my father would always say. At the age of seventeen my imaginative spirit was as strong as ever. Scenes and events filled my head as I let the story blur reality, the contents taking a life of their own.

We left the park later that afternoon and a young heart vowed to put this adventure down on paper before any traces of it vanished forever in the obscurities of life. Its nuances followed me for many years after that fateful day. In 2000 the topic came up again and after talking with a good friend of mine, I decided to finally put it to paper. Four months later I had my first draft. I handed the manuscript to Jonie...prouder than punch, I was on cloud nine.

She brought me back to reality by quickly pointing out the numerous errors and grammar mistakes. I was crushed, the manuscript sat for another four months before I had the courage to look at it again. Needless to say I had never written before and the work was horrendous. With her help and guidance I revised the manuscript and learned.

It was another six months before I had the nerve to show it again. When I finally did, it came back with mixed reviews. It needed work....a lot more work. So I put my nose to the grinding stone and reviewed, rewrote...and rewrote again and again until I was satisfied that it was the best it could be.

Now I had a manuscript but no publisher. I wrote and sent query letters after query letters...after 8 months still no lucky break. A friend of mine brought Trafford self publishing company to my attention, my ears perked up and I listened. I found a wonderful editor through them and Emily Jacque put the finishing touches on my manuscript. I was very impressed with her work. Her suggestions appealed to me and brought my story up another level. Now in the year two thousand and four....my story is finally being published. I'm ecstatic, dreams do come true.

I'd like to thank all of those who helped make this dream a reality. Jonie, thank you! If it weren't for you...this may have never been published. You gave me the drive and desire needed to see this through.

John...words cannot describe the appreciation I feel for all the hard work you did with me on this project. Pierrette, thank you for all the support you gave me during the writing process.

My best friend...Karl, thank you for all of your constructive input. Your input was invaluable in making this project the best it can be.

I'd like to thank Allan and Sofia. Let's not forget their little guy Nicholas, full of energy and life with a personality of giants. Their photo contribution helped make the cover as fantastic as it turned out to be.

To all of you who are struggling to fulfill your dreams...don't give up. Work harder; see it through...never give up. It will pay off in the end.

Joshua's Journey

Shattered Innocence

Prologue

Long ago, before we humans existed, before creation of this planet, and before the universe itself, there was a very powerful entity made of pure energy—a single thought. Powerful but alone...this entity felt like a king with no kingdom. Many millenniums passed while this entity pondered its existence and purpose. To fill his emptiness, he tore from his being twelve elements of energy. He nurtured each and every element until consciousness awoke within them. From that date, this powerful entity was known as Saavatha.

As his sons awoke, he named them. First came Merthor, then Symraay, Myrey, Thaabar, Baltaseim, Phaalor, Bartholomew, Qwenthrey, Bayrthraa, Raphael, Piatre and Zallier.

With a renewed sense of purpose, Saavatha began the everlasting education of his sons. He never violated the most important gift ever given to them, their freedom of choice. He taught them the difference between right and wrong, the essence of loyalty and the importance of truth from its most basic to its most complex form. As their education progressed over billions of years the Eternals began to multiply as their creator multiplied, and began to teach their children the importance of Saavatha's doctrine.

Now in his kingdom, there are multitudes of Eternals that are always growing and evolving. Their ultimate goal, to have the privilege of bathing in Saavatha's life-giving energy, the Garden of Life, where thoughts, emotions, and pleasures above any human's tolerance are experienced as one—beyond love and tenderness. Entering their creator's plane of existence is the greatest of privileges. Eternals of all different levels of evolution willingly put themselves in peril to achieve the necessary perfection that Saavatha demands of them. The Garden of Life is every Eternal's desire, their final destination.

To return to the energy from whence they came is every Eternal's fondest wish. Saavatha cares and nurtures all of his creations, giving each and every one the chance to evolve.

For the love of his children, Saavatha created the world of the Solids. Eternals can Journey to this realm to test their newfound knowledge. In the hopes of moving one step closer to their goal, an unending number of Eternals visit the world of the Solids to learn and grow closer to their creator.

Joshua is one of those Eternals; driven almost to a fault, he always strives to better himself. This being has seen his share of struggles since his inception into consciousness, but always managed to eventually overcome them and come up victorious. This is his story.

Chapter One

In a small and crowded study of his home, a frail-looking Eternal worked feverishly, absorbed in his own thoughts. At the tender age of four billion years or so, his hair once blond, was now bright white. The smell of burning candles permeated the room as he wrote his final words on the parchment covering most of his desk. *Finally I am done!* he thought, putting the last period on the crisp paper with his long white quill pen.

"Now I can go and spend some quality time with my favorite book," he said, a smile coming on his tired face. Looking at his work with satisfaction he rolled the parchment and put away his ink-bottle in one of the top drawers. His seat creaked loudly as he got up and organized the few books and items on his desk. *I will have to fix that,* Joshua reminded himself before exiting the room.

He sauntered lazily to his library when something out of the corner of his eye struck him odd. *Baltaseim's curse,* he rubbed his white beard. *I'm sure I closed that door when I left.* Entering, Joshua stopped suddenly when he realized that he was not alone. *What in Baltaseim's pride are they doing here?* He gave the small group who dared to invade his personal space a questioning look. *Shawn of course, I should have known.*

"Hello Shawn," Joshua said, his annoyance coming out loud and clear. "What are you doing here?"

"I'm sorry to intrude," the tall and slim Eternal began.

"I was doing a class on the history of this kingdom when Master James dropped by and suggested that a high-profile Eternal like yourself would have a lot to offer to a class of this nature. I agreed, so here we are. My class would love to hear some of your past heroics, after all if I remember correctly you single-handedly saved this kingdom from the clutches of Baltaseim some time ago."

Joshua grimaced. He would like nothing better than to forget the whole affair. *Won't he ever forget?* he thought. *I was lucky that the little stunt I pulled paid off in my favor; I could have landed in a heap of hot water. Baltaseim is no fool, I'm sure that he has been plotting his revenge for quite some time now.*

"I see," Joshua replied flatly.

"I hope you don't mind," Shawn said with an amused eye. "We can do this at another time if we are intruding."

The idea of sending Shawn and all of his little brats away appealed to Joshua immensely. He loved his solitude and he never felt all that comfortable around children. But he decided against it. If Master James suggested Joshua could help, who was he to argue?

"No, that's fine." Joshua replied with annoyance seeping through his voice despite his best effort.

"Are you sure?" Shawn asked, his dark and bushy eyebrows rose questionably, wrinkling the skin on his oddly high forehead.

"You are here now," he sighed. "Frankly I didn't expect you. It might be a good idea next time to let me know ahead of time so I can be better prepared."

"Sure, I will keep it in mind," Shawn replied, his smile revealing dark and crooked teeth.

Joshua had never seen an inkling of consideration in Shawn. All of this talk was just Baltaseim's song and he knew it. *Won't you ever change? I find your little games annoying and exhausting.*

"I'm sure you will," Joshua said, his voice dripping with sarcasm.

"Looks like you have everything under control," the bald Eternal replied with an amused smirk on his long face. "I will leave you with these wonderful children."

"Thanks!" Joshua shot him an unamused glare.

"Have a good time." Shawn told him on his way out the door, his giggle sounding like an ass in agony.

Yeah, I'm sure I will. Joshua thanked his lucky star that Shawn had finally left.

Taking a deep breath he looked at the children that were sitting quietly around his favorite sofa-chair.

"Alright children," he said, resigning himself to his fate. "We should get started. Come on little one, you can sit on my lap," he told Carla, surprised at how light the small child was as he picked her up.

"Now, I will tell you a story," he said, sitting the small red-headed child on his lap. "You must be very quiet and listen carefully." Hushes and murmurs echoed quietly amongst the children.

Collecting his thoughts, Joshua's mind reeled back to the very beginning of his Journey. *If these children were a little older,* he mused. *I could tell them this story with all of its true color and nuances. I better not,* he decided. *They're too young to be exposed to this kind of truth. I will have to keep it tame, for their sake.*

"Long ago," he began, looking at all the children hanging on his every word. "There was a child no older than you Carla, and he was called Joshua."

"Joshua?" she asked, her surprise glittering through her emerald eyes, "a boy with the same name as you?"

"That's right," Joshua replied, his warm smile catching him by surprise. "Now be very quiet so that everyone else can hear the story."

"OK," she answered, her small frame fidgeting in anticipation. "I will be very quiet, I promise."

"After attending one of elder Shawn's classes," he continued, "Joshua being the curious and mischievous child that he was, decided to look for the Damned Hall."

"The Damned Hall?" Tim, a scrawny kid with dark hair piped up as Carla, scared out of her wits, covered her mouth with both of her tiny hands.

"That place is scary..." Thoomaa said louder then he wished, "Elder Shawn told us all about that place; he said that it used to belong to Baltaseim."

"Yeah," John interrupted, wanting to make sure that he put his two cents in. His large blue eyes seemed too big for the size of his head. "Saavatha kicked him out when he turned bad. Now he lives far away."

"That's right," Joshua replied. He was impressed with the amount of knowledge these youths possessed. "Baltaseim used to live in this hall. Now it represents the wickedness of his ways.

He was banished from the kingdom many years ago, long before any of us were ever created. Now to return to my story," refocusing their attention. "Joshua set out to find this hall at all costs. He had made a bet with one of his playmates that he could find and return with a piece of this hall as proof of his success.

Unaware that the hall was guarded at all times, he still managed to locate and enter this dark place undetected. There were shards of broken crystal everywhere. The dome was reduced to pieces on the floor. Every fragment turned black like Baltaseim's heart. Joshua picked up a piece of crystal and put it in his pocket."

In the midst of his storytelling, Joshua's thoughts overshadowed his words. The account told to the children was overly simplified. Not wanting to shock and traumatize them, this version was a lot tamer than what he remembered. Lost in his own thoughts, Joshua's memories took a life of their own, revealing the true nature of the actions that shaped his life. Even after all this time, the old Eternal still had a clear and vivid memory of the events that occurred so long ago.

****

"Joshua, son of Gabriel, what are you doing here? This place is off limits."

Joshua froze as his heart skipped a beat. *Oh no!* A cold sweat came over him suddenly. *What is he doing here? I can't let him catch me! If he gets a hold of me, I'm done!*

Without looking back, Joshua bolted before the guardian took another step.

He's making a run for it, Sons of Saavatha! The guardian could not believe his own stupidity. *I should've grabbed him before saying anything.*

Wait until I get my hands on that little hoodlum. "Joshua, STOP!" he screamed.

In a desperate attempt to evade the guardian that was close on his tail, Joshua entered the dense evergreen forest. *Maybe I can lose him in this underbrush,* His mind raced, trying to outwit the experienced guardian. Petrified of being caught, Joshua could barely stay ahead of the predator that was snapping at his heels. "I have to run faster," he muttered under his breath, surprised by the agility and speed of his pursuer. "He's catching up to me. I have to lose him, but how?"

A brilliant plan formulated in Joshua's mind when he saw the Hall of Wisdom through a clearing, *I will cut through the hall and if I am lucky I can lose him on the other side.* Running with all his might, Joshua veered to the left and set his sights on the great hall.

"Gees he is close to me," he said, as panic set in. "I can feel his footsteps right behind me. One more step Joshua, come on one more step and we're home free." He glanced over his shoulder momentarily before leaping over the last of the twelve crystal steps.

"Joshua, NOOOO!" The guardian screamed, leaping after him.

He turned his head back momentarily and plowed over the Master who was in the middle of his daily thanks. Tumbling head over teakettle, Joshua knocked the white-haired Master flat on his back.

Gwen, the custodian of this hall was dazed, angry and confused. He gave them an angry glare.

"What in Athraw's domain is going on here?"

Grant froze in terror as he witnessed the scene before him. *Oh no... Why do these things always happen to me?* "I'm sorry Master," the dark-haired guardian replied quickly trying to remedy the situation. "Joshua, look what you did!" he screamed at the frightened and confused child. He grabbed Joshua by the scruff of the neck and yarded him off the Master forcefully. "Apologize now!"

"I'm sorry." Joshua stared at Grant's frightening glare.

"Master," Grant asked. "Are you alright?"

"My pride is a little bruised," an annoyed and embarrassed Master replied. "But other than that I am fine. Don't just stand there and ogle like Athraw's minions," Gwen said, his facial expression making his frustration crystal clear. "Help me up will you!"

"Hum, sorry," Grant replied, embarrassed by his lack of action. Leaning down he grabbed Gwen's right hand and pulled him to his feet.

"Now," said Gwen, patting the dust off his long white robe. "Could you tell me what in Baltaseim's pride is going on here?"

"I caught Joshua snooping in the Damned Hall." Grant explained.

Gwen's face went white. Even after two-millennium the memory that plagued him was still fresh in his mind. Gord was the last Eternal to enter this cursed place. He was young and naïve, much like Joshua. Gwen had warned him to stay away but Gord ignored the Master's warning.

He was never seen again. Since that day, guardians have been posted near the hall around the clock. *Baltaseim is probably still feeding on him,* the Master thought.

A shiver ran up his back as he pushed that terrifying thought to the back of his mind. *I remember when you fed on my energy dear brother. I never thought that I would ever recover from that.*

"I see," Gwen's eyes took a distant look.

"I've been chasing him all over the countryside. I was hoping to stop him before he slipped through here, but as you can see I was not very successful."

"Don't remind me," Gwen replied, a hint of sarcasm overshadowing his voice. "We need to keep him away from the Damned Hall. What was he doing there anyway?"

"I have no idea," shrugged Grant. "Why don't you ask him?" Gwen turned his glare on Joshua. His shoulders were slumped forward, and he was staring at the floor. The silence was almost deafening. "Well?" he asked, expecting an answer.

Joshua could feel a lump forming in his throat. His heart thumped; his knees almost gave out from under him. Never in his young mind did he ever imagine being caught.

What am I going to tell him? His mind raced to give the angry Master a satisfactory response. "It's all the Elders' fault," Joshua nearly screamed.

"The Elders?" Gwen could not believe what he just heard. "What do they have to do with any of this?"

Joshua looked up at the white bearded Eternal and answered hesitantly, "They want to kill me."

A giggle escaped Grant's lips. *In all of my existence, I have never heard anything so stupid.*

Gwen shot a glare in Grant's direction. He could not believe that a guardian would find this amusing. Death should not be mocked.

Grant felt his face go flush. "Sorry," he felt himself shrink to nothingness.

Certain that Grant understood, Gwen turned his attention towards the frightened child. "Joshua, you are an Eternal; you cannot die."

That's impossible. Joshua's face went blank; an expression of disbelief washed over him. *Peter knows-he Journeyed before. He would never lie to me.*

"I don't believe you!" he shot back. "They want me to Journey to the Solids and Peter said that going there would kill me. I don't want to die! So I ran away and I came across the black hall by accident, I swear. I didn't mean to break any rules, I'm sorry."

Gwen sighed and bent down to Joshua's level. It had been a long time since he saw this kind of fright.

Fear is a powerful force. Some fears are good, but most are not, Baltaseim can attest to that. "So that's what this is about," he said looking at the child's frightened blue eyes. "Peter was lying to you."

"No he wasn't!" He replied, taking his friend's defense.

"Yes he was." Gwen insisted.

Joshua looked into Gwen's gray eyes. A calming peace blanketed his being, making him feel safe and secure. There was gentleness in Gwen's eyes, something reassuring. Not knowing why, a feeling of trust overcame him. He was almost positive that the Master wasn't lying.

"Are you sure?"

"Yes I am sure," Gwen replied. "We are Eternals like Saavatha; we do not die."

A stunned look washed over Joshua's face. For a moment the child didn't know if he should laugh or cry. *Why would Peter lie to me? I don't understand, I thought he was my friend. All this time he was lying to me.* Sadness and anger swelled in his heart. The thought of his friend's betrayal was almost too much for this youngster to bear.

"Joshua," Gwen said to the despondent child. "You must promise me never to enter that place again."

Caught up in his own turmoil, the Master's voice faded to a whisper. Putting his hand in his pocket Joshua's rising anger was turned towards his playmate. He could feel the only thing that could provide the proof he needed. *I will rub it in your face,* he thought wanting to prove his superiority. *You think it's funny? You lied to me and pressured me to enter that dark place. I will show you that I'm a lot braver than you ever were. I went there, and I will go in again.*

When the youngster failed to respond, Gwen shook him. "Joshua! Listen to me! It's really important that you stay away from there."

Gwen's words brought him back to reality. He looked up at the old Eternal. "I will never go in there again, I promise," he lied.

"Master," Grant interceded. "I'm sorry about all of this. I will make sure that he doesn't bother you again." *The Master may be willing to let this go, but I won't.* Grant was fuming. *You're in for it kid.* "Come on Joshua!" He held the child's collar tightly. "We have wasted enough of the Master's time."

Shock, surprise and panic came over Joshua. *What's going on?* He struggled to get free. "Wait!" he screamed. "Leave me alone! Let me go!" Grant, ignoring the child's plea, turned and walked toward the stairs.

Gwen stood and observed the guardian leaving his premise silently. He could feel the anger and embarrassment that the child caused him. *He will not treat the child fairly. I should not interfere. The child surely deserves whatever he is going to get. No, I cannot do that. If I do I will not be able to think about anything else. Athraw's curse! It would be a lot easier if I didn't have a conscience.* "Grant!" Gwen interceded. His voice boomed across the open space. "Leave the child here."

Nearing the crystal pillars, Grant stopped. It *looks like your luck is holding out kid.* Grant gritted his teeth from frustration. "Master, are you sure?" he asked, turning to face him.

One scolding is enough. He doesn't need another one from you. "Yes Grant, I'm sure." Gwen replied. "Let him go, I will take care of it."

Grant sighed, unable to hide the disappointment he felt. *There's nothing he would like better than to show some manners to this little hoodlum. Lucky kid,* he glanced down at the struggling child. *Looks like you got yourself out of this mess after all. I will be keeping a close eye on you. Your luck won't hold forever.* Letting go of Joshua, he turned on his heel and departed.

The child got to his feet and looked at Grant who was descending the steps of the great hall. Then, very still, he faced the Master. Bowing his head, looking at Master Gwen from the corner of one eye, Joshua wondered if he would have been better off going with Grant, regardless of the punishment.

Chapter Two

Gwen looked at the timid child and could not help but feel sympathy towards him. *What am I going to do with you? I couldn't let you go with Grant; he would have enjoyed punishing you too much.* "Child...come," he said, his voice flat and monotone.

Gwen's words echoed in Joshua's mind as he stared at the old Master before him. His long white hair, the long wavy white beard and those piercing gray eyes gave him the menacing quality that demanded respect. Shivers ran down his spine as he walked uneasily towards the Master. He looked up at the intimidating form before him.

His apprehension melted away slowly when he saw a warm smile come over his stone cold face.

"I know that right now you don't like the Elders," the Master said, picking him up gently. "One day, however that will change."

"I don't think so," Joshua replied timidly.

"We will see."

Feeling a little bit more at ease in the Master's arms, Joshua took in the scene before him. Having never entered a Hall before, he was captivated by all the things surrounding him. The twelve crystal columns around him supported a large marble ring at the base of an enormous crystal dome. A huge crystal ball was sunk halfway into the dome, right above a glittering crystal throne. "What's that?" asked Joshua, pointing to the throne in the center of the hall.

"It's where I sit and teach," Gwen replied. "Would you like to go up there and see it up close?"

Joshua nodded silently.

Gwen smiled, walked to the throne and sat down. "What do you think?" he asked his smile radiating throughout his face. "Pretty nice, is it not?"

Joshua nodded and a faint smile came across his face. He turned and snuggled back shyly against Gwen's chest, resting his head just below the Eternal's chin. Tilting his head up, he noticed energy radiating from the sunken ball.

"Master it's beautiful, what is it?"

What is what? Gwen looked up momentarily before answering. "It represents Saavatha. You know who Saavatha is, do you not?"

"Yes Master I do," the child replied. "Elder Shawn told us all about Saavatha."

"Tell me about him. What you can remember?"

"He's the creator of all things," Joshua began nervously. He hoped to remember it all. "I know that he loves us and he wants the best for us, right?"

"You are right, he does love us." Gwen replied. "One day if you work hard you might get the chance to see Saavatha."

"I will see Saavatha?" Joshua's excitement lit up his cute face. "When, Master, please tell me?"

Gwen listened to the child and lost himself in his own thoughts. *I remember being this young. Life in this kingdom was much simpler then. He talks about Saavatha with such admiration. It's been a long time since Saavatha made me feel this way. I admire his innocence, but innocence is weak. One day he will have to leave his naivety behind and move into the world of good and evil. I do not envy you child, facing evil and coming out victorious is the hardest thing that you will ever have to do.*

"Master!" Joshua did not like to be ignored. "Are you listening to me?"

"What?" Gwen asked, the sudden leap to reality left him confused. "I'm sorry, Joshua," he composed himself. "What were you saying?"

"When am I going to meet Saavatha?" he asked with exasperation. "Please tell me."

"When you are ready," Gwen quickly replied.

"When I am ready? When is that?"

"When the time is right you will know."

I don't understand, Joshua thought, looking at the old Eternal oddly. "I don't know when I will be ready," he said and wrapped both of his arms around the Master's waist. "But you will tell me when the time is right?"

"If you wish," the Master replied.

Gwen observed Joshua for a moment. He couldn't understand the apprehension that Joshua felt toward Journeying. *He should take to it like Baltaseim does to hatred. After all Journeying is the reason for our existence. From the look of him, he should be well into his fifth or sixth Journey by now. His fear seemed to be too deeply rooted to be recent. His fear of dying doesn't help, but I'm sure that there's more to it than what he is willing to admit. Maybe I should pry a little and see what gives.* "Joshua, why are you afraid of Journeying to the Solid's realm?"

"I don't want to go there." Joshua felt another shiver run up his spine. "That place gives me the creeps."

"You don't have to think about that right now." His tone was full of reassurance. "I will talk to the Elders and tell them that you are not ready for that step. Would you like that?"

Relief washed over his worried face. For a brief moment he thought about kissing the old Eternal.

"Oh, thank you! I would like that very much."

Whatever scared him is pretty powerful: I've never seen a child so afraid of Journeying since my inception. Gwen felt his heart sink with worry. He knew too well the power that fear could wield over someone. *This could be a serious crutch for him. It could interfere with his evolution. I will talk to the Master of his house*, he reasoned. *Between the two of us, I am certain we can find a way to help him get over this fear.*

"Joshua, what House do you belong to?"

"Let's see, hum," Joshua felt awkward. "Qwenthrey, I think. Yeah, that's it. I belong to the House of Qwenthrey."

He belongs to the House of Qwenthrey. Interesting, it will be nice to see James again; it has been a while since we met last. When was the last time, let's see? It can't be—it's been almost twenty years. Goodness, I need to get out more often. All of this work and no play Gwen. This is probably why you are so cranky. Seeing him will do you some good. I can't wait to surprise him: boy will he be shocked.

Joshua was hugging Gwen like his life depended on it. *I'm glad I found this Master*, he snuggled tight. *He will protect me from the Elders. I hate them. I will never like them, no matter how hard the Master tries, that's for sure. I want to stay here with this Master. I like him...even if he looks grumpy. Grown-ups are weird. I can never tell how they will react. I really thought that this Master would be the death of me. Look at me, all snuggled up with the grumpiest Eternal I've ever met in my whole life. I wish I could stay here forever.*

Joshua's entrance into the Damned Hall worried Gwen. *One casualty is enough. No Eternal should suffer Gord's fate.* The guilt that had lain dormant for many years returned with a vengeance. *I won't screw up this time. Now I'm well prepared. No other Eternal will get lost in that labyrinth, not if I have anything to do with it, I swear on the Garden of Life! Joshua*, he took the child's small hands in his. *What am I going to do with you? Maybe I can use your fear for Journeying to my advantage. If this works, you won't ever want to set foot in the Damned Hall.*

"Joshua, are you aware who Baltaseim is?"

"Shawn told us about him, but I don't remember much of it."

"You weren't paying attention in class now were you?"

"No," He felt his cheeks went crimson red. He hated being put on the spot.

"Baltaseim is the fifth son of Saavatha," Gwen began. He hoped that this little lesson in history would be to his benefit. "He was the apple of Saavatha's eye. He excelled at all his studies, and like most studies there comes a time when the student's knowledge becomes as vast as the teacher's. At that point the student has earned the honor to become a Master in his own right.

However, Baltaseim thought that the time had already come for him to become a Master. False pride made him believe that he was a better leader. He was secretly plotting to overthrow Saavatha and take over the kingdom. The holy one became furious when he heard of Baltaseim's desire. Saavatha didn't want to believe his pride and joy could possibly be plotting against him.

When reality finally set in and Saavatha realized that his son secretly envied him, he banished Baltaseim from this kingdom. From that date on he was known as Athraw, the lord who reigns over the world of the Solids. Of course Baltaseim was furious. He vowed to turn everything Saavatha holds dear, against him. Saavatha could have destroyed him in an instant if he desired, but he still loved his son. Saavatha hopes that one day Baltaseim will mend his ways and come home."

Joshua's blood ran cold. *So those stories are true.* His face lost all color. *Peter was right. Oh no, I stepped into Athraw's home. The crystal! Athraw's curse! I have an evil crystal in my pocket. I have to get rid of it NOW!* Searching his pocket desperately looking for the damned crystal, Joshua felt his spine go cold as he wrapped his fingers around the dark stone. His heart wanting to beat out of his chest, Joshua threw the stone as far away from him as possible.

"Joshua, what did you just throw away?" asked Gwen surprised.

"Nothing," he hoped the Master would drop the subject.

"Joshua, don't lie," Gwen scolded. "I saw you throw something, now tell me what it was!"

"You'll get mad at me if I tell you." Joshua met Gwen's angered gaze and quickly looked away. *Those eyes, how could anyone not be terrified of those eyes...?*

"I will be angrier if you do not tell me." Gwen raised his snow-white eyebrows in expectation.

"A black crystal," he mumbled hesitantly. "I threw away a black crystal."

"I see," replied Gwen, satisfied that his tactic worked.

"I picked it up when I was in the hall." Joshua felt his fear burn and tighten his stomach. "I wanted to keep it as proof."

"I'm glad that you got rid of it. That crystal could have harmed you. It is one of the reasons why The Damned Hall is off limits to all Eternals."

"When you told me who Baltaseim was, I got scared and I wanted nothing to do with anything that belonged to Athraw. I hate him, he gives me the creeps."

"Joshua!" Gwen voiced sharply. "One of Saavatha's rules dictates that you should not have hatred in your heart, not even for Athraw. He..." Gwen continued in a softened tone, "...is lost and one day he will repent for the wrong that he is doing."

I don't care. I hate him I wish he never existed. "All I know right now, I'm happy that he is nowhere near me." Joshua snuggled against the Master. "I hope that I never see him." *And if I think hard enough,* he plotted silently... *maybe I can find a way to rid us of this menace once and for all.*

Chapter Three

Joshua shivered lightly, his skin felt the coolness of the faint summer breeze that flowed through the open columns of the sacred hall. The sun at its zenith, reflected its rays through the crystal dome. The light danced along the thousands of etchings covering the surface like a river flowing to the sea. Thousands of colorful specks of light glimmered over his hands, captivating him. They shimmered aimlessly on every surface it touched. Looking up to investigate the origin of these wonderful little miracles, he noticed something odd.

"Master, what are those scratches on the ceiling?"

"Those scratches are writings." Gwen replied. "The name of every Eternal that belongs in the Kingdom of Saavatha is etched on the dome's crystal."

"Why?" Joshua asked with an odd look on his face.

"Saavatha wanted to keep a written record of all the Eternals who are part of his kingdom."

"Oh, that means that every Eternal's name is up there?"

"No Joshua," replied Gwen. Sadness filled him as he was reminded that not all choices are righteous, "only the ones who belong to this kingdom."

"Not every Eternal is part of this kingdom?"

"No, not everyone."

"They're not? How come?"

"Because they chose not to."

"Where do they live if they are not here with us?" Joshua asked dismayed.

"They are with Athraw," Gwen replied flatly.

A sense of dread overcame him. He never thought anyone would go to Athraw willingly. "Isn't Saavatha angry?" The thought of living with Athraw made Joshua nauseous.

"It makes Saavatha sad, but it's their choice." Gwen sighed. "Saavatha has given all Eternals free will, he cannot take it back just because he doesn't like the choice they made."

"Why not? I would, if I were him," Joshua voiced with disgust.

"I know you would," the old Eternal chuckled, "but it would be wrong to do it your way."

"I don't understand why it would be wrong."

"One day you will understand why Saavatha does things this way," Gwen added, forcing a reassuring smile on his unsure face.

The sheer number of names displayed on the dome's surface overwhelmed Joshua. Searching aimlessly for his name, frustration overtook him and he gave up quickly.

"Master," he asked. "Could you show me where my name is?"

"Your name is in that section of the dome." Gwen pointed to Qwenthrey's section of the dome with his right hand.

"Where?" Joshua voiced with discouragement. "I can't see it. I'm sorry but it's too far for me to see."

"That's OK," Gwen's eyes smiled at him. "I will help you. On the marble ring that the dome sits on, look for the name of your house."

Josh scanned the room and looked at the base of the dome and to his amazement he found the names of all Saavatha's sons stamped in gold on the face of the marble ring. He quickly looked for the house of Qwenthrey and was overjoyed when he found it.

"There's my house, I found it!" he exclaimed triumphantly.

"Now look up at the pie section that is above the name Qwenthrey," Gwen told him.

"There it is! I see it!" Joshua shouted, his young voice full of excitement.

"That section of the dome," Gwen began, "represents the house of Qwenthrey and all of your ancestry beginning with Qwenthrey himself at the tip of the triangle."

"Wow, there are a lot of Eternals that are part of my house."

"Now," Gwen continued, "in the center of the dome lays the sunken ball representing Saavatha. Remember you asked me about it earlier?"

"Oh yeah I did! I remember."

"If you look closely, the twelve pie sections of the dome, which represent each house of this kingdom, meet in the center where Saavatha is located."

"Why is that section black? Oh, I know," he replied before the Master had time to answer. "The black section of the dome is for Athraw, right?"

"Yes." Gwen wanted to forget the betrayal that Saavatha suffered at Baltaseim's hand. "It's black because he represents all that is dark and evil." Gwen looked around his hall and he still felt an overwhelming sense of euphoria. *Even after all these years, I'm still filled with awe when I look at all the Eternals who are part of the kingdom. I remember when this hall was created. The kingdom wasn't that big when I took over as custodian.*

I knew that Saavatha had a plan but the thought never crossed my mind how prosperous those plans would turn out to be. It still amazes me.

"Master, could you help me find my name?"

"Sure, I can do that," the Master replied, slowly returning to reality. He closed his eyes and asked Saavatha silently; *Help me grant the child's simple wish.* The sunken ball started glowing extremely bright. One by one in order of birth the name of every son of Saavatha stamped in the marble ring started to glow. The house of Merthor was the first, then the house of Symraay, Myrey and Thaabar. Saavatha's fifth son Baltaseim was skipped. Phaalor, Bartholomew, Qwenthrey, Bayrthraa, Raphael, Piatre and Zallier completed the cycle. A white light started emanating deep within the pillar's core and expanded towards the column ends.

Completely enveloped in energy, the pillars released a horizontal beam of light in the same sequence as the previous cycle, at the throne's crystal base, energizing it. The light merging in the base produced a radiating nucleus that built up energy until it discharged a vertical column of light, gently lifting the throne towards the center of the dome.

Stopping a few feet from the energized ball, Gwen opened his eyes and looked at Joshua who by this time was overwhelmed by the sequence of events. His mouth dropped and for a brief moment the words would not come.

"Unreal," he managed to say under his breath "all this to find my name."

Look at him, the simplest thing seems to make him happy, Gwen thought. *I hope that in your Journey towards perfection you never lose this aspect of your personality. It would be a shame.* "Well I'm ready to find your name, are you?"

"You bet I am," he replied enthusiastically.

Gwen closed his eyes and concentrated. *Qwenthrey, my brother...*he asked silently. *Show me the way to Joshua's namesake through his ancestry.* Qwenthrey's name lit up momentarily. The energy followed Joshua's lineage down, illuminating every one of his ancestors one after the other until it reached the child's name.

"There it is I see it! There it is!!" Joshua exclaimed, pointing and fidgeting on the Master's lap.

Looking right at Joshua's name, Gwen fixed his eyes on it. *Come closer, and reveal yourself to me.* The writing brightened and a stream of energy discharged directly in line with Gwen's gaze. Stopping a few inches from the Master's gaze, the energy turned into a three dimensional holographic replica of the original writing.

"Master, it's so beautiful," Joshua said, mesmerized. He felt a little overwhelmed by the events surrounding him. *This Master is so cool,* he thought. *Shawn never did anything like that before. Shawn is so boring...I like this Master much better! Maybe only Masters can do these neat things...Shawn is no Master.* "I have never seen anything like this before, thank you!"

I love this kind of innocence, however fragile it might be. Gwen looked at the child with amazement. Closing his eyes, the holographic image vanished and the throne started its descent back to its base. "Oh you are very welcome," Gwen replied, his smile warming Joshua's heart.

When the throne settled, the horizontal beams of light retracted, the energy deep within the columns dimmed and all trace of the event was gone.

"Did you enjoy all the things that I showed you?" Gwen' heart filled with tenderness towards the youngster.

"Yes Master, it was great!" Joshua could hardly contain the excitement he felt. "It was awesome!"

"I'm glad you enjoyed yourself." Gwen picked up the child and walked down the throne's crystal steps.

"We have to go now," he said with regret.

"Where are we going?" Joshua asked, disappointment clearly showing on his face.

"We are going to the house of Qwenthrey," Gwen replied, "where you belong."

Joshua looked up. The last thing he wanted was to go home. "No! I want to stay here. I don't want to go," Joshua protested. His lips curled into a pout. "I like it here."

The Master bent down to Joshua's level and took both of his little hands in his own. "Joshua," he said, hating to disappoint such a young heart. "You know that you should not be here. This is not your house, the house of Qwenthrey is where you belong."

Joshua lowered his head. *It's always like this...I hate it!* His face gave way to the sour expression that displayed his displeasure so well. *When I start to have fun, I have to leave. It's not fair!*

"I don't want to go back," he complained. "I'm having so much fun here."

Gwen looked at the child with compassionate eyes. "Joshua," he said squeezing his hands gently. "You can come back anytime."

The child's face lit up like a Christmas tree. "I can? Really?" he replied, his eyes lit with joy.

"Yes Joshua, really." Gwen got up and took the child's hand and walked towards the entrance to the house of Qwenthrey. He stopped briefly and asked, "Are you ready to go?"

Joshua felt like a leaf pulled in any direction the wind would blow. He conceded that the lack of control he felt in his existence would change one day. He looked up at the gold engraving that marked the entrance of his house. "I guess, if I have to."

Gwen took a deep breath; he hated disappointing children but he knew it was the right thing to do. "OK then," he said, "Let's go." He walked slowly with the boy past the crystal columns and they both vanished in a blinding flash of light. Unexpectedly the crystal ball radiated momentarily, leaving a faint whisper echoing softly throughout the hall. "Joshua, son of Gabriel your destiny awaits you, go." Silence overtook the room once more...no one heard Saavatha's testimony.

Chapter Four

In the afternoon the House of Qwenthrey was unusually busy. Thirty Eternals were sitting on red silk pillows in a semicircle facing the throne. Master James rested his elbows on his knees, cradling his head in his hands while he listened to one subject's question.

They were all here today to learn self-sacrifice. To put oneself in peril, to protect or help another was the foundation of Saavatha's morals. If you could completely forget your needs and wants and put everyone else's before your own, you were on the right track to learning this very important lesson.

Thank goodness this is over, James thought. *I'm beat.* "OK folks, we are done for today," he told the group. Tired and numb from sitting so long, James couldn't wait to stretch his legs. *I will have to fix that,* he thought. His glasses slid halfway down his nose and he pushed them back, bringing the room into focus. "Next class is in three days so don't forget. Class dismissed. Thanks for coming John," he said to the dark haired Eternal walking towards him. "I hope that you got something out of this class."

"Yes I did. It was very informative. I'm looking forward to your next class," John replied. His voice was full of enthusiasm.

"Great, we'll see you then, take care." You could see a satisfied gleam in his eye. *Perfect*, he thought as he observed the last straggler exit the hall, *everyone is leaving on time for once. I guess I should go and prepare the next course; I am so far behind you'd think that I was in first place.* A brief flash caught his attention. *Great...who's here now! I don't need this...I'm busy. Whoever it is I hope that they don't plan to stay long.* He looked up and he recognized the form walking towards him. His mood lightened immediately. *Gwen! I can't believe it, it's been a long time since I last saw him.* "Gwen! It's good to see you old friend."

Gwen looked at him oddly. *He changed his appearance,* he thought. *I hardly recognized him.* "James," Gwen replied with a vivid smile. "It's been ages since I saw you; you look good for an old fart."

James scoffed silently. *He hasn't changed a bit. Same twisted sense of humor.* "I wouldn't talk, look who's got white hair."

"Better than that dark brown of yours! Anyway what's with the goatee and the ponytail?" Gwen asked teasingly.

Ponytail? James raised an eyebrow. "It's a French braid," he corrected, an amused smirk came forth. "Not a ponytail. I decided that it was high time for me to look younger. At my age I have to use everything that will give me an edge. So that's where you've been!" James cried out, noticing Joshua by Gwen's side, "Elder Shawn has been looking all over for you."

Joshua felt his face go red with embarrassment. "I know," he replied not having the courage to look at James.

"He was running away from the elders." Gwen explained.

James shot Gwen a confused stare. He wasn't sure if he heard Gwen correctly. "What?"

"Joshua ran away from the Elders," Gwen repeated.

"Joshua, is that true?" James asked.

Joshua lowered his head in shame. "Yes," he replied sheepishly. "They wanted me to Journey to the Solids and I got scared."

"I don't think he is ready to Journey yet," Gwen interrupted.

James looked at Gwen and then lowered his gaze to the trembling child. *I wonder what got him this riled up. This kind of fear is unusual at his age.* "You're probably right. I will talk to the elders myself and tell them to hold off on that for now."

"Joshua," James said while bending down to the child's level, "The next time you don't feel comfortable with something you don't need to run away. We are here to help you, not to hurt you."

"I'm sorry. I didn't mean to worry anyone."

James smiled at the child. "I know you didn't. You just need to trust us a little."

Joshua's guilt got the better of him. "I'm sorry. When I get scared, I panic and do stupid things."

"I know," he replied, stroking his rosy cheeks. "Fear is a powerful emotion—mastering it can take many Journeys."

Joshua turned to Gwen. "Thanks for showing me all those neat things Master," he said

Gwen smiled back. With the long white beard and all, he looked pretty jolly. "You're welcome," he replied. He rested his gaze on James. "It's not very often that I get a chance to see you, it's kind of refreshing actually. I'm really glad that this is settled. When is Joshua's next class?"

"You know," James replied looking thoughtful. "I can't remember right now, but I'm sure that either Shawn or Paul will teach the class. I will ask them, and then I'll let you know."

"That would be great. If you want I can come and visit you in your class sometime," the old Eternal suggested and turned to Joshua, "Would that be OK?"

A wide and joyous smile came over Joshua's face. The thought of seeing Gwen again put a twinge of excitement in his voice.

"That would be great! I would just love that." He hugged Gwen's leg tightly.

Gwen glanced down, and lifted the child's chin to his gaze. *Such tenderness, may you never change* "I love you too, child." Gwen looked past the crystal pillars and noticed the natural light dimming slowly. "I should be going," Gwen said looking at James. "I still have a lot of things on my plate."

Joshua hugged the Master's leg tighter. "Do you have to go, can't you stay?"

Gwen looked at the pleading child with compassion. "Josh I'd love to stay," he sighed, "but I can't. I have too many things to do. They won't get done without me."

"Please, stay. Pleasssse, I'll be good!"

A moment of silence passed while Gwen juggled his conscience. "Tell you what," he said. "I promise to come and visit you often OK?"

Crushed, Joshua lowered his head and his face scowled into an unhappy frown. *He won't come,* he thought. *Grown-ups always forget their promises.*

Gwen said, a little saddened, "I have to go. It was nice to see you again, James. I promise not to be so long next time. Take care."

He then walked through the entrance of his house and disappeared in a blinding flash of light.

Alone with James in the Great Hall, Joshua could hear every breath. For a long moment the quiet was deafening.

"Well young one," James said, breaking the silence. "It's time that you and I go see your founder. He is probably worried sick."

Joshua's heart jumped. *Oh no! I totally forgot about him.* "Do we have to? He's going to be really mad at me, and I don't want to be in trouble."

James looked down at him and adjusted his glasses. "You should have thought of that before. You can't run away from your problems. You have to deal with the consequences of your actions." Joshua dragged his feet close behind James as they exited the hall. The beauty surrounding the sacred hall would normally mesmerize Joshua, if he weren't so distracted. The hall sat in a beautiful green meadow with a half-dozen trails that led in every direction. There were many varieties of fruit trees adorning the field.

Birds of all sorts flocked from tree to tree; some earthly, some of other worlds, returning to the kingdom after a cycle in the solid's realm to enjoy the rewards before them. A Vegonian chameleon flew near them and landed in a maple tree, blending almost perfectly behind the large leaves. The scent of wild flowers that grow sporadically throughout this land permeated the air.

James looked at Josh, who seemed to be in his own little world. His trance was interrupted when he felt the Master's hand on the top of his head. Looking up, he heard "We should take the trail on the left, don't you think?" Nodding his approval they took the trail that would bring Joshua home.

"Tell me Joshua," James asked trying to distract the child, "what did you do with Master Gwen?"

"Master Gwen showed me where my name is on the crystal dome," he replied, kicking a stone near him. "He also told me about Athraw and the section on the dome that represents him. He was not too happy when he found out that I went to the Damned Hall."

James took a deep breath. His protective instinct took over. He stopped and put a hand on the child's shoulders. "Joshua," he began, his riveting eyes trained on the unsuspecting child.

"It is very important that you never step foot in that Hall again!"

Joshua looked up with trepidation. From the look on the Master's face he knew that he wasn't happy. "Oh don't worry." Joshua tried to sound reassuring; his mind was more on the trouble ahead than on the present conversation. "I promised Master Gwen that I would stay away from there."

James sighed. *I wonder how he found it, the Hall I mean. It is quite a ways away and to find it you almost have to look for it. The underbrush usually conceals it very well.* "Joshua," he asked, "how did you find the Hall?"

A heat wave washed over Joshua. "I don't know how I found it Master," he replied, trying to evade the question. "I just stumbled onto it."

James felt a flash of anger course through him. He didn't like to be made a fool of. *He is lying!* He clenched his teeth trying to suppress the rage he felt. *I can tell. Look at his face, it says it all.* "Josh," he asked suspiciously. "Did you run into any guardians?"

"Yes Master," Joshua replied evading James' eyes. "I ran into Grant. He chased me all the way into Master Gwen's Hall. I was running fast, I tripped and knocked the Master on his butt."

I knew it! James thought feeling vindicated. *This Baltaseim's minion is lying to me. It takes a lot more finesse than that to fool me. Does he think I've lost the way to the Garden of Life?* "Joshua, don't lie to me. There is no way that you could just stumble on that hall, it's too well concealed."

Joshua's eyes opened wide. He looked at the ground trying to think his way out of this mess. "Athraw's tricks!" he swore under his breath. *I don't understand: I never told him anything. It must be that sixth sense Peter told me about. What do I do now? I can't tell him the truth but if I lie again he is going to see right through it. I don't have a choice—I have to tell him the truth. I might be able to use sympathy to get me out of this corner.* He took a deep breath and looked straight at the Master. "I'm sorry Master," he said, feeling the tremors inside his chest. "You were right, I lied. I didn't want to get in trouble."

James exhaled and looked away, his gaze fixed on a distant point. He didn't want to look at the child. "How did you find the hall Josh?" James asked, the hurt in his eyes betraying his anger. "This time tell the truth."

"It's Peter from my class," Joshua sighed, conceding defeat. "He told me about the Damned Hall. I thought that he was pulling my leg until he dared me to go in there. I promise I won't go there ever again, just don't tell my founder." Josh begged, sobbing.

"Josh, you should know better. I have to tell your founder. I won't lie for anyone: there's no other choice."

Joshua felt the tears swelling in his vivid blue eyes. *Maybe I should run away, but I love my home. I don't want to leave. What am I going to do?* "Master, please don't tell him," he pleaded as fearful tears flowed down his cheeks. "I am going to be in big trouble."

"I'm sorry Josh, I can't help you. I have no other choice. You should have thought about that before you went ahead and lied. Now you will face the consequence for your action. Next time maybe you'll think twice before lying."

A burning in the pit of his stomach rose forth. Joshua knew how his founder would react to James' news. His founder is quite strict. He's not looking forward to facing Saavatha's truth.

He better curb this bad habit, James thought, walking beside the young child. *Saavatha doesn't take lying lightly. He nicknamed Baltaseim the Master of Lies for a reason. If he stays on this road, he will have to deal with Saavatha's justice. I wouldn't want to be him.* "You know Josh," James said to the upset child. "There is no good reason to lie. You had better change your ways. If you stay on this road, you'll find it very unpleasant. Trust me, I've been there. It's not worth it."

Joshua rolled his eyes, making sure that James didn't see him. *What does he know? I'm a better liar then he ever was. I wish he would just shut up.* "I know," Josh replied flatly.

James looked at the child and knew that nothing he said was getting through. *I almost feel sorry for you child. The road you've chosen is not an easy one. I tried, my conscience is clear.* "Josh is your founder home?" James asked as the rancher came into view.

"I don't know," Josh replied, shrugging his shoulders uncaringly. James walked past the trees decorating that front yard and took the trail that led to two massive oak doors framing the arched entrance.

Reaching the stoop, he knocked on the naturally finished wood. As he waited patiently, he admired the craftsmanship before him. The door's edges were lined with carved angels looking upwards to the glory of Saavatha.

Two centerpiece carvings of life-size angels playing the trumpet greeted them. The facing trumpets formed the door handles.

Moments later, the door on James' right opened slowly. A blond curly head poked out. "Yes, who is it?"

Chapter Five

The door opened slowly and a small Eternal with thinning curly hair greeted them. "Master James!" Gabriel looked on surprised that such a high Eternal would take the time to visit with him. "Welcome to my humble home Master," he said graciously.

James looked at Gabriel and could see the family resemblance. *In his younger years,* he mused, *he must have been quite a handful.* "Greetings," James replied. He smiled at Joshua's founder, certain that Joshua's return would be good news. "I am here to return your son Joshua. May we come in?"

Gabriel felt himself go faint. "Joshua..." His voice crackled. "...you found him?"

James nodded and brought the missing child forward.

Tears flowed down his cheeks as waves of emotions washed over him; relief, happiness and finally anger. "Where in the Damned Hall have you been?" Gabriel shouted in anger. "I've been worried sick!"

"Maybe I can answer that." James volunteered.

"I can't wait to hear this!" Gabriel replied, unable to restrain his anger. He gave his son a glare then rested his gaze on the Master. "I'm sorry," he said taking a deep breath, "How rude of me. Come on in." He pulled the doors open and waved them in. He pointed to the living room as he closed the doors behind them. "Let's go and sit down."

James could feel the coolness of the stone as he walked across the jade tiles that spanned the entire home. He barely had time to sit on the sofa-chair before Gabriel started in on Joshua.

"Joshua, where have you been?" he asked with rising hostility. "I've been looking all over for you. When you failed to come home after your studies, I didn't know what had happened."

Josh bowed his head in shame, not wanting to look into his founder's eyes. A cold sweat took over. His skin felt clammy as he waited, expecting the other shoe to drop at any moment.

James studied the pitiful-looking child and wondered what was going through his head. *I'm sorry to do this to you kid. I hope that you won't hold it against me too much.* "Your son," he began, staring at the child, "was snooping around the Damned Hall."

Gabriel's eyes shot open from shock, his mind started to spin and his skin began to dampen. "HE WHAT?" Feeling lightheaded, he rubbed his temples until the discomfort vanished.

"He was caught inside the Damned Hall by one of the guardians." James continued. "When Grant approached him, he decided to make a run for it. He would have gotten away with it too if he hadn't run into Master Gwen, literally."

Gabriel looked at his son horrified. His mind raced, searching for something to say, but words couldn't describe the emotions that were passing through him. *Boy, are you in for it! I can't believe this.* His face went blank. "Oh no," Gabriel said "is he alright?"

"Yes, he is fine," James reassured. "His ego is a little bruised I'm sure but he didn't seem too worse for wear."

"What is the matter with you?" Gabriel yelled and cuffed Joshua upside the head. "Don't you ever think about anyone else but yourself? What were you thinking? I can't believe you did this, unbelievable!"

"I'm sorry," Josh replied meekly. "I didn't know whose house it was."

James' eyebrows went up in both surprise and shock. "He's lying," James pointed out with disappointment. "He knew exactly what he was doing. Peter from his class made a wager with him. My guess is that Joshua wanted to prove to this kid that he wasn't afraid of the Damned Hall."

"Is this true?" Gabriel asked astounded. "Did you just lie to me? Joshua, answer me now!" Gabriel's anger was reaching a new level. His brow knitted into an angry scowl, he glared at his son expecting an answer.

The intensity in Joshua's eyes would have sent chills to the most seasoned Eternals. "Yes Founder," Joshua replied, maintaining his glower towards James. "I lied. I'm sorry, I won't do it again, I swear by Saavatha's elements!"

Frustrated, Gabriel's head dropped in his hands. *Out of all my children Joshua is the most difficult. The hostility that he is exhibiting towards James is not unusual. He's used to getting everything he wants. Now I'm paying the price. I don't know what I'm going to do with you, I really don't.* He looked up at his son, and his face spoke of pain and disappointment. "I don't believe you," Gabriel finally said. "Now get out of my sight before I do something that I'm going to regret."

Gabriel didn't have to repeat himself. Joshua made a hasty exit, thankful that James was in the room. His founder had a violent temper.

Gabriel observed his son leaving the room. He took a deep breath and looked at James. "Master," he voiced exasperated. "I'm sorry about all of this. I didn't mean to involve you into my problems."

James gave him a timid smile. "It's alright," he assured. "Been there, done that. Probably a million times by now. With having to deal with ten thousand or more children since my inception, there is not much I haven't seen or dealt with."

Gabriel leaned back into his seat. Just the thought of having that many children was enough to give him nightmares. "You are a better Eternal than I," he replied, in disbelief. "The four I have give me enough grief as it is. Anyway thank you for bringing my son home. I am eternally grateful. I wish there was something I could do to make up for all of the trouble Joshua's been to you." Gabriel sighed. "Wait, I've got an idea, why don't you stay for dinner?"

James looked at him oddly. Not needing sustenance, it had been years since he indulged himself in the pleasures of dining. "Dinner?" He asked unsure if he heard right.

"Yes, dinner." Gabriel replied with a sly smirk. "It would give me a chance to thank you properly. I know that we don't have to eat. It's a habit that I picked up from my days as a Solid. I have very fond memories of moments I experienced during dinner.

Every once and a while I like to eat to remember them. It takes me away from all of this," he said, waving at his children.

James' eyes twinkled with amusement and a broad smile came over his face. "I would be honored," he replied. "What are we having for dinner?"

"Arthra stuffed with miutos weed served with heltha, costus and kemtra."

Goodness, it must be at least two or three thousand years since I have had arthra, James mused. He had once Journeyed as a boy named Costuniad on a planet called Vegonia. It was during Coustrad, a time of giving and thanks. The fowl they had that night tasted wonderful. *I drowned in the river near my home the next morning. I was only fifteen when I returned to the kingdom. How time flies, I still can't believe it has been that long.* James suddenly felt grateful to be an Eternal, especially now that he was going to eat this fowl. One degree off in the cooking process was enough to kill any Solid. It still baffled him how many Solids were willing to take their life in their own hands for the pleasure of eating the sweet-tasting flesh.

Gabriel observed James for a moment. "Is that satisfactory to you?"

James was suddenly brought back to reality by Gabriel's voice. "Sure, yes! That would be wonderful. Sorry about that: my mind was drifting a bit."

"Understandable—I'm sure that you have a lot on your mind." Gabriel's smirk radiated his round face. "Make yourself at home, while I go into the kitchen. I have some tesulos wine if you like, very old vintage, 3000 years at least. Dinner should be ready in twenty minutes."

James walked to the cabinet and poured himself a drink. He chuckled as the glowing green liquid swirled in the bottom of his glass. As a Solid he enjoyed this delicacy. Made from tesulos, a very rare plant on the Audruckra planet, this Audruckrian jewel was prized for its aphrodisiactic qualities. James sighed with disappointment. It had no effect on Eternals. *Oh well,* he thought. *Thanks for the memories.* He started to browse through Gabriel's large library looking for something interesting to read while dinner was being prepared. Finding a book to his liking, he sat down and casually leafed through the binder.

It seemed only moments before James was interrupted by Gabriel's voice. "Dinner is served, come sit down to eat."

James sighed with regret. He was actually looking forward to reading this book. *Damned Hall, I wonder if Gabriel would let me borrow this for a while.* His disappointment was short-lived. The sweet smell coming from the kitchen enticed his senses with long-forgotten pleasures. James sauntered into the dining room and was astounded by what laid before him. On a crystal table that seated six, was an arthra baked to perfection. Three gold candelabras decorated the table, one in the center and the other two sitting near the ends. Six silver settings with matching plates and goblets were evenly placed on the table. Three bottles of milk white darsthos wine sat beside the candelabras.

"Sorry." Gabriel said, bumping his guest holding the last bowl of heltha on his way to the table. "I know, I know, with a mere thought I could have had the dinner done in seconds. Call me sentimental but I like to do things the hard way. It makes me appreciate all the difficult work I do."

James acknowledged his understanding with a smile, and marveled at the table setting. "Gabriel, it looks delicious. Where do I sit?"

"You can sit at the other end of the table if you like." In the midst of this conversation the four boys filed in one by one and took their places at the table. Gabriel acknowledged the boys as he finished the last dinner preparation, "Boys, meet Master James. Master James, here are my boys. The redhead on your right is my oldest. His name is Carl, he is in level four, section six."

James smiled at the mischievous looking child who looked about fourteen.

"The child beside Carl is Thomas," Gabriel continued. "He's in level four, section one." James' attention was drawn to Thomas, who was dressed in a blue shirt and pants. This child looked about twelve. He had brown hair and piercing blue eyes. The child smiled shyly.

"This one is Steve," he said, rubbing the top of the child's head. "He's in level three, section eight."

James turned to Steve and noticed that he was dressed like his brother Thomas. He looked about ten and had curly blond hair like his founder.

"And last but not least, there is Joshua whom you've already met. He is my youngest and also the most curious. I'm sure that you can attest to that."

"Absolutely." James gave him a sly grin.

Gabriel looked at his boys, "Pass me your plates and I will give you some meat. You boys are responsible for dressing up the rest of your plates." Gabriel looked at James who still looked a little overwhelmed at the amount of food laid before him. "Master," Gabriel asked once everyone was ready to eat. "Would you do us the honor of saying grace?"

James looked up and smiled. "I would be honored."

They bowed their heads respectfully and held hands while James started the blessing. "Saavatha, bless this house and the Eternals within it. Honor us with your presence of mind. We give thanks for this food that we are about to receive and for the fellowship of these friends. Forgive our transgressions and help us understand the true meaning of your love, Saavatha be praised." The sound of utensils and the chiming of glasses began to fill the room as everyone started to eat.

"Master," Joshua asked while chewing on a piece of miutos weed. "Can Athraw force you to do something that you don't want to do?"

James looked at the child suspiciously. "No, Athraw can't hurt you or make you do things that you don't want to do. Saavatha does not allow that to happen."

Joshua tried to suppress the faint smirk that came over his face. "What if Athraw ignores the rules and does what he wants anyway?"

"He can't," James replied. "He has to follow Saavatha's rules. Breaking those rules could put his existence at stake and he knows it."

Joshua couldn't restrain the excitement he felt. His face was glowing. *Interesting, even Athraw has to obey Saavatha's laws or he will be punished. Maybe I can use this to my advantage. What if I could get Athraw in trouble? If I do this right, I may even be able to get rid of him altogether. How do I make Athraw do something that will anger Saavatha, I wonder? I got it! Athraw you are done. I'll dare him. I'll dare him and in his pride Athraw will do what I want him to do, and Saavatha will get rid of him.*

A sly grin came over his face. He loved his newfound scheme. *Joshua,* he thought. *You are brilliant. It's so simple I wonder why I didn't think of it sooner. If my plan works, Athraw will be destroyed and I will be looked upon as a hero! Every Eternal will love and respect me. Saavatha might even allow me in the Garden of Life.*

Excited, Joshua daydreamed of the glory to come. Determined to follow through, he knew what he had to do. He had to Journey with the sole purpose of daring Athraw. *What could I do to make Athraw die?* He smirked when it came to him. *Saavatha's honor, this is good. I will force him to break my freedom of choice. That's it, it's Saavatha's most sacred rule, that should do it, I'm sure.*

James observed Joshua's demeanor. He didn't like what he saw. "Josh did that answer your question?"

"Yes, it's crystal clear," Joshua replied with a gleam. "I know exactly what I must do."

James choked on his mouthful. "What do you have to do? Joshua, I really would like to know!"

Joshua's face went white. *Athraw's despair,* d*id I say this out loud? Joshua, you've got to be more careful.* "Hum," he said, his mind racing to find something plausible to say. "I have to Journey to the Solid's so that I can grow closer to Saavatha. Yeah, that's it. That's what I have to do."

James put him under intense scrutiny. *I'd give a year of my freedom to know what you are really up to.*

Joshua was not aware that Saavatha had knowledge of his plan. The Holy one sensed his thought as only he and a few could and he was not amused. The child came from a long line in Qwenthrey's lineage. It's been a long time since Qwenthrey had learned this lesson, and it cost him dearly.

****

A faint giggle was heard throughout the Solid's realm as Joshua's plan was revealed to a darker and more sinister Eternal. Baltaseim touched his creator's core energy moments before being ousted from the kingdom long ago. He stole from Saavatha a very important part of his element—the ability to read thoughts-every Eternal's thoughts.

Baltaseim snickered; he remembered the day well, his proudest moment. *Trying to get rid of me?* He chuckled slightly as he sat on his dark throne. *Foolish boy,* he mused. "I am succeeding in making Solids fall into my grip." His voice boomed across the dimly lit room.

"What makes you think that such a young and naïve Bright like yourself can outdo me?" *If this was not so insulting, it might actually be funny.* "Joshua, son of Gabriel," he growled sadistically. "Come to me if you dare! Come to me child," Baltaseim cried out with fury. He looked up, towards the kingdom. "I am ready for you!"

Chapter Six

Gabriel was suspicious, he knew his son too well. "Joshua, what are you up to?"

"Oh nothing." Joshua stared at his plate, hoping Gabriel would drop the subject.

Gabriel sighed, and his anger flared. "Really?" He piped up, his voice revealing his true feelings. "Then why can't you look at me? You do this when you are up to no good—I know you."

Joshua felt his face go red and a wave of heat came over him. His eyes shifted, avoiding his founder's stare.

"I'm just curious that's all," he replied quickly. Getting the courage, he looked at Gabriel. "After all I was the one who entered the Damned Hall, remember?"

Gabriel groaned. "I don't like it!" Joshua knew more than he was telling. "If I find out that you're lying to me, Baltaseim is not going to be the only one that you're going to be afraid of, trust…"

"May I make a suggestion?" James asked, interrupting Gabriel in mid-sentence. James shifted in his seat and leaned forward.

Gabriel sunk back in his chair and waved his arms up in resignation. "Certainly it couldn't hurt."

James fixed his eyes on Gabriel's anxious face. "We're just about done with dinner, why don't you and I talk. The kids can go play outside."

Gabriel turned to his son, eyeing him with a desperation he hadn't known for a long time. He was losing control and he knew it. He needed a new perspective and James was offering one. *Maybe he is right.* He looked at his son. *I need to talk to someone. I'm getting way too hostile.* "That's an excellent idea, actually…" he muttered to James.

"Children," Gabriel announced, wiping his hands with the napkin close to his plate, "outside, all of you. I need some private time with the Master."

The children begrudgingly made their way out. Gabriel was about to walk to the living room when he noticed Joshua, standing by the table his hands behind his back waiting.

"What are you still doing here? Go outside and play with your siblings. When I said, children go outside I meant all of my children—that includes you I'm afraid."

Joshua looked up for a brief moment. "I have a question for Master James," he replied stubbornly.

"You try my patience," Gabriel answered, glaring at him. "You have a question for the Master? Make it quick."

Joshua walked past his founder with a smirk of victory on his face. He stopped a few steps away from the Master. "Elder Shawn taught us that Saavatha gave us freedom of choice so that we may climb towards the Garden of Life willingly. Is that true?"

James looked at him for a moment before answering. "That's correct," he said. "Why do you ask?"

"I'm curious, that's all," he replied with a suppressed grin. "What would happen if Athraw broke that law and took away your freedom to choose?"

James cocked his head a bit surprised with the question. "I don't know Joshua. No Eternal has ever dared to break that rule. They would have to be pretty foolish to do so. It's Saavatha's most important rule. If Athraw broke that rule, Saavatha would most likely destroy him I guess. Why are you asking?"

"Oh nothing," Joshua replied as innocently as possible. "I was just curious. I never quite understood the importance of that rule. I'm just trying to put things into perspective."

"Well I hope so," Gabriel said, "I would hate to think what might happen if for some reason you decided to do something foolish, like break rules."

Joshua eyed him coyly. *I'm sure that you would get mad at me. It will be too late before you find out what I'm going to do.* "Oh no," he replied. "I would never do anything like that."

"I sure hope so, for your sake," he warned. "I would not want you to have to deal with the law of return and the kind of consequences associated with it."

Consequences—that word hit Joshua like a brick wall. *Receiving tenfold of what you sow is not something I want to get. I can't think of that now. There will be enough time to worry about this later. Athraw has done too many misdeeds. He must be stopped. It's obvious that Saavatha does not have the guts to do what is right. So I will force his hand, he won't have a choice. I hate doing this but it's for the good of the kingdom. I must get rid of Athraw at all costs and what happens to me afterwards won't matter.*

****

Baltaseim was listening very carefully to Joshua and Gabriel. He remembered that fateful day when Saavatha exiled him to reign over the Solids.

I was Saavatha's finest son, he thought, still feeling the sting of betrayal. *No other Eternal could outshine me. My beauty was unique and surpassed even Saavatha himself. That is...until I was banished here!*

"I was destined to take your place!" he screamed, the fury burning in his emerald eyes glowed as red as hot pokers. He looked up towards Saavatha's kingdom. "You took my birthright away from me!"

Standing there before him was the only remnant of what he used to be: a façade, a mirrored image of a tall and handsome Eternal with jet-black hair and dark eyes to match his complexion. Baltaseim's stature could ease the sorest eyes. His beauty had been renowned throughout the entire Kingdom. He caught a glimpse of his reflection; he winced as his own monstrosity appalled him.

Half man, half corpse...I used to be so beautiful, so handsome. Now look at me! He did this to me! Why? I don't understand—I was his favorite. Then he turned on me and did this. The stench of rotten flesh overwhelmed Baltaseim's senses. *Oh yes, let us not forget this stink!* "Saavatha!" he howled as tears of rage streamed down his bleached cheekbones. "Why did you do this to me?"

"Your stupidity Saavatha" he said, sobbing uncontrollably..."helped me. I found out about the plan that your little protégé has in store for me. He does not know who he is dealing with.

By the Garden of Life! I will show him what I am truly capable of and when I am done; there won't be much of this insolent child left."

In a fit of rage Baltaseim got up and knocked over the only semblance of what he used to be.

"You will pay for this, I promise you Saavatha!" he exclaimed, giggling.

His resonating laughter echoed in the room and he disappeared into the darkness.

****

"Right," Joshua told Gabriel, "I wouldn't want that kind of consequence either."

"Good, I'm glad that we finally agree on something. Now if that was all, go play with your brothers."

Joshua reluctantly obeyed and left Gabriel and his guest alone.

Gabriel sat down beside James. "Finally, he is gone. He sure drains me. I don't know what I'm going to do with him. Now we can finally have some peace and quiet."

"Yes, silence is golden," James replied. "These children take a lot out of you don't they?"

"You don't know the half of it."

"Yes I do." James replied with a smile. "I raised at least ten thousand of these little monsters."

Gabriel shook his head in disbelief. "I don't know how you did it. I couldn't do it."

James gave him a warm smile. Secretly, he envied Gabriel's accomplishments. "You'd be surprised what you can do once you put your mind to it."

"Joshua worries me. He's always plotting and scheming. I don't know what to do with him."

"There's not much you can do," James replied. "You can't force him to change; change has to come from within."

"I know, I know," Gabriel sighed. "I see the road that he is taking and I want to reach out and scream at him before he hits that brick wall."

James shrugged his shoulders. "To some Eternals, it's the only way they can learn. When he has dealt with Saavatha's justice, he'll straighten out, you'll see."

Gabriel felt his stomach tense. Saavatha's justice was harsh. He didn't want his child to go through what he had endured.

If only he would listen. All of this could be avoided. He's too stubborn. He felt useless. He took a deep breath and eyed James. "That's what I'm afraid of," he replied. I know he will revolt and get worse."

"He will be fine," James assured. "We all went through this, and in the end we came out OK. You can't spend your time worrying: he will advance at his own pace."

"Yeah I guess you're right. I just feel so inadequate."

"You're doing just fine. After raising a few hundred more, all of this will be old hat to you."

Gabriel laughed. "A few hundred more?" He rolled his eyes and pointed a finger from side to side. "I don't think so. Once these four are out, that's it. No more, it's too hard on my—"

"Hello, is there anybody there? Hello?"

Gabriel jumped slightly. "Did you hear something?"

James leaned over and eyed the door. "Someone is at the door I think." Gabriel frowned and looked around. "Someone at the door? At this time?" He got up and answered the door. A nervous looking individual waited impatiently on the doorstep.

"Hi, hum…sorry to bother you, especially at this time," the pale man said. "Something terrible has happened. I have to find Master James. Is he here? I was told that he might be here."

"Yes he is here." Gabriel was a little surprised. "What's going on Shawn? Come on in, please."

When Shawn saw the Master he felt immediate relief. "James, finally!" Shawn said in exasperation and walked towards the Master. "We have a major problem!"

James stood up and greeted the visitor. "We do?"

"Yes we do," Shawn replied nervously. "It's Baltaseim—he has done it again. We are officially at war."

James froze. *Saavatha's honor!* "What?"

"Saavatha is calling an emergency meeting at the Hall of Journeys."

James face went totally blank "Now?" he asked, not quite believing what he heard.

"Yes right now!" Terror showed on his pale face. "The troops are assembling already. Saavatha wants this dealt with immediately."

In the midst of all this chaos, the children heard the ruckus and gathered around Gabriel, hoping for some reassurance. On the outside they seemed calm.

We really didn't need this right now. James thought. *You can always count on Baltaseim to stir things up. He will never learn.* He looked up at Gabriel, almost panicking. "I have to go," he said. I hate to cut my visit short, but this situation has to be dealt with right away."

"Let us come with you."

"What? All of you?"

"Yes," Gabriel replied, holding James gaze, "All of us. After all it does concern us all."

He looked at Gabriel with surprise in his eyes. He shrugged his shoulders. *After all,* he mused, *Gabriel is right.* "OK, fine." James said in resignation. "But we must leave now."

"Children gather around." Gabriel said with authority. "We're going to the Hall of Journeys."

Impatiently, everyone gathered in a circle taking each other's hands. James looked at the lot and hoped that he was doing the right thing. *In these extreme circumstances, it probably won't matter anyway.* "It looks like we are ready to go. Is everyone ready?" James looked at the faces around him as each nodded in turn.

"Now bow your heads and think about where you want to go."

James lowered his head. *Saavatha, take us to the Hall of Journeys.*

A brilliant light appeared suddenly in the center of the circle. The light quickly enveloped the Eternals and they vanished.

Chapter Seven

Joshua stood in the middle of all the chaos and stared in awe. "Wow, look at all those Eternals. This place is huge. I've never been here before." Joshua was astounded.

"Yes it's big," James replied. "It looks somewhat like the Hall of Wisdom, but it's at least ten thousand times bigger."

"There has to be millions, even billions of Eternals here," Joshua said. "I didn't know the kingdom was this size."

"There are a lot of things you don't know kid." James smiled at him.

Joshua looked around. He felt odd. *Something is missing; I can't quite put my finger on it. Wait, the throne...that's what's missing!* "Where is the throne?"

"There is no throne." James explained. "This place is not to teach, but to facilitate the metamorphosis Eternals must go through in order to Journey."

Joshua stared at him with a blank look on his face. "Metamor..." he said, trying to repeat the word. Finally he gave up and looked at James with disbelief. "Say what?"

"Metamorphosis," James said, unable to restrain a chuckle, "are the changes that an Eternal goes through in order to Journey."

"Changes?" Joshua did not like the sound of that. "What kind of changes?"

"All kinds of changes," James said with a slyly. "You'll find out soon enough."

"I don't like it." Joshua was a little frightened. "That's great. Now I have something else to look forward to."

"Don't worry, you'll be fine," James reassured. "Now I have to leave you."

"You're leaving? Why?"

"I have to join the other Masters." James pointed to the platform that was in the center of the hall. "Gabriel," he said putting his hand on Gabriel's shoulder. "I'm sure that you can find your way around this place."

"Absolutely," Gabriel replied. "I've been here many times. You go ahead, I will take care of my little brats."

"I'm sure you will." James smiled warmly. "I will see you later."

Gabriel nodded as he watched James join the other masters.

James took his place at the head of the House of Qwenthrey. Facing the twelve-foot sunken emerald jewel in the center of the platform, the eleven masters waited patiently for further instructions.

The sunken ball in the center of the crystal dome started to glow. "Children of this kingdom," Saavatha began, his voice thundered over the crowd. "We face a grave situation that could overthrow the balance of good and evil. Baltaseim, my lost child, has it in his mind to undermine the progress that all of you have achieved.

It is time for battle. Baltaseim must be driven back to where he belongs. The time has come again to enslave Athraw and all of his minions. You who are the closest to me will fight this battle. Prepare yourselves children, for the transformation that will enable you to fight."

The ball pulsated brighter and discharged a vertical column of white light, hitting the center of the twelve-sided jewel. The light separated into eleven beams, hitting each master in the center of their being, transforming them into their true selves in battle armor.

In the place of James stood a muscular blond warrior: his name was Qwenthrey. The form fitting golden chest armor that he wore, contrasted well with the white of his short tunic. The sleeves and hem were embroidered with golden thread that matched his open toe sandals.

Qwenthrey stood with legs apart, and stared straight at the crowd. He leaned both hands on the jewel-adorned handle of his double-edged crystal sword that came to his midsection. The sword was called Saavatha's Despair. It had seen many battles. It's long and slender blade seemed to almost disappear when tipped on its thin edge.

This was Qwenthrey's blade. The blade's dull glow illuminated his ancestry, which was etched from edge to edge. Following the blade to the tip, the etchings glimmered to demonstrate Qwenthrey's deep lineage. In the middle of its golden hilt, two teardrop jewels were embedded.

On one side a peridot twinkled, the stone of Qwenthrey's house. The transparent yellowish-green properties flashed when the light hit its surface. A sardonyx was set into the other side of the sword, Master James' stone. Its milk white stripes contrasted against the fire-red surface on the jewel, giving it a candy quality.

A crystal clear grip held the pommel sphere in place. Saavatha's energy swirled within. The light blue clouds swirled slowly and lightning struck within, moving toward the surface of the sphere. At the equator, the Twelve Stones of Life representing the twelve houses were embedded. Saavatha's energy reflected through the equally spaced gems, giving them a twinkle of their own.

The garnet was the first stone laid in the sphere. It represented the first house of Saavatha, the house of Merthor. Portraying the house of Symraay was an amethyst. This was followed by an aquamarine representing the house of Myrey, a diamond for the house of Thaabar followed by an emerald for the dark lord himself.

Baltaseim's jewel turned from green to black on the day of his betrayal. An alexandrite was laid for the house of Phaalor and a ruby for the house of Bartholomew. Peridot represented the house of Qwenthrey, sapphire for Bayrthraa, opal for Raphael, topaz for Piatre and a zircon finishing the cycle for the house of Zallier.

Qwenthrey's fingers roamed over the surfaces of the stones. He felt every single one. Then he touched the dark emerald. *So this is what it has come to* Qwenthrey thought sadly...*my dear brother. May Saavatha take pity on you...*

"I am the first born." Merthor declared, lifting his sword above his head. "My house supersedes all others. Children of the House of Merthor, prepare yourselves for the transformation."

Lowering his sword towards the crowd, a blanket of light shot out from it and covered the House of Merthor. Every Eternal in this house was transformed into war attire. One after the other, in the order of births, the sons of Saavatha repeated Merthor's action. Three hundred billion winged Eternals stood near the platform. Two hundred billion archers stood behind then. The remainders were foot soldiers for a grand total of eight hundred billion Eternals per house.

Gabriel went pale. He lowered his head in shame. *If I only knew. James is actually Qwenthrey himself. I had no idea. If I only knew...I would have paid him the respect that he deserves.* "Stay close to me," Gabriel said to his children. "I wouldn't want to lose any of you in this crowd."

"Founder," Joshua asked, "where did Master James go? I can't see him anymore."

"You have no idea what happened, do you?" Gabriel said. "Master James transformed into our forefather Qwenthrey.

"He did?" Joshua said in surprise. "When? I didn't see it." *Athraw's despair!* He thought. *I always miss the cool stuff.*

"Yes he did," Gabriel said.

"Cool! Master James is Qwenthrey. I like that." Joshua said, nodding in agreement with his statement.

"Don't you understand what that means? No, not cool! Don't you get it?"

"Get what?" Joshua replied.

"Get what?" Gabriel repeated with annoyance in is voice. He couldn't believe the statement that came from his son's mouth. "If James is Qwenthrey, guess who will be at the front lines organizing the troops?"

"I don't know." Joshua shrugged his shoulders. "Who?"

"Who else?" Gabriel shook his head. "James...James will be at the frontlines."

In that moment, all of Joshua's aspiration came crashing down. He could feel a faint tremor overtaking him. *Oh no! If Master James is at the front, then Master Gwen will be too! If the enemy takes them they will be sent to exile! Not cool, I have to stop this somehow.* "No, this can't be happening," he said, his voice trembling with terror. "It's not fair! What are we going to do?"

"There's nothing to do but watch and hope that James will come home once this is all over."

Meanwhile the sons of Saavatha faced the jewel and prepared to open the gateway. "In the name of Saavatha," they chant together, lifting their swords over their heads with both hands. "We the sons of the holy, command this entrance to open."

Lowering the white-hot tip of their swords, they barely touched the jewel and it energized instantly. A green column of light shot up towards the ceiling.

"Children of Saavatha," they began in unison, facing the crowd. "We are about to go to battle for the sanctity of this kingdom. Many of us will not see our families for a millennium. Our sacrifices will not be forgotten. Many eons from now our names will be chanted in remembrance of the sacrifice that each and every one of us is making this day. Our hope is that we will be worthy of your respect. We the sons of Saavatha salute you!"

"Baltaseim's army is stronger then ever," Merthor voiced passionately.

"It will take all of the courage and strength that each and every one of you can muster. Let us ask Saavatha for strength and victory."

"Let us pray." A hush fell over the crowd as they lowered their heads in prayer. "Saavatha," the army chanted. "Give us the strength to restore the balance of this kingdom. Lead us not into temptation while we do battle with your enemy. Help us forgive the trespasses that will be done against us and lead us to victory, may Saavatha be blessed." The sons of Saavatha raised their heads and stared at the crowd. "VICTORY TO SAAVATHA!" they chanted. "VICTORY TO SAAVATHA!"

You could feel the energy in the crowd. Weapons rose towards the sky, they were thirsty for blood—Baltaseim's blood. The sons of Saavatha stepped aside to give way to the winged Ethernals. Half of them went through the column of light. Each house entered in single file. The remaining winged Ethernals stayed behind to organize the troop's entrance to the battlefield. Each house representative went through the facet of the jewel that named their house. The archers followed suit, like moths to light, the sea of Eternals were drawn to the column of light from all directions.

Joshua was beside himself. He couldn't believe that Gabriel wouldn't get involved. *Master Gwen would be lost. Can't he see that? Doesn't he care? I can't let this happen, I just can't.* "Founder," Joshua asked his plotting mind racing. "Could we get closer to the platform? I can't see anything from here."

"We don't need to be any closer; we can see everything from here just fine."

"No, I can't," Joshua lied. "I can't see the armor that the sons of Saavatha are wearing from here. They look really neat; I'd like to see it up close, pleasssse!"

Gabriel sighed as he looked at his son's pleading face. *How can I refuse a face like that?* "Alright," he said smiling. "We'll get closer, but you must promise to stay close to me. Promise!"

Joshua looked at Gabriel with a deceptive gleam. "I promise," he lied. "I'll be good, you'll see."

"Don't make me regret this." He gave Joshua a stern look and took his little group closer to the platform. Squeezing through so many Eternals was not easy but he hoped that it would provide adequate distraction for his youngest son.

Joshua looked nervously around. *Good, they are not paying close attention to me. Patience Joshua, patience—you have to time this right. There's my chance, the last of the winged Ethernals is about to enter. Wait...wait...a little longer...now!* Joshua took off and ran with all of his might.

Gabriel's stomach felt like someone took a round out of him as terror set in. "Joshua," he screamed. "Get back here! What are you doing?"

Joshua quickly leaped on the winged Eternal's back moments before he crossed the green barrier.

By the Garden of Life! He's going through the gate! Gabriel thought, horrified. He bounded with all his might, slamming in vain, on top of the jewel as the gate dissipated behind the last winged Eternal.

"Oh noo! What have I done?" he sobbed in desperation. "My baby, it's all my fault. I looked away for one moment and now he is gone! Why couldn't I stop him? Why couldn't I stop him?"

Carl walked to his founder and bent down. This was the first time Carl had seen Gabriel cry. Feeling the need to comfort him, Carl kneeled down close to Gabriel. "Founder, it's OK." He put his hand on the trembling shoulders. "We'll find him, you'll see."

Gabriel sniffled a few times, trying to regain control. He lifted his chest off the cold surface and kneeled on the jewel. Wiping the tears that were running down his cheeks, he looked up and saw three little worried faces.

"Oh I'm so glad that I have you three." He wiped his tears. Gabriel took a moment to collect his thoughts.

"Let's go home." His body vibrated as exhaustion took over. "I have to think this through. Somehow I will find him...somehow." He took the hands of his remaining children and bowed his head.

"Saavatha," he said with a slight quiver remaining in his voice, "take us home." In that instant the light of the sunken ball brightened and their names started to glow. A stream of energy touched each one, and in that instant, they were gone.

Chapter Eight

The sun rose on the Kellsic plains, warming the dew on the open field. Bartholomew looked at the red sky. *Just what we need, a storm is on the way: I can feel it.* He felt a mild breeze on his face. Ignoring his damp feet, he took a deep breath and inhaled the sweet aroma of the wild flowers. *Look at all those colors. You could almost feel at peace here—if it wasn't for this damn war.*

"Bartholomew?" A winged Eternal cried out, waved his hand in a friendly gesture and moved slowly towards the leader.

He did not expect to be interrupted. "Michael, don't do that," he said, startled.

"Sorry," the dark-haired Eternal replied. "I didn't mean to sneak up on you like that. Anyway, all of the troops are accounted for."

Bartholomew took a deep breath and closed his eyes for a moment. *I don't want to be here. All that violence, must we all suffer because of him? What does he hope to accomplish? Win this war? Oh dear brother, how soon we forget.* Opening his eyes, he looked at Michael with a vacant stare. "Finally!"

"Everything is ready for you to take command."

The warrior felt an enormous burden settle over him. *All this responsibility,* he thought with dread. *I'm not ready for this. Why me? Why couldn't Merthor take this role? After all he is the first.* Bartholomew knew the answer to his question. A vote was taken and he got the job. *Saavatha, please take this away from me.*

"Alright," the tall and muscular Eternal sighed, not showing any signs of weakness. "Let's get to it. We don't have that much time."

The sound of raised voices caught his attention. He looked towards the commotion and found to his amazement two soldiers bickering. He could see that if something was not done soon, the argument would soon escalate to blows. "Excuse me! What are you two doing?" *The last thing I need is to have these two morons strengthen our enemy.* "We don't have time for this," he said glaring at them. "With all this negative energy that the two of you are expelling, you may as well be working for Baltaseim himself. He would be proud of you two. Now break it up and get back to your post."

Surprised and ashamed, they gave their leader a pitiful look before returning to their post.

Bartholomew ran his fingers through his flaming red hair. *How am I supposed to win this war with these bumbling idiots? Unbelievable!* He took a deep breath to calm his nerves. He remembered something essential when he saw Stand a few meters away. "Stand!" he bellowed above the crowd to the blond warrior. "I want those archers on the front lines now! The last thing I want is to be caught unprepared."

The broad-shouldered Eternal's nod made Bartholomew smile. *I know I can count on him. His attention to detail has always been impeccable.* He turned his attention to Michael who was still at his side. "Sorry about that. I hate babysitting. Now where were we?"

"Everybody is here and accounted for."

"Ah yes," Bartholomew sighed, rubbing his forehead. He tried to appease the nagging feeling that he had forgotten something very important. "Very good."

"Do you think he knows we're here?" Michael asked, keeping pace with Bartholomew's gigantic strides.

"Who? Baltaseim?" he asked, looking back at Michael's worried face. "Most likely."

"How much time do we have?"

"Not enough, I'm afraid," Bartholomew scoffed, feeling the pressure of command waiting to crush him. "And to make matters worse, this forsaken Cooma is holding us back. If it wasn't for the limitations it imposes, we'd have this war over and done with in no time."

"Yeah, being stuck between realms is not making things any easier. Half Eternal, half Solid. What a way to have to fight."

Bartholomew chuckled. *Eternals fighting a war with Solid's rules, can't fly, feel pain, or even experience death. Well at least the death of this temporary body. What a way to even up the odds.* He shook his head. Bartholomew couldn't understand Saavatha's logic. "Yeah, while you're up there playing flying hero," he said pointing to the sky, "I will be stuck down here in the mud, having to dance with Baltaseim's minions."

"You should have asked Saavatha for some wings!" Michael mocked in a playful tone.

"Nah, I'm needed down here. Baltaseim could pounce on us at a moment's notice. Have you got a count yet?"

"No I'm still working on it."

He tried to control his panic. A scowl appeared as he tried not to think of what could happen if Baltaseim caught them by surprise. *Baltaseim's Pride!* He felt a sharp spasm behind his aching eyes. "Get it done!" he snapped at Michael with more authority than he wished.

"I want the troops to have mounts. Once you have a number, summon as many as you need."

"You can count on me," Michael reminded him. "It will be done."

"Oh, Michael," Bartholomew said, wrinkles on his forehead becoming more prominent.

"Yes?"

Shattered Innocence

"I needed those mounts yesterday!"

"Understood," Michael nodded and resumed his duty.

As hard as he tried, Bartholomew couldn't shake the feeling that they were running out of time. He caught a glimpse of his brother in the crowd. "Qwenthrey!" he shouted over the voices around him. "I need to talk to you!"

His brother acknowledged him with a smile while signaling him to be patient. Bartholomew walked to his brother. His impatience was more than apparent to Qwenthrey. He noticed his brother's frown and he gave the last-minute instructions to his lieutenants.

"What's up?" Qwenthrey asked.

"Finally," Bartholomew said sharply. "Any news on the size of our dearest brother's army?" he asked.

"Yes," Qwenthrey replied with a solemn look on his face. "It's not good."

Another crack appeared in the fragile control he had over his fears.

"Spill it." He sighed, wishing he could be anywhere but there.

"As of the last report," Qwenthrey began. "His army is three times the size of ours."

"This is not good." Bartholomew replied looking at his brother.

Qwenthrey could see the despair in his brother's eyes. "There's a good chance he might win this one," Qwenthrey said, confirming Bartholomew's fears.

"That won't happen! I won't allow it!" Bartholomew snapped in anger. "Drain all of the animal kingdoms," he said in a last minute attempt to even the odds. "We're going to need their help."

"All of them?" Qwenthrey asked with a hint of anxiety.

"I understand your concern. I share it," Bartholomew replied. We don't have any other choice. Once they are summoned, brief them of our situation."

"Alright!"

"Oh, one more thing," Bartholomew said to his departing brother.

"Yes?"

"Make sure the troops understand the importance of direct hits," he said, gazing over his army. "The heart is the only target we should be concerned about. Anything else is a waste of time and energy, understood?"

"Crystal clear, I will get on it right away."

A couple of unsuspecting Qwellinians mounted on Scorpthian beasts rode through the chaos unaware of the events brewing under their feet. Qwenthrey looked at the strolling couple who were mounted on the giant longhaired scorpions.

"They can't see a damned thing, can they?" Qwenthrey asked.

"Not a thing," Bartholomew replied, surprised that his brother was still there. "Solids can't see this realm—you know that!"

"Yes, it never ceases to amaze me. Here we are preparing for the biggest fight this kingdom has ever seen and they are totally unaware of what is at stake."

"Well, that's the way Saavatha wants it," Bartholomew said, felling little hope. "There's no need yet to tell them that if we lose this fight, their world and all other worlds in the Solid's realm will go down Baltaseim's lane."

"I see your point; no need to push the panic button yet."

"That's the way I see it." He rubbed his temple. "One more thing..."

"Shoot."

"Make sure that the elements that you bring down here can be summoned as flying horses and unicorns. I want equal numbers of each. Anything else would be a waste of time."

"Yes sir."

An uneasy feeling overcame Bartholomew as he watched his brother attend to his orders. Looking up at the teal sky, Bartholomew couldn't stop from wondering if he would see his brother return to the kingdom. As much as he hated to admit it, if Baltaseim's luck held out, they may all be in exile this time tomorrow.

"Bartholomew?"

"Yes?" he replied, putting aside those unpleasant thoughts.

"How are things coming along here?" Zallier asked.

"About as good as expected," he told the white-haired warrior. He tried to sound more optimistic than he felt. "I just broke up a screaming match between two soldiers. They have to keep their negative emotions in check. The last thing we need is to strengthen our enemy with our inner conflicts."

Zallier raised an eyebrow. "I agree" he replied flatly, "we have enough to deal with without this kind of hassle."

"We can't fight amongst ourselves," Bartholomew said, frustrated. "To win this war we must stand united."

"I sent a couple of scouts to locate Athraw's army," Zallier replied, hoping to raise Bartholomew's morale. "They should be back in a couple of hours."

"Perfect!" Bartholomew cried out, happy to know that someone was finally using his brain. "The sooner I know where Baltaseim's army is, the better I will feel." He plucked a piece of wheat from the ground and stuck it in his mouth. "I've talked to Qwenthrey," he said. He chewed the stem, unconsciously trying to release his stress. "He's going to summon all of the flying horses and unicorns that he can."

"Good thinking!" Zallier replied with a comforting pat on Bartholomew's back. "The unicorns should do very well. Their firepower should even up the odds a tad."

"That's what I'm counting on. I would hate to spend the next millennium in exile."

"Baltaseim sure picked a fine time to force this war on us," Zallier said with a hint of disbelief.

"It's the perfect time," Bartholomew replied. "More than three quarters of our troops are away Journeying. He picked the most vulnerable time for us to be in this mess."

"The frightening thing is," Zallier added, "if I was in his place, I would have done the same thing."

"I know, so would I. That's what scares me the most." Bartholomew scanned the horizon looking for a hint, anything that would give up Baltaseim's position. Being nowhere near ready, he feared the worst. The knowledge that most of these loyal Eternals would be in exile by the end of the day, didn't sit well with him. Suddenly, he was nauseous. He recognized the stench that the wind blew in from the west. *Damn! I'm not ready.* "He's close," he said, staring to the west.

"Who?"

"Baltaseim," Bartholomew replied. "I can smell his stink!"

"By the Garden Of Life! We're nowhere near ready."

A cloak of desperation covered him. *What am I going to do? Saavatha help us in our hour of need.* "We'll have to deal with him with what we got," he said, masking as best he could the slight tremor in his voice. "Let's hope that Qwenthrey brings those damned unicorns soon!"

"Let's go tell the others to prepare for the arrival of the dark one."

Bartholomew stared in the distance and noticed the dark lining of the cumulus clouds moving in. The breeze picked up. His eyes flickered; he felt the sting of rain on his face. *Damn you,* he thought turning his head away as the slight drizzle turned into a downpour. *Where are you? One more day, all I needed was one more day. We'll all end up in exile I can feel it!* "Damn you!"

"Bartholomew, did you hear me?" Zallier asked, putting his hand on his brother's back. "We have to alert the others."

"Yes we do...let's go," he said bravely. "It's time for us to dance."

In a last gesture of hope, Bartholomew gave one more glance over the horizon before joining his brother. He walked back to his troops, painfully aware that their fate was sealed. Many Eternals would lose their freedom today...and he would most likely be the first one to go.

Chapter Nine

Upon arriving on the Kellsic plains, Baltaseim surveyed the landscape for the best plan of attack. Smiling to himself, gloating at his own brilliance he was almost giddy. *This will be an easy win. I will have to thank Saavatha personally when I take over his precious kingdom. It's his stupidity that's giving me his kingdom on a silver platter. What do you know? The old fart is losing his marbles. What do I care if he is willing to throw everything away. Fine by me, my revenge is at hand...finally! Saavatha made a grave mistake in calling this war. I will pulverize him and everything that he believes in.*

He rested his right hand on the pommel of his sword. *Soon my pretty you'll send them all in exile for me.* With a gentleness that even surprised him, he pulled the blade out of its sleeve and rested the sword across the palms of his hands, cradling it like an infant. Joy filled his eyes as he admired the object before him. His sword was the only thing that would never betray him.

He caught a glimmer of the Kellsic sun reflecting on the long black crystal blade. His eyes scanned over it and came to rest on the two onyx gargoyles that made the hilt. The gargoyles wings were stretched out towards the tip of the blade that passed between them. Their dewclaws tangled together in what seemed a deadly dance of will. The gargoyles red eyes glared at the blade that separated them. Ears flattened against their skulls, their lips snarled back as they held the blade tight with their powerful paws. The gargoyles held on tightly to two snakes. They appeared helpless as the jade reptiles wrapped around the grip.

Fangs out, the snakes seemed frozen in time, staring into the swirling black energy within a crystal ball held tightly by a raven's talon. Baltaseim took a deep breath and held his lover's gaze for a moment before returning his love to its sleeve. He caught out of the corner of his eye one of his minions trying to sneak away unnoticed.

"Fred!" Baltaseim called out. "Get over here!"

The soldier froze when he heard his name. "Yes Master, I'm coming!" Hurrying as to not anger his lord, Fred tripped and fell at Baltaseim's feet."

"Get up! You idiot!" Baltaseim screamed, exasperated by the stupidity.

"Sorry my Lord," Fred replied embarrassed. "I got a little overexcited."

A smirk came over Baltaseim's grotesque face. *A little petrified maybe. I will never know where these idiots get their brains.* "Report!"

"Hum…well…we have a small…problem," Fred replied, sweating profusely.

"A problem?" Baltaseim spat impatiently. "What now?"

Fred jumped nervously before answering. "Hum…well…you see…I kind of forgot to arm your legion Master."

"What!" Baltaseim screamed and raised his hand at him. "You idiot! I should send you in exile personally!"

"Oh, no…don't do that…I'm fixing everything as we speak," Fred cowered under his Master's menace. "You'll still be able to launch your attack on schedule."

These morons try me. Well at least everything is moving along as planned. "For your sake I hope that you are right. Fail me," Baltaseim warned with a sadistic grin, "and you will feel the full extent of my fury!"

"Oh, I understand perfectly." Fred swallowed the hard lump in his throat. "Master, I will not fail."

"Good! Now for the other business at hand."

"Yes Master, anything you'd like I can do," replied the small humpbacked underling.

"I'm counting on it. I want all the gargoyles and giant ravens you can summon."

"All of them?" Fred asked, shaking nervously.

"Are you deaf? Yes all of them." Baltaseim replied with a burning stare. "My victory must be final."

"Oh yes my lord," the minion giggled. His giggle sounded more like a coughing fit than an actual laugh. "It will be done."

The rotting dwarf scurried off to do his Master's bidding. Baltaseim sighed heavily.

I cannot underestimate Saavatha's army. They are relentless; my victory must be complete. I can taste it already, he anticipated. *Unlike the failure I suffered by their hand many eons ago…this time victory is mine!* "They won't be so cocky after spending a thousand years in exile," he scoffed.

"Master! We have something for you!"

"Must you always interrupt me?" Baltaseim's displeasure seeped through his rasping voice. "How am I supposed to think with you idiots always bothering me?"

"Forgive us Master," the minions replied, frozen by his Master's icy stare. "This time I think you'll be pleased."

"I doubt it. Well, what do you have?"

Smirking, they pulled the two scouts in front of them. "We caught them snooping around."

A boisterous laugh escaped Baltaseim and then faded. *Things are looking better every minute. Dear brother you really must be desperate. To send these two to spy on me—shame on you. Well it's time for me to teach you a lesson that you won't forget.* "Well, well, well," he said, circling the two like a stalker ready to strike. "What do we have here?"

"Scouts I think," the minion replied.

Baltaseim whipped his head around. "Oh shut up!" he screamed, his anger approaching the boiling point. "I know what they are you moron!"

"Oh...sorry," the Shadow replied, recoiling in fear. "I didn't mean to insult you...Master."

"You low lives sicken me," Baltaseim said. "How pathetic—no spine. Bring those two closer to me."

The scouts were shoved and held down as Baltaseim walked to them. "Well," he began, "it looks like you got yourselves into a nasty predicament. If I would have known that you were so eager to meet me," he mocked and brought his hand to his chest bowing fully. "I would have prepared the way. But as you can see...I wasn't expecting your company. As pleasant as it may be to find you here, I find myself wondering, why? Oh never mind...I know why! He gave them a wide grin. Tell me...which of my dearest brothers sent you."

The scouts stared silently at the dark Eternal.

"Who sent you!"

"Saavatha is with us!" they replied, lowering their heads.

He leaned closer to them. "Saavatha cannot protect you from me!" he whispered. The scouts stared into Baltaseim's sunken globes and saw the malice in his eyes, pure evil. In that instant they knew that their existence in this realm was over.

"Prepare yourself," one of the scouts shouted. "Exile awaits you."

In a fit of rage, Baltaseim pulled his black crystal sword out of its sleeve and plunged it into the scout's chest, piercing his heart.

"You first!" Baltaseim's hand shook as pure and overwhelming hatred took control over his being. "Go and prepare the way for all of Saavatha's army!"

Falling to his knees, the scout held the invading blade with his hand. "I forgive you." Unconsciousness overtook him.

Baltaseim sneered and kicked the limp body off his blade. "Fools, they're all fools. Keep your pity for yourself!" he wiped the blood off his sleeve.

He turned to the remaining scout and grabbed him by the scruff of his neck. "Tell me who sent you!" The scout stood there, staring at the demon. Baltaseim backhanded him forcefully as his anger flared one more time. "Tell me who sent you!"

The stare continued, Baltaseim's eyes seemed to bulge out of his head. In his rage the dark leader was drooling profusely on his chest and feet. Even the green puss on his open sores seemed to ooze. The scout felt a wave of nausea and he heard Baltaseim speak. "And I may spare you!"

"I have nothing to say," the scout replied as he witnessed his friend's body disappear.

Baltaseim stared at his captive. For the life of him, he couldn't understand the loyalty this fool had for Saavatha. *Fool! I gave you a chance to save your life. Now I cannot be held responsible for what happens next.* "Then you my friend," Baltaseim said while raising his sword, "just sealed your fate."

Seeing the dark blade rise above Baltaseim's head, the scout prepared himself to die when he heard a scream behind him.

"Wait!"

Baltaseim froze. Rage built within him as he stared at the fool who had the audacity of interrupting him.

"What?" He replied in mid stride. "How dare you interrupt me!"

"I'm sorry," His minion started to shake. "But I think that sending him in exile now...may be a...how could I say...a mistake?" He winced and brought his hands over his head, protecting himself from the blow that did not come.

The prince of darkness was shocked by the reaction from his loyal subject. It was not like him to countermand orders. Baltaseim eyed him with suspicion but decided that maybe he should at least listen to what he had to say. *This had better be good or you're going with him!* "What did you just say?" Baltaseim said, still holding his sword over his head.

He slowly regained his posture and continued, "well...if you exile him now, our enemy would never know what happened to them. If you sent him back with a message..."

"Yes," Baltaseim replied thoughtfully cutting his minion off in mid-sentence. "A message from me might be useful. I see where you're going with this, their morale is everything. Take it away...and they come crashing down!"

He turned and looked at the scout. "I would thank him if I were you," Baltaseim pointed out. "He just saved you from exile, for now. Prepare him to return to his people," Baltaseim snarled. He leaned close to his captive. "And you my friend," he said with his rotting face only inches from his prisoner, "tell your Masters that I am coming. Tell them to prepare themselves for exile. Here in my domain Saavatha cannot help them." He gave a sigh of disgust before waving him away. "Take him away! I cannot stand the sight of him a minute longer."

The scout could still hear Baltaseim's malicious laughter. As he was lead back to the perimeter, Athraw's laughter faded to nothingness.

A tall and slim soldier approached the dark one. "Master," Jase cried out, waving to get his attention. "The horses are here."

Baltaseim stood straight and proud. He fixed his gaze on the incoming soldier. "You did well," he said, breaking into a smile. "I will not forget."

"Thank you Master."

Don't thank me yet! He looked at him from the corner of his eye. "Did you check on Fred's progress as I asked?"

"Yes Master," he replied. "All is ready. The gargoyles and the ravens you asked for have arrived."

Keep this up my friend, Baltaseim reflected, *and you will go far in my reign...not too far however. The overly ambitious like yourself usually become a thorn in my side. I'm going to have to keep a very close eye on you.* "Perfect!" he said and grinned as best as his deformed face would allow. "Brief them all on our plan of attack. We will leave shortly before the scout has time to alert them."

"As you wish my Lord."

Baltaseim was pleased with himself. *Perfect! Everything is falling into place. Finally after all these years I will have my revenge! The army of truth doesn't stand a chance. Saavatha! Prepare to meet your doom. Soon all that is yours will be mine!* Baltaseim surveyed his army with satisfaction. There were gargoyles, ravens and soldiers as far as he could see.

Baltaseim waited with anticipation for the moment he had been lusting over since he was banished from the kingdom. Raising his hands over his head, he hollered to get his troop's attention.

"Children!"

A hush came over the crowd and they focused their attention on their leader. Baltaseim waited patiently for complete silence before he began. "Children! The time has come for us to be recognized. When this battle is said and done even Saavatha will have to take notice." In a symbolic fashion he mounted his horse with sword in hand. "Then we shall have our revenge and send all those who oppose us in exile for all eternity."

A cheer came over the crowd as he smiled to his troop. "SEND THEM INTO EXILE!" shouted one lone soldier. Many picked up the call until the whole troop was caught up a lustful yearning for revenge.

"My children," Baltaseim declared and lifted his sword over his head. "We have waited many billions of years for this moment, revenge is finally ours! It is time for us to take what is rightfully ours and teach those who oppose us a lesson that they will not forget."

He pointed his sword towards the enemy. "There is our enemy," he exclaimed. "Ride with me and make them pay for what they did to all of us!"

With his army cheering behind him, Baltaseim galloped towards his destiny.

Chapter Ten

The ground shook under their feet. Bartholomew could hear the rumbling of the behemoth that was thundering towards them full gallop.

"Here they come!" Qwenthrey cried out, sword rose towards the rainy sky.

Saavatha help us all, he thought sadly. *It begins.* "WINGED ETERNALS," Bartholomew bellowed over the clashing thunder, "YOUR TURN HAS COME FOR BATTLE!" A swarm of Eternals took flight. And once over the enemy, their arrows covered the skies. The Shadows were forced to stop and take cover.

Baltaseim looked at the incoming hail and anger rose forth.

"Get those things out of the skies now!" he ordered the gargoyles. The beasts rushed towards the winged Eternals, only to be met with a sea of arrows. Most found their marks. The winged Eternals could not deal with the sheer volume of opposition confronting them. Their bows, now useless, were dropped in favor of swords.

The gargoyles were met with a slashing force. Many lost their wings and fell on the army below. The gargoyles were frustrated. With no other weapon than the razor sharp claws on their feet and hands, they had to resort to volume if they wished to dominate the skies.

A gargoyle caught an unsuspecting Eternal by surprise. He grabbed his opponent by the throat and squeezed his windpipe closed.

The gargoyle's hate filled eyes stared at his struggling victim. "You...bastard, are mine!" he spat; revealing his white fangs.

Fernando went white. His pulse raced. He knew that soon he would lose consciousness. He tried in vain to loosen the iron grip suffocating him.

"It will be a lot easier on you if you stop struggling," said the beast ironically.

The pressure tightened. Out of options, Fernando realized that the time on this plane was over. *Saavatha,* he thought, looking at his enemy with defeat. *Forgive me.* "Do with me as you wish," he strained to say, gazing into dark eyes.

"Your wish is my command," snarled the gray beast, lips curling back. With his right hand he ripped through the Eternal's armor.

Fernando's face strained in silent agony as he felt his ribs snap one by one. An involuntary spasm went through his body. A suffocated whine escaped Fernando's trembling lips when the beast ripped out his heart with one swift jerk. "I forgive you," his eyes seemed to say as his life was ending.

In a cruel show of victory, the beast raised a bloody hand and showed his victim his still beating heart. "It was nice knowing ya," the gargoyle said and dropped him from the sky. The gargoyle took a salivating bite into the heart, and observed the body disappear moments before it touched the ground.

One hundred billion Eternals lost their freedom before they were reinforced with two billion soldiers on flying horses.

****

Meanwhile on the battlefield, the army of truth was losing precious ground, fast.

"I want another volley on my mark," Merthor bellowed to the archers. They waited anxiously, aware that the enemy was closing in on them fast. "Steady, steady, NOW!"

The enemy took cover, trying to shield themselves from the incoming hail of arrows.

"Qwenthrey!" Merthor ordered. "Line up the unicorns beside the archers!"

"Yes sir!" Qwenthrey yelled back and prepared the unicorns. "That should slow them down a bit!"

"Come on Qwenthrey! We don't have much time here! I need them now!"

"They're all yours!"

"You have all earned a place in this battle," Merthor told the animals quickly. "Make your masters proud today by making every burst count. Aim for the hearts of the wicked so that we may finally be at peace."

The beasts recoiled momentarily as the white-hot missiles were launched from the crystal horns of the unicorns. Nothing could protect Baltaseim's army as it were forced to stand ground and take the oncoming punishment.

Baltaseim caught himself watching the fireball race towards him. "Duck!" he screamed as the burst of energy whisked by him and struck a soldier on his right.

Screams of agony echoed around him. He cursed Saavatha as he desperately tried to make his way towards the front. *My minions are being slaughtered*, he thought watching helplessly. One of his favorites was struck. He was trying to pat out the white-hot cherry burning its way to his heart. His eyes rolled back and he dropped moments before he disappeared.

Saavatha's plight! I've lost a third of them. How could that be? They're cheating! His rage boiled over. *Damn you Saavatha! Damn you! Saavatha's decadence!* Baltaseim leaped just in time to avoid been crushed by a raven's carcass dropping out of the sky. *That was too close;* he thought looking at the broken body sprawled out at an odd angle. *You'll pay for this I promise you! I have to gain more ground or I will have nothing left to fight with! Here comes another one!*

He dove off his horse as another volley struck them. He fell face first into two inches of mud and looked up to find his horse gone. "I've had enough of this!" he cried out trying to stand up.

The slippery slope was unforgiving. Trying to steady himself, his feet gave out from underneath him and he fell flat on his back. He took a deep breath and wiped his face. Getting up, he managed to steady himself on the slippery clay. "This must end now! We need to overwhelm them NOW!" Baltaseim screamed in frustration, grabbing another horse.

Tired and discouraged, he prompted his horse towards the enemy at full gallop. His army followed at full speed, weaving from side to side trying to avoid falling corpses. Most of them succeeded. The gap between the armies was closing fast. Baltaseim finally leaped over the unicorns and plowed into the enemy.

Merthor was knocked down violently when Baltaseim's mount struck him in mid-stride. "Baltaseim's hide!" he said falling back.

"Saavatha help us! They're on top of us." Bartholomew screamed, afraid that his premonition was coming true.

"To your swords!" Commanded one soldier.

Pulling his sword from its sleeve, Merthor defensively studied every square foot around him. Feeling his pulse in his temples, he paced in circles looking for a scent. The downpour was making any tracking next to impossible. Merthor got a break when the wind shifted and brought with it the unmistakable smell of his enemies.

Man they stink! He thought and winced. "There's one!" he said under his breath. "Wait, not yet. Come on…a little closer my friend. Now!" He plunged his sword in the unsuspecting beast. He heard the animal whine as it fell to its knees holding the blade with both hands. Once the animal had fallen to the ground, he pulled his bloody sword out of the carcass. He swung it left, cutting another demon in half.

"Athraw's revenge! May he spit on the Garden of Life and all that belongs to it!" the demon cursed.

"Forgive me and may Saavatha take pity on you," Merthor said before finishing the demon off with a swift blow through the heart. He noticed a shimmer on his left.

"Nooo! Thomas!" he screamed in horror. Down came the blade, beheading his best friend. Staring at his friend's body, tears gently streamed down his round wet face. *Saavatha protect him; exile is a miserable place to be! Don't they ever stop?* He noticed a gargoyle run towards him. *Don't they realize that they will not win!* Merthor swung his blade up and brought it down forcefully, slicing off the beast's right arm at the shoulder. Screaming in pain the beast launched in vain for his throat with the remaining hand. With one swift blow of his sword, Merthor amputated the beast at the elbow and pierced its heart.

The battle was fierce; both sides suffered severe casualties, half of their complement was in exile and from the looks of it...there was no end in sight.

Zallier, a mighty warrior with white hair, was pounced upon by two gargoyles.

"Hey!" he said with mock insult. "Two on one! Where is your sense of fair play? Figures, No such sense. Well then take this!" He plunged his blade into the closest beast.

"One down, one more to go!" Zallier's face went blank as he felt a curious sensation through his back.

"Oh, this is good!" he said with sarcasm, looking at his bloody heart still beating in the beast's hand.

Michael's eyes hardened as he got caught a glimpse of his dying friend. "Zallier!" he screamed as his friend's body fell to the ground. *Bastard! You are next!* Michael raised his bow. A single tear trickled down his face as he took aim. "This one is for you Zallier." He whispered under his breath.

"Beast, I am Michael of Saavatha's kingdom," he cried out, winding the string tight for a forceful entry. The beast looked up and one could hear the thump of the arrow plunging deep in its chest. "Remember me!"

Falling backwards, the beast gave a last effort before becoming limp. An unholy rattle left his lungs moments before he disappeared.

Chapter Eleven

Qwenthrey gave his surroundings another passing glance. His long blond hair brushed his cheeks moments before being blown by the torrential winds. He blinked to clear his eyes from stinging rain. Drenched to the bone, he held his sword up defensively. *This is not the best time to lose a horse!* He looked at the enemy soldiers that were slowly approaching. *I need to get out of here.* Out of the corner of his right eye he saw a lone unicorn. "Ah! Salvation! Someone is looking after me."

He paused, momentarily assessing the situation before starting to run for the mare. The mud clung to his feet, slowing him down. His left foot slipped from under him and he fell flat on his face.

His head hit a boulder with a loud crack. Almost knocked out, he cupped his head with both hands and wished that the intense headache would go away. He lifted his head, trying to focus, when he saw the shadow of a soldier behind him.

Dizzy and confused, he rolled on his back to face the enemy. He could just make out the features of the soldier who was ready to impale him. With his sword raised above his head, the soldier aimed for a fatal blow. Qwenthrey's mind was racing. *I'm not going into exile; not like this.* His right hand searched for his sword that was nearly out reach. Straining to grip the handle, he stared into the dark and cold eyes of his enemy.

With a sadistic laugh, the soldier plunged his sword through Qwenthrey's chest. A gurgling scream echoed in his ears as the blade passed through him—missing his heart. Its handle rested on his chest and the mud swallowed the blade in earnest.

Stunned and furious at himself for being so careless, the soldier tried to pull his blade from his victim. But like a jealous lover, the mud was not willing to let go.

The soldier went for his blade. Qwenthrey finally was able to get a good grip on his sword and plunged his blade through his enemy's heart. The soldier looked at Qwenthrey with rounded eyes as he fell over.

Now look at you! Qwenthrey tried to sit up. *You are pinned in this mud like an insect in a display case. I've got to get out of here before more of them show up.* He tried to sit up once more. His screams of agony thundered through the storm as the blade twisted oddly in his chest. Exhausted, he laid back down and felt for the blade. *Athraw's demise! It won't budge. I've got no choice. I have to pull this cursed thing out.* He gritted his teeth and pulled upwards with all his remaining strength.

The intense pain took his breath away. Three of his ribs snapped. The handle was lodged tightly in his ribcage and the blade was extracted slowly. *I can't pass out.* He gritted his teeth and sweat poured over his face. "Come on Qwenthrey!" he grunted. He winced as the pain reached a new level. "It's just about out."

An ear-piercing cry left his lungs as the mud finally gave up her prize. He fell over on his side. *It's free! I can't believe it.* With one last effort, he got up and stumbled towards a unicorn.

"One more step Qwenthrey and we're home free!" he muttered to himself always keeping his eyes on his goal. The stocky Eternal jumped onto the unicorn with the blade still protruding from his back.

"Hey! What do you think you're doing?" The unicorn was surprised by the sudden weight.

"Straddling your back," he replied, looking around nervously. "What do you think I'm doing, horsy?"

Her nose flared in anger. "I am not a horse!" the unicorn scoffed. "Horses are useless! Unicorns serve a greater purpose."

"Whatever." Qwenthrey leaned forward and held on to the unicorn's neck for dear life. Qwenthrey winced. The pain was becoming unbearable.

The unicorn rolled her head back, trying to get a good look at the intruder on her haunches. "Whatever!" she cried out in disbelief.

"What do you mean whatever? To top it off you didn't ask permission to ride on my back!"

The pain took his breath away as he straightened up. "Now is not the time to discuss this!" Qwenthrey replied, wincing as he pulled the sword out of his chest.

"Wrong!" the unicorn said stubbornly. "Now is the perfect time! You ask now or I will throw you back to those unhappy soldiers that are following us!"

He wiped the bloody sword on his sleeve. Qwenthrey swallowed his inflamed pride. "Fine, you win. I'm sorry. You are not a horse; you are a unicorn...now can I?"

"Can I what?" The animal asked, enjoying her position of power.

"I don't believe this!" he said under his breath. He took a deep breath to calm his nerves. "Could you please let me ride on your back? Please!"

"No!"

"What!" Qwenthrey cried out in disbelief.

"I don't want you to!"

"That's it!" he screamed red-faced. "I've had about enough of you! If you haven't noticed we are in the middle of a war! Stop this nonsense. That's an order!"

"Fine, fine you win grumpy! I was going to let you stay anyway."

When this is over, I'm going to have a talk with Saavatha, Qwenthrey thought. *These animals are way too emotional for me. Something has to be done.* "Now that this is settled, would you mind taking care of our friends

...if that's not asking too much? You know, the ones that are following a bit too close."

"Certainly!" she agreed joyfully. "Hold on tight! It will be a bit bumpy."

The animal reared up and turned 180 degrees. Lowering her head, she took aim and fired three shots just as the archer wound his bow and shot two or his own.

One of the bursts hit a demon in the chest and burned right through him, continuing its trajectory until it hit another in the face. Screaming in pain, the Shadow tried to pat out the fire as the energy incinerated his brain. All that was left was a gaping hole, radiating red-hot flames where his face once was.

He fell to the ground and started to convulse until a passing soldier of truth put him out of his misery.

"See!" she said taunting him with her large brown eyes. "That was easy. All you had to do was ask."

"Great," Qwenthrey replied shaking his head "a horsy philosopher."

"I wouldn't go there if I were you," the unicorn warned. She felt her pride bruise. "You might end up flat on your ass."

"So hypersensitive," he chuckled with a mocking tone. His tone turned serious. "Thanks for saving my butt back there. For a moment I thought that I was...."

"Don't mention it." The unicorn replied in mid sentence. "My name is Alexia. What's yours?"

"Qwenthrey," he replied looking over his shoulder.

"Qwenthrey son of Saavatha?"

"The very one."

Alexia took a deep breath. She almost gave this son of the holy back to the enemy.

"I'm sorry." If unicorns could show shame she would have being glowing.

"For what?"

"I didn't know"

"I know... I'd love to continue this chat," he said looking behind him. "But it looks like we picked up more company."

"I see them!" Alexia lowered her head as she turned and galloped toward the enemy. Her horn fully charged, glowed bright as the energy burst built within. She discharged it towards the enemy. *Athraw's despair! I missed him!* She panicked. *Oh no! His arrow... Qwenthrey!* She reared up, shielding him from the incoming missile.

Alexia cried out in agony, feeling the arrow burying itself deep in her chest. She fell on her back and Qwenthrey was thrown off his saddle.

From the ground he looked up at the fallen unicorn. Panic set in as he stood up and ran to her. "No! Alexia!" he screamed. "You stupid horse! Why did you do that?" Looking up at the archer that was preparing to take another life, his anger turned to rage when he sensed the enjoyment his opponent was experiencing.

"You!" he cried out with vengeful eyes. "You will pay for this! Your time on this plane is over! Die you bastard!" In a fit of rage he threw his sword at his enemy. With luck on his side, his blade found its mark and the soldier collapsed. He dropped to his knees and cradled her limp head, looking for any signs of life.

"Alexia," he pleaded caressing the side of her face. "Answer me! You can't go yet! You haven't had time to get even with me for calling you horsy."

There was a spark of hope when he saw her tearing eyes open.

"Alexia! You're alive!" he exclaimed with relief.

"Not for long…I'm afraid." She fought to stay conscious.

"Why did you do this?" he asked, still baffled by her actions. "You hardly know me."

"I have my reasons, Qwenthrey," she whispered. "Take care of yourself…Son of Saavatha; I will see you again."

Tears streamed down Qwenthrey's cheeks as Alexia took her last breath. He petted the bridge of her nose as if soothing a crying child and held her until she disappeared.

I will not forget you, he thought. He wiped the moisture in his eyes. Qwenthrey reminded himself that a thousand years was not an eternity. "Until then take care of yourself Alexia—the greatest Unicorn I ever had the privilege to know."

Chapter Twelve

Pinned on his back, Bartholomew could feel the raven's talons squeeze the life out of him. He took a breath, trying to overcome the pressure on his ribs. He winced while the raven cocked his head sideways at an odd angle, staring at him. Bartholomew swung his sword, missing the bird's head.

"Stop struggling!" the raven screeched. "You're only delaying the inevitable."

Bartholomew found himself wondering why he ever agreed to join this war. He longed for home. He missed his books and the tranquility that the Hall of Wisdom brought to him. *Is this the end?* An eerie calm overtook him. *Are these eyes the last thing I will see before I enter exile?* An overwhelming urge to fight surged through him. *I can't go like this. I won't! If there ever was a time when I needed your help Saavatha, now would be it.* "Never!" he stubbornly screamed at the beast holding the upper hand. "I will never give up!"

"Have it your way," the raven replied. With uncanny agility, the beast lowered his head and ripped open Bartholomew's armor with its razor-sharp beak. "If you have any last words to say to your maker, now would be the time," he said and cocked his decaying head to get an eyeful of his victim.

Well...this is it. So much for leadership, forgive me Saavatha. "That would be a little premature," Bartholomew replied, sounding more confident than he felt. "Don't you think?"

"We'll see about that!" the bird scoffed, diving for Bartholomew's heart. As hard as he tried Bartholomew knew that he wouldn't be able to keep this bird's beak at bay forever.

"OK, now I'm angry," the bird screamed, ripping the sword out of Bartholomew's hand. "No more games. We finish this now!"

The beast's wild eyes struck a chord deep within Bartholomew as he forced himself to die with his eyes open.

So much for winning this battle, at least this is over for me—no more fighting. I don't know what is worse: watching the demise of this temporary body or spending a thousand years in exile. I guess I will find out any moment now!

"Bartholomew!"

This familiar voice seemed so far away. "Hold on! I'm coming!"

He looked over and saw his brother running to his aid. *Qwenthrey! Sorry, you're too late.*

"By the Garden Of Life, don't you give up on me now!" Qwenthrey gave his brother a worried look before jumping on the raven's back.

"Hey! Get off me!" the bird shrieked.

"Sorry to spoil your plans," Qwenthrey replied, steadying himself on the excited bird. "But my brother isn't going anywhere!"

Finally getting a good grip, Qwenthrey plunged his sword through the raven's rotten carcass and pierced its darkened heart. The animal screeched, whipping his head up in pain.

"I'm free!" The words came to him despite himself. Bartholomew watched helplessly the animal whip his brother around like a rag doll.

Hold on a little longer Qwenthrey. This damned bird will run out of steam soon...I hope! He held on for dear life.

In a last act of defiance, the bird turned his head and tried in vain to peck the invader off. Out of energy and time, it fell on its side and catapulted Qwenthrey a few feet away. Qwenthrey waited patiently as the bird's breathing became labored and stopped altogether before retrieving his sword. He walked to his brother and helped him up to his feet.

"You'd better be more careful whom you invite to dinner," he teased and slapped him on the back, "you may end up being the meal."

Bartholomew looked at his brother and a smirk came over his face, "I thought for a moment that you would have to continue fighting without me."

"We couldn't have that now, could we?" Qwenthrey answered.

"No...that would not be a good thing."

"I didn't think so. Anyway let's walk back to the front. We have many more Eternals to send in exile dear brother."

An uncomfortable scowl washed over his tired face. *I wish that it was all over and done with. All this violence sickens me.* He eyed his brother. "Let's go and get it over and done with."

"I couldn't agree with you more." Qwenthrey said trying to lighten the mood. "No better time than the present I always say."

Bartholomew stared at his brother as they walked back to the front. *I'm grateful for what you've done for me brother. However I can't help but wonder if I'd be better off in exile—at least the fighting would be over. I'm tired, so tired of this battle and of this stink! When this is over if I ever have to smell them again it'll be too soon.* He took a deep breath and hoped that weakness would not overtake him and swallow him whole.

Chapter Thirteen

Above the clouds the battle was still going strong and the army of truth was keeping the winged demons at bay—barely. His sword up in defense, Tom-a dark-haired warrior was mounted on his trusted steed, a mighty flying horse called Saur. Having witnessed the demise of his two friends, Tom was determined to stop this menace at all cost.

"Saur don't let him get away!" His heart pounded in his chest.

"Not a chance," Saur replied with a confidence that could easily be mistaken for arrogance if you didn't know him. "He's mine." Saur dove after the gigantic bird.

His six-foot wings tight against his muscular flanks, the black horse dropped like a rock with Tom holding to his mane for dear life. *Bird, don't even try it!* He noticed his pray veer left defensively. *Give it up. You are mine!* Just as Saur was about to touch the fleeing creature, he was catapulted upwards, almost losing his passenger to the mercy of the open sky.

"Saur!" Tom cried out. Gooseflesh appeared on his neck when he noticed the sudden appearance of a gargoyle on Saur's soft underbelly.

"I can't get him off of me!" Saur screamed hysterically, kicking the gargoyle that had latched on him.

The gargoyle took the abuse with determination. He was not going to let this one get away. His face bloody and savagely beaten, he managed to give his assailant a sly grin while staring into Saur's wild and terrified eyes. "You can't get rid of me that easily," the gargoyle said.

He gurgled as he swallowed his own blood. His once white and pristine fangs were now stained with blood. "Prepare to meet your maker!" the beast declared with a cockiness that rose the fine hair in the back of Tom's neck.

He threw his head back and roared-a long and fierce roar-anticipating his kill. With a shake of his head he sunk his four-inch fangs into Saur's muscular chest.

The pain took Saur's breath away. He felt his ribs snap as the beast ripped him open. "You first!" Saur screamed with fierce determination. Defiantly he reached over and severed the beast's hand at the wrist with his powerful jaw.

An ear-piercing screech was heard. Throwing his head back suddenly, the gargoyle shook his head violently before resuming his screams. Blood was pouring from his open wound. "You'll pay for this!"

Saur spitted out the severed hand. "I won't go willingly! You want me? You've got me. Now you'll have to deal with me!"

The gargoyle felt his wound throb to the beat of his own heart. Out of his mind with pain, he clamped his razor sharp claws around Saur's flanks.

With his amputated arm wrapped tightly around Saur's neck, he plunged his remaining hand into Saur's open chest.

Saur breathed in short and rapid intervals. He felt the gargoyle rummage through his open cavity. Saur struggled against the beast's iron grip. *Saavatha, forgive me!* It was over...he realized and accepted his own fate.

"This can't be happening! No!" Tom cried out, panic creeping in his voice. In a desperate attempt to save his friend he lashed out in a frenzy. "Leave him alone!" he hollered, kicking the demon's head repeatedly.

The moist environment of Saur's chest warmed the invading hand. With surprising gentleness, the beast searched for the object of his interest.

"Where is it?" he asked out loud, "there it is....listen...it's thumping. Thump, thump, thump, thump." He glared into Saur's eyes. "Now I'm going to deal with you!" With little effort, he tore out the heart with such delicacy-for a gargoyle from Saur's chest. "Look!" the beast cried out, his glistening fangs clearly visible as he attempted his best smile. He showed Saur his beating heart before breaking into a laughter that only a gargoyle could appreciate.

Tom, hysterical at this point, was kicking the gargoyle mercilessly. Irritated, the gargoyle gave Tom a look that would freeze Baltaseim's domain.

"I've had enough of you!" He screamed, reached up and pulled the source of his irritation off his dying mount.

An expression of shock and disbelief came over Tom's face as he plunged into the open skies. *I can't watch!* He felt his heart race. *By the time I hit the ground I'm going to be but a small bloodstain on the face of this forsaken planet. Maybe I will be lucky and something will pierce my heart on the way down, sparing me the agony of been stuck in this soon to be useless body. Tom your luck has run out. Here it comes!* He closed his eyes tight and waited for the inevitable to happen.

After what seemed an eternity, confusion crept into Tom's mind. *What's going on? I haven't hit the ground yet, or did I?* With the last bit of courage he had left, he opened his eyes. To his amazement, he found himself floating about two feet above the ground.

"Looks like I came to your rescue just in time," Tom heard as sweat poured off his brow. Looking up he chuckled in disbelief.

"You're the sweetest thing I ever laid eyes on!" he cried out.

"Thanks, it's nice to know that I'm appreciated."

"You have no idea. I'm Tom. I would shake your hand right about now, but as you can see I'm in a bit of a predicament."

"You don't say?" The winged Eternal said smiling. "Maybe you should ask Saavatha for some wings?"

"Believe me, after today, I'm giving it serious consideration."

"Maybe we should find you another mount. What do you think?"

"I'm all for it..." Tom replied, looking up at his rescuer. "...unless of course, you are willing to carry me by the scruff of the neck like this for the remainder of this war."

"Not likely."

"I didn't think so," he sighed. "Another mount sounds good right about now. If we stay here any longer, I will be soaked!"

"Well," we couldn't have that!" The Eternal replied with a hint of amusement. His wings flapped forcefully against the wind. As they gained altitude, Tom was assaulted by gusting winds, which blew the downpour sideways. *I wouldn't want to be on the ground right now. It must be horrible down there.*

Suddenly, the winds brought a familiar stench. *We are getting close to the battle,* he thought. *They could never take anyone by surprise. Their smell would give them away.* The Eternal's heart pounded heavy in his chest when he noticed a cream-colored flying horse nearby. "I found you a ride!" he announced.

"I see it!"

"Her name is Sonia," the Eternal said, looking down at him with an expectant eye. "I hope that you will take better care of her."

Tom looked at him with rounded eyes. *What does he mean by that?* "Hey! That's not fair!" Tom protested loudly. "I can't be responsible for who those Shadows pick for a victim!"

"I know, I'm sorry, I didn't mean anything by it." The Eternal replied feeling uneasy. "It's just...you see...she's a good friend of mine. That's all."

Tom looked at him, then at Sonia. *What's going on between those two?* He thought suspiciously. *He couldn't mean...Nah, that's not allowed. Saavatha doesn't allow interspecies joining.* "I see," he replied, letting the words trail in his voice.

The expression on Tom's face made the winged Eternal nervous. "Hum," he said, trying to break the embarrassing silence. "Let me make the introduction," he said lifting Tom onto Sonia's back. "Sonia this is Tom. He's in need of a ride. I hope you don't mind."

"It's nice to see you again," Sonia answered coyly. She was thankful that her soft facial fur concealed her blush. It would have been a most embarrassing moment. "Of course I don't mind. You should know me better than that!"

"I do but I would never want you to think that I'm taking advantage of your good nature," he replied with an uneasy smile.

"I know you would never do that," she said, trying to conceal the obvious. "I appreciate the respect you're giving me."

A warm smile came over his face.

"Take good care of her," he said turning to Tom.

"You can count on me."

"Good hunting until we see each other again." The Eternal waved them goodbye and turned to fly back to the battle.

Sonia heard an object whiz by her ear, moments before the familiar thump of the penetrating arrow registered in her brain. "No! Francis!" she screamed. *This can't be happening! H*er mind raced to understand the recent events. *I've got to save him.* Her mind made up, she dove for the fallen hero.

Saavatha protect us, Tom thought as he hung on to her mane for dear life. "Sonia!" he screamed close to her ears. "He's gone! Let it go! Chasing after him won't make him come back."

"No, this can't be real. I must be dreaming! Sonia, wake up! He can't be gone!" she cried out. "He promised me! Damn you Francis you promised!"

"Sonia," Tom said. "I'm sure that he didn't mean to break his promise. We are in a battlefield."

"Don't remind me," she replied bitterly. She paused trying to focus her thoughts. "I hate losing friends—I have so few of them."

"Well, now you have me!" He gave her mane an affectionate pat. "We have a job to do. Let's get to it."

Sonia knew that Tom was right. She took solace in knowing that the last face Francis saw was hers.

"Sonia! There is an Eternal in distress."

"Yes, I see him."

"I know this may be of little comfort, but even though you could not help Francis, there's someone else who needs you. I think that Francis would have wanted that."

"I know." She knew that Tom was right. Taking a deep sigh she dove to the rescue of an Eternal who had taken on more than he could handle.

Tom noticed that Sonia was closer to the raven than he thought. "Good girl. I knew you'd do the right thing."

Sonia ignored Tom's last comment as she approached the raven.

"Sonia, whip around his back. I will take the wind out of his wings."

Tom waited patiently. Sonia circled the beast, anticipating the right moment to approach.

A little closer…closer…perfect! With a wide arc of his sword Tom severed the beast's left wing at its base.

The raven, too focused on his prey, failed to notice the company that was approaching until he felt the sting of Tom's blade.

The beast screeched, unable to stop his wing from falling away from him. With only one to support him, he dropped out of the sky like a stone, taking with him his intended victim.

"Sonia!" Tom screamed.

She knew what had to be done. She brought her wings tight to her slender body and dove headfirst after the beast that was coming closer to the ground. Like an eagle after its prey she caught up to the raven.

"Sonia, get closer to his legs!" Tom screamed over the deafening sound of the wind swirling wildly around him.

With one flap of her wings she got as close as she dared to be…too close and it could spell disaster.

"Hold it right there!" With both hands on his sword he severed the talon that was gripping his friend. The beast, screeched in pain and knocked the blade out of his hands. Tom helplessly witnessed his blade tumble to the ground below.

Now free, the winged Eternal shook the severed talon off his waist and stretched his wings to stop his spiraling decent.

He watched the predator hit the ground below, thankful that someone was watching over him. "Thank you. For a moment I thought that I was gone," the winged Eternal said smiling.

"It's been a pleasure," Tom replied.

"I am forever in your debt."

"You are a valiant soldier my friend," Tom said proudly. "Now go. There is still much to be done."

With a nod the Eternal retreated and returned to the battle.

"You did very well Sonia. Francis would be proud," Tom said, caressing her white mane.

Sonia felt pride and joy for what she had accomplished. "I think you are right. I did well. We did well together."

Tom smiled inwardly; he was proud of her. "Yes we did."

"Now if you're going to save Saavatha's kingdom single-handedly, we need to find your sword don't you think?"

"I couldn't agree with you more! Let's go find it."

Remembering the general area where she had seen the blade fall, Sonia hurried and circled above hoping to locate it from the air. She saw something shiny on the ground and turned to investigate.

"There it is!" she told him excitedly.

"I see it!" He smiled from ear to ear when he recognized the glimmer.

Stroking Sonia's mane excitately he whispered, "Let's go down and pick it up."

Sonia extended her wings fully, gliding to a slow descent. "Hang on, it's going to be a bit bumpy."

Tom felt the vibrating rumble of Sonia's full weight as she finally made contact with the grassy plain. She slowed to a full stop and stretched her wings a few of times before closing them tight to her flank.

"We're here!" Sonia cried out.

"Great! You keep a look out for uninvited guests while I go fetch my sword."

"I can do that. Don't take too long," she replied, looking around nervously. "I'm a sitting duck over here."

He looked around nervously. "I will make it quick." He didn't like being this vulnerable. "Don't go anywhere."

Tom hurried to his sword. As he picked it up, he heard a scream.

"Tom!"

He whipped around and saw Sonia surrounded by a number of enemy soldiers.

"Sonia! I'm coming! Leave her alone!" he yelled out, running as fast as his stride would allow. Lassoed around her neck by four soldiers, she was flapping her majestic wings wildly trying in vain to pick up some altitude.

"You bastards—if I wasn't tied down I'd show you a thing or two!" Sonia yelled at them and struggled wildly.

"I'm sure you would my pretty," the soldier replied grinning, his infested boils bursting under the strain on his rotting skin. "That's why we're not taking any…"

The soldier arched his back, and cried out in pain as he felt the sting of a blade through his ribs.

"I said leave her alone!" Tom insisted and twisted the knife into the soldier's rotten carcass.

Falling on his knees, the soldier dropped the rope before falling flat on his face.

That was all that Sonia needed. She flapped her wings forcefully and lifted the remaining soldiers off the ground.

"Now you're going to pay!" she declared, circling the field with two soldiers still clinging to the rope. Thinking the better of it, they released their grip and dropped fifty feet to the ground. Stunned, Tom used that advantage to finish them off.

"Die!" he screamed, wildly impaling one through the heart. Like a cat, he pounced on the last one.

"Sonia! I've got them all. Come and get me!"

Tom waited until she landed safely before making a run for it.

"Tom! Behind you! Hurry!" she warned.

Baltaseim's Pride! Where did they all come from? Run Tom run!

"I'm coming…one more step." Tom said out loud. He felt a burning in his back.

"Nooo!" Sonia shrieked, galloping towards Tom with all of her might. When she reached him, she found him on his knees with an arrowhead protruding from his chest.

"Hold still!" She told him, "I will remove the arrow."

"Sonia, don't bother," he said, looking at her with downcast eyes. "It's through my heart. I will be dead any moment."

"Noo! You can't go! You can't leave me!" she sobbed.

"Sonia, it's not like I have a choice in this matter."

"Yes you do! I will pull this arrow out of you and you'll be just fine," she said, not wanting to accept the severity.

"Sonia!" Tom screamed, forcing his gaze on her. "Face it, when this body dies I will be sent into exile. I will see you when I return to the kingdom." Reaching up he stroked the bridge of her nose tenderly. "You've been good to me. Leave me here and save yourself."

"No! I won't leave you!" She watched helplessly as Tom lost consciousness and died by her side. Fury was building inside of her of the likes to which she had never known before. With forbidden hatred, she looked up at the archer who cockily sauntered by her side.

"You!" she spat, defying the arrow pointed at her heart. "You'll pay for this!"

"Not today I'm afraid," he smirked.

Losing control of her anger, she pounced on him with unknown agility. She snapped his neck like a twig with her jaw. She maintained a grip of steel around the victim's neck and took flight, climbing higher than she had ever been. She wished that she could kill him, but she knew that only a damaged heart would do that.

I may not be able to kill you, she thought, her hatred seeping over. *But you won't hurt anyone else. Being trapped in a useless body until this war is over is worse than dying.* Dropping him, she listened with satisfaction to his fading screams as he fell to the surface. "I will see you when you return to the kingdom," she said teary-eyed, glancing down to the very spot where Tom lost his life. "I won't forget you." She observed a moment of silence before returning to the battlefield.

Chapter Fourteen

Soaked and cold, Joshua wished that he never entered this cursed place. He longed for the comfort of home, he missed his family. He blinked as a lightning bolt struck the darkened sky in the distance. He felt the strong wind as the rain belted against his skin. His blond hair was limp and stringy. He lowered his face, attempting to shield himself from the storm and bundled up as best as he could; Joshua was fully aware of the importance of his anonymity.

He had to keep his distance from any living creature if he wanted to survive. For once, he felt fortunate for his small stature. He never thought that being unnoticed would be this important.

I've never seen so much blood in my life. I thought that we couldn't die. Master Gwen lied to me! We can die...I've seen it. He could feel a lump in his throat. The memories of the recent events were still fresh in his mind. *Those horrible creatures with the long batty wings—they're viciously cruel. They stink too. This whole place stinks.*

Suddenly Joshua noticed something out of the corner of his eye. *Maybe if you're still he won't see you!* He stopped dead in his tracks. Not more the twenty feet away, a gargoyle had a winged Eternal pinned on his back.

"Prepare to meet your maker!" the child overheard the beast say with a raspy growl. Before the Eternal had time to reply, the gargoyle ripped his victim's chest open. Shivers ran through Joshua as he heard the winged Eternal's bones snap one after the other over the beating rain.

I think I'm going to be sick! Joshua felt a wave of nausea. *Saavatha! Help me! I'm sorry! I will be good from now on. Please help me. I don't want to die here.*

Convulsing violently, the Eternal was held down while the gargoyle buried his head in the open cavity. The child heard the beast slobbering as he proceeded to devour the beating heart. Joshua gasped. The gargoyle stopped and lifted his bloody head, almost as if he had heard the child's silent plea.

Joshua and the beast locked eyes. The animal's face was covered with blood. An eerie coolness raised the fine hairs on his body when he snarled. Gooseflesh rapidly covered his skin when he realized that the beast noticed him. *This is not good...not good at all!* He suddenly became aware of his uncontrollable shivering. *He's looking right at me! I've got to get out of here.* Hoping to save his skin, he bolted before the gargoyle had time to react.

Joshua's heart skipped a beat when a bolt of lightning struck only a few feet away from him. In the temporary flash of light, he perceived movement to his left.

Not again! Will this ever stop! I have to hide somewhere quick...but where? Nervously he looked around for the closest shelter. *There! That burrow on the side of this mound—that should do it.* He quickly scurried into the damp hole. In his panicked state he failed to notice that his safe haven was already occupied. He turned towards the exit, laid low and stared, mesmerized by the scene before him.

I have to find the Master before one of those get me! That was way too close for me. I hope he didn't see me. That poor Eternal... His eyes took on a distant look. *Gross, I can't watch this.* He looked away as a gargoyle beheaded a winged Eternal with his bare claws. *I hate this war. I don't understand why Saavatha doesn't just end it...*

A kurthious-a large lizard-like creature with short fur-dashed out of her burrow and passed through the unsuspecting child. He screamed and, jumping back, hit the tunnel wall with his head knocking himself out. When Joshua awoke, all was quiet outside the burrow.

He reached for the throbbing at the back of his head and rubbed a large protruding goose egg. Turning around nervously to confirm his suspicions, he gasped when he saw the kurthious nursing her litter of young. *That thing! It ran right through me. How is that possible? By the Garden of Life! It's coming this way!* He raised his arms to shield his face and felt a curious sensation when the animal passed through him on her way out to search for food.

I felt that! I felt her! She can't see me! How's that possible? She thinks that she's alone in this hole. She obviously can't touch me. This is getting a little creepy. What's going on? Her head came through his chest. The kurthious had returned with some tharths-glowing worms-to feed her young.

"This is too weird," he whispered, intrigued by the tharths' blue hue reflecting on the young's faces as they devoured them whole. Joshua stayed with the kurthious and her family for a few hours. The beast seemed less frightening, even playful in its own strange way.

He stopped near the mouth of the burrow and scanned the area. *The rain has finally stopped. I should be safe now.* Slowly he exited the safety of his hideout. Getting up on his feet, he felt the painful lump on his head. *I can't believe how much this hurts. I've never hurt myself in the kingdom. The sooner I'm back home, the better I will feel.*

Nothing seemed familiar in the dark landscape. Anxiety was setting in. "You're lost now, aren't you?" he said to himself, not believing his own stupidity. "In your haste to save yourself you didn't notice where you were. Now look at you, you're as stupid as a knocking bird! Now what am I going to do?" He sighed heavily as he scanned the horizon.

Wait! Salvation, I think. That tree in the distance—I could get my bearings if I climbed high enough.

Three hours passed before he finally reached the tree's trunk. His eyes followed the enormous trunk up to the top which swayed gently in the wind, its bear branches seemed to go on forever. He sat down, took his shoes off and rubbed his sore and tender feet.

I'm exhausted. I feel like I could sleep for eternity. I don't know what's wrong. I used to walk a lot further than this in the kingdom. He sighed and looked up at the branches near the top. *It's a lot higher than I thought,* he concluded, not sure if climbing this behemoth was still a good idea. *All this rain is sure going to make it slippery.* He took a deep breath and set forth. With his shoes back on, he climbed to the highest branch that would support his weight.

Grabbing on a large branch for stability, he looked down momentarily. *Saavatha help me! It's a long ways down.* "Branch," he said, tightening his grip on the limb that was giving him stability, "you're my new best friend." A light breeze came from the west and caressed his face. He looked up at the cloud formations in the sky. *It's going to rain again...that's not good. In fact if I really think about it nothing that I've seen from this place is good.*

Joshua's face scowled suddenly as a pungent odor whisked by him. His eyes watered from the unpleasantness. *I must be close to the battlefield.* He scoured the horizon, scrutinizing every tree, hill and valley—anything that remotely resembled a battleground of any kind. "There!" he shouted with excitement. "I can see it from here. I knew this would work! Now, to find the Master." He concentrated his efforts on the frontline, the most likely place where he would be.

There's the battlefield, he thought. *Look at all these Eternals: there has to be millions of them.* "Finding the Master in this chaos won't be easy," he sighed. Suddenly the tree shook violently.

Joshua tumbled forward into nothingness. Out of pure instinct he grabbed at anything that came near him. With the ground coming towards him fast, his body jerked suddenly as he managed to grasp a branch. His heart raced as he bounced, his body suspended in mid-air. Slowly his movement slowed to a gentle sway. He looked up at the limb that was moving slightly and wondered how long this slim twig would support his weight. He swallowed hard and took a few deep breaths, trying to calm himself.

Athraw's despair! What was that? He looked down. His stomach tightened into knots when the severity of this situation dawned on him. He felt the blood drain from him. *What ever you do Josh don't fall. Hold on—here it comes again!* The tree shook again as an Eternal threw a gargoyle against the trunk.

"Give it up! You can't win against Athraw!" the gargoyle cried and leapt at the soldier, knocking him off his feet.

"Never! I will never surrender to the likes of you!"

Locked together, trying desperately to finish the other off, they rolled in the mud. The stalemate was over when the soldier managed to free himself long enough to swing his sword and chop off the beast's right arm at the elbow.

The beast let out an agonizing groan. Joshua was trembling and still swinging helplessly, halfway up the tree. The gargoyle's eyes hardened and his whine turned into a low and frightening growl. His catlike ears flattened against his head. His lips peeled back showing his opponent menacing fangs. A pool of drool was accumulating near his foot as the beast recoiled momentarily, striking towards his enemy.

An ear-shattering shriek broke the silence as a crystal blade penetrated the creature's chest. He gasped in horror as he tried to hold it in vain. His grip of steel was not enough. He could only watch in horror as the cold crystal slipped through his bloody fingers.

The soldier retrieved his sword and watched the blood drip from his blade, unaware that Joshua was watching him. However a raven circling above, was stalking him, waiting for the right moment.

Joshua looked up and noticed the bird. "Look..." Joshua started to yell, but stopped suddenly. *You idiot! You will only bring attention to yourself.* He heard the soldier's cries as the beast's talons gripped him tightly by the shoulders. With blood pouring out of his open wounds the soldier was whisked away.

"That was close!" His body shook uncontrollably; he closed his eyes as a pang of remorse washed over him. *I should have said something!* He felt his eyes moisten. *I could have saved his life but I didn't. I'm a coward...*he took a breath of resolution. *I'm alive and that's all that counts.* "Nothing you can do about it now—just calm down. Right now I have to get to the top of the damn tree."

He reached for a larger branch near him and grabbed it with uncertainty. He took a breath, fully aware that he would fall if he lost his hold. Before he could change his mind, he let go of the twig that saved his fall, hoping he had made the right choice.

The small branch swung back to its original spot. Joshua gave a sigh of relief when he climbed back to the main trunk of the large tree. He reached the top and sat down nervously in his original spot. Looking around to assure himself that there were no more surprises, he resumed his scan.

"I have to find the Master," he said, still shaking. His eyes opened wide and he went pale. "By the Garden of Life!" he yelped. *There's Athraw...Yuck! He's more repulsive than any picture I ever saw. And that stench—I can smell them from here—gross! I hope that he didn't see me.* Joshua's gaze moved from soldier to soldier, hoping to spot the Master in the sea of Eternals. "There he is!" he said triumphantly.

Joshua took a breath and held it. *That soldier of death is coming up behind the Master,* he thought. *He doesn't know Athraw's there.* "Master, behind you!" he yelled at the top of his lungs. A feeling of helplessness came over Joshua when he realized that no one could hear him.

"What am I going to do? He can't hear me. I've got to do something!" Joshua lurched forward almost losing his balance when he saw the soldier raise his sword ready to strike. "Master, look out!" he screamed louder, desperately trying to be heard. *That unicorn*, he thought, noticing her amongst the crowd. *She sees the danger. Please Saavatha, I beg of you. Help her to save the Master.* Joshua's face paled when he realized that the unicorn wasn't going to arrive in time to save him.

"Oh no...not the Master, it can't be. Wait! He's turning around; the Master is turning around! He saw the soldier!" He let our a scream of optimism. "That'll teach him to mess with us! Saavatha is the best!" Joshua watched the soldier lurch backwards as the unicorn rammed her horn through his back. He was picked up off his feet and tossed twenty feet away.

"You go and get him girl!" His eyes followed the unicorn as she rushed the soldier and pinned him down with her front legs. "You're going to get it now. Say goodbye to this war and hello to exile!" he said as her horn glowed brightly. The fireball entered his chest and incinerated his heart.

"Saavatha's plight! I heard that from here!" Shame overcame Joshua when he suddenly realized the severity of his actions. *That must've really hurt,* he thought. *I'm sorry Saavatha. I shouldn't be cheering any Eternal's misery. Pain is pain, no matter what side you're on.*

"What's he doing?" he asked out loud, confused about Athraw's actions. *He's going after the Master! Saavatha protect the Master.* Deep down inside he knew that if Athraw got to the Master, he didn't stand a chance. Joshua's knuckles were going white as the grip around the branch tightened more than he realized.

Joshua watched helplessly as Baltaseim approached the Master. *Saavatha help us all.*

Chapter Fifteen

Baltaseim looked around, dismayed. Two-thirds of his legions were dead or dying. Tears slowly streamed down his face as rage built quickly, hiding his bruised ego. "How dare you take this victory from me!" he spat resentfully. "You started this war and when you realized that you couldn't beat me, you cheated. Saavatha I despise you!"

The confidence he previously exuded died when he realized that his once colossal legion was reduced to a few measly followers.

Those unicorns, he vibrated from anger. *If it weren't for them I would have won by now! Curse you father! You banished me to this realm and when I'm finally ruling it...you do this!* "Saavathaaaaa! I spit on you and yours! If it takes me all of eternity I will send every one of your deluded followers to exile personally, starting with your darling son Bartholomew!" Blinded by his lust for revenge he marched over to his opponent and shoved him violently knocking him off his feet. "Bastard...you are mine!"

Bartholomew saw his brother standing over him, sword in hand ready to strike. *I can't afford to lose my temper.* He stared him down. *He hasn't changed a bit...still as arrogant as ever.* "You're a sore loser dear brother!" he said, getting back up.

"I am not your brother!" Baltaseim circled him slowly with his sword raised ready to strike.

"You can't dismiss us that easily," Bartholomew smirked. "We have the same father. Sorry to disappoint you brother. But you're still part of Saavatha's hierarchy."

"Keep your wishful thinking for yourself," Baltaseim said, glaring at his brother. "I stopped being a part of your cult when Saavatha banished me, remember?"

"I remember," Bartholomew replied, following his brother's glare. "If only you'd repent Saavatha would forgive what you've done and would welcome you back with open arms."

"I was winning this war until he cheated. Now I will most likely be exiled."

"Yes you will," Bartholomew reminded him. "You put yourself in that situation!"

"Keep your lectures for those who need them."

Baltaseim was still encircling his brother. His eyes focused on him, overflowed with hatred.

"Pity," if you had listened to those lectures as you call them, you wouldn't be alone in the darkness. Tell me brother, how do you survive without bathing in Saavatha's life-giving light and feeding on his everlasting love?"

"I manage just fine!" His voice hissed with contempt.

"Really? That's not how I see it. Just look at yourself brother! From where I stand, you don't look so well. I'd say that you look like you've been dead for a few million years. And that stink!" Bartholomew fanned the smell with his hand.

"You should really consider having a bath some time soon."

Bartholomew's last comment had the desired effect. It hit Baltaseim in his most tender spot—his pride.

"You will pay for what was done to me!" His sword struck his brother's blade. "And when I'm done with you, I'm going after Saavatha myself!"

"You are welcome to try." Bartholomew replied, staring into his brother's sunken glare. "But I doubt that you'll get anywhere. Remember, Saavatha is also your creator!"

"When his entire following is in exile," Saavatha will have no other choice but to surrender to me!"

"Living in this darkness has changed you. You can keep this delusional dream of yours alive," he said, shoving his brother back. "Or you can do the sensible thing and surrender before it's too late."

"Never!" Baltaseim clenched his jaw. "That bastard will never get the satisfaction of seeing me weak and on my knees before him."

"It's too bad." Bartholomew shook his head in disbelief. "You might have learned something from his wisdom."

"Wisdom?" Baltaseim struck again. His voice was full of anger. "If he was that wise he would have surrendered his kingdom to the better leader."

"And let me guess," Bartholomew chuckled, "that would be you?"

"Don't look so surprised. I am a far better ruler than any of you."

"Why am I not surprised by that answer?" Bartholomew scoffed. "Saavatha is our creator, our father. He can run his kingdom as he sees fit. We were not created to rule but to serve the greater purpose."

"How pathetic!" he mocked. "Don't you have a will of your own or does our dearest father dictate all of your thoughts?"

"We have free will dear brother, you know that! If we did not, you would not be allowed to be so ungrateful."

"He didn't give me freedom. I took it. That's when he ousted me from his precious kingdom!"

"It amazes me that after all this time you still don't understand." Bartholomew sighed, blocking his brother's blade. "Our purpose is to grow and evolve so one day we may choose to return to Saavatha... not to become Saavatha."

"Your purpose...not mine! I refuse to be brainwashed, to become one of his automatons. Because of my views I was punished. I will always hate him for that!"

"Don't you get it? All of this hatred has made you who you are today—a pathetic Eternal with a superiority complex."

"All of this hatred," he seethed, "has made me a strong and unyielding Eternal. I am ruler of all that is Solid. I am ruler of the flesh!"

"Rotting flesh maybe. The Solid's realm was created to help us evolve. Not for your personal playground."

Baltaseim started to laugh. "Saavatha should have thought about that before he exiled me here."

Baltaseim was about to strike again when suddenly he sensed something out of the ordinary. Someone was not supposed to be here. "Joshua!" he cried under his breath. "He's here!" He could not believe his luck.

"What?" Bartholomew replied, confused. "Joshua?"

Baltaseim enjoyed the effect that Joshua's name had on his brother. "Yes Joshua is here."

"What! It can't be! I left him at the Hall of Journeys."

"Well, it seems that he made his way here, and to top it off," Baltaseim said, breaking into a hysterical laugh. "He's here to save you!"

Bartholomew's heart sank. This was the last place that he wanted to see Joshua.

"Oh no! Joshua what have you done?" Bartholomew said. Suddenly, a morbid thought came to him as he studied his brother's gleaming face. *He's going after Joshua; I've got to save him, somehow.* "Leave him alone! He has nothing to do with this war."

A wide grin came over Baltaseim's decaying face. He could not hide the pleasure he felt. Seeing his brother in such distress delighted him.

"Perhaps you're right. After all he is still a child. I will let him be, I promise."

The sincerity in Baltaseim's words struck Bartholomew as odd. "Thank you," Bartholomew replied, eyeing him with distrust.

Baltaseim smiled thinly and turned his attention to one of his beasts nearby. "Beast!" he screamed. "Get that child now!" The gargoyle looked at his master and with a nod took flight in search of the child called Joshua.

Bartholomew looked at his brother wide-eyed. *I should've known. He had no intention of keeping his word.* "What are you doing? You promised not to involve him!"

"I lied," Baltaseim replied, finding the moment sweetly satisfying.

Chapter Sixteen

Joshua huddled up, trying to stay warm in his perch high above the ground. The constant assault by the northern winds made it almost impossible. With his teeth chattering and his body trembling, Joshua stared at the battlefront, mesmerized by the two Eternals who confronted each other.

I wonder what they're saying. Athraw sure seems to be upset about something. Probably because he is losing this war...I think. Something moved. It was a gargoyle flying in circles. Looking lost and out of place in the midst of the ongoing battle, the beast seemed to be looking for something. Joshua's skin was crawling. He could not take his eyes off the monster. Suddenly he realized who the beast was most likely hunting. *Athraw's despair! He saw me!* Terror flashed across his face. *Oh no, he is coming this way. You'd better find a really good place to hide before that monster gets here.*

Mud splattered high up the massive trunk when Joshua's knees struck the ground. The thirty-foot drop cracked his kneecap. Searing pain registered in his brain as he cried, holding his leg. He stared at the swelling, not understanding the pain that he felt. He had never been away from the kingdom and was not ready for the reality of becoming a Solid. Physical pain was one of the many limitations that the Solids' realm imposed on the Eternals who visited it. Summoning the last of his strength, he got up and hobbled to a hollow log a few feet away. Upon reaching the log, Joshua frowned. *This log looks too small!* No time to debate—the beast will be here any minute now. Ignoring his aching knee as best he could, he scurried inside hoping that his entrance went unnoticed.

Meanwhile high above, the gargoyle noticed a slight movement to the west and flew in to investigate. He circled above the mighty tree. He scrutinized every inch of it and surrounding area. His forehead wrinkled in confusion. *Where did he go? I thought I saw a child in this here. He's got to be around here somewhere.* Flying around the tree one more time, he opened his ten-foot wings to slow his descent. His feet sunk in twelve inches of mud before hitting solid ground.

He looked down at the quicksand he was standing into and growled, discontented. *The sooner I find this child, the better I will feel. I can't afford to disappoint the master again. It would be the death of me. There's no way that he could have fled. I would have seen him. He's got to be *hiding...but where?* His gait was hindered by the mud's suction. Tired and disgusted, he stopped momentarily to rest.

Joshua could hear the commotion outside. It started to rain again and the sound of the drops hitting the hollow log filled his ears.

The soothing music of the rain was calming the terrified child, until a pair of horrible-looking legs passed by the opening. Unable to restrain himself, he gasped aloud.

The beast stopped moving. His fine-tuned ears picked up something unusual. Turning his head slowly, he strained to hear the light shuffle that seemed out of place in the midst of all the sounds that surrounded him. He lifted his feline nose and sniffed the air, hoping to get a scent. He looked down and frowned lightly, wondering why he hadn't noticed the half-submerged log a few feet away. *I wonder?*

The gargoyle bent and put one of his powerful paws on the log to keep his balance. Squinting his catlike eyes, he bent his head and peered inside the log. Inside he found a frightened child, huddled and shivering. "Are you the child called Joshua?" he asked, his voice a deep growl.

Joshua felt faint. A monstrous face looked at him. He could see the gargoyle's warm breath rising in the cool air. *He knows who I am!* He stared into the terrifying eyes that were locked on him. *How is that possible?* "Please don't hurt me...I don't belong here."

A low growl rumbled. "Are you Joshua?" he repeated impatiently.

"Yes." Joshua trembled.

"Good," the beast said, smiling.

A bolt of lightning struck suddenly, outlining his feline features. The sight of the beast's long fangs threw Joshua into a state of shock. Never in his young life had he come so close to one of Baltaseim's creatures.

"Then my search is over," he continued flatly. "We can do this two ways: you can come willingly and no harm will come to you or I can rip this log apart to get to you. Either way is fine with me, the choice is yours."

Paralyzed by fear, Joshua's mouth opened but nothing came out. He could feel his heart beat in his ears. His quick and uneven breaths were increasing to the point where he was about to hyperventilate. "I...will go...with you...willingly," Joshua finally managed to answer between breaths. Not being able to feel his legs, he started to shuffle slowly toward the beast's salivating mouth.

The beast snarled with his lips back, trying to imitate a human grin. "A wise decision," he growled. "Now come to me and we can return to my master." When Joshua poked his head out of the log, the gargoyle picked him up and held him close to his chest.

Joshua looked up at the form that was holding him tight. *I'm going to die.* He shivered. *I know it. Why else would Athraw want to see me? He must have found out about my plan to get rid of him somehow.*

The beast craned his neck down to look at the frightened child. "Hold on tight!" Joshua could feel the wind created by the creature's batlike wings as he prepared to take flight. Joshua looked in amazement as the ground disappeared before his eyes.

"Are you going to eat me?"

"I should," he replied with a giggle, "but I won't."

"Good I would hate that," Joshua said matter-of-factly. "What is your name?"

The beast looked down at him with surprise. "I have no name," he replied, squinting his eyes with suspicion.

"You don't have a name?"

"No."

"Why not?"

A low rumble vibrated in the beast's throat from exasperation. "My master never saw it fit to give me one," he curtly replied.

"Oh. I've never seen your kind before I entered this war. What are you?"

Pleeease Athraw spare me the agony! The beast took a deep breath. "I am a gargoyle," he replied flatly. "I was created by my master to fight the Brights."

"The Brights? Who are they?"

Joshua's question caught the gargoyle off guard. *Is it possible that he doesn't know who he is?* He craned his head down, bringing his cold stare only inches from the frightened child. "You!" the beast scoffed with amusement. "Those who belong to your precious kingdom are Brights. We are Shadows."

"Because you don't live in the light?"

"Yes."

"Why is your kind so mean?"

The beast's head snapped back as he broke into an ear-piercing laugh. "Because we enjoy it!" he cried out.

Joshua could smell the repugnance of his breath. He couldn't ignore the deadly fangs lightly touching him. Only the slickness of the beast's drool protected Joshua's vulnerable skin.

"I loathe them," he said passionately. "Your kind are so self-righteous. The thought of frightening the Brights gives me insurmountable pleasure. To watch them suffer as we inflict pain on them is very satisfying. One day we will rule and when that day comes we will destroy all of your kind. For what other purpose would we be created?"

An eerie calm washed over the child. Not bothering to answer, Joshua turned his head and stared straight ahead. He could feel the breeze in his hair as he approached the battlefield. Tears welled in his eyes, as he was unsure of what the future held.

I'm sorry Founder. I should have stayed home with you. Now it's too late for me to be saved from Athraw. If I ever make it back home I will make it up to you I promise.

Chapter Seventeen

Bartholomew looked up and saw Joshua in the arms of the demon who was ready to deliver the child to the dark master. His stomach tightened at the thought of leaving this child to Baltaseim's mercy. "I will not allow you to harm that child!" With a swift strike of his blade he severed his brother's right hand at the wrist.

Baltaseim howled in agony as he watched his hand twitch on the ground near him. Blood was pumping out of his wound to the tempo of his own heartbeat. Whining from pain, he grabbed his stump trying to stop the blood flow. He glared at him and growled like one of his minions. "How dare you do this to me! YOU WILL PAY FOR THAT, I PROMISE YOU!"

Weakened, he fell to his knees. He whipped his head in the direction of his minion. "BEAST," he screamed, the pain overshadowing his words despite his best effort. "BRING THIS INSOLENT CHILD TO ME NOW!"

In a last effort to save the child, Bartholomew leaped towards Joshua's captor. "No!" A rapid blow from a gargoyle sent him flying backwards. "Baltaseim! Leave him alone. It's between you and me, remember?"

"You can't distract me from this!" Baltaseim gave his brother a conceited smile. "I've waited some time to meet my slayer."

"Slayer? What are you talking about?"

"You don't know?" Baltaseim asked, grabbing the terrified child by the collar.

"Know what?" Bartholomew's shock seemed to surprise the Dark Lord.

"You didn't tell him?" Baltaseim asked Joshua. When the child failed to respond Athraw continued. "It seems that your protégé had plans to get rid of me."

"Get rid of you? I don't understand."

"Oh I'm sure that you do not. However those who cross my path must pay the price," he said, glaring at the child mercilessly.

"Joshua, what have you done?" His tone hung heavy in his throat. Bartholomew knew it couldn't be good. Otherwise his brother would not have had so much interest in him. "Baltaseim! You can't expect a child to be held responsible for his actions!" Bartholomew yelled, struggling against the strong arms that held him back.

"I can and I will," he replied, turning his burning gaze to the child. "I can feel your terror child. It's quite nourishing actually."

"I'm sorry," Joshua managed to say, his voice resonated with fear.

"Oh you will be. Look at this brave child." he said to his brother tauntingly. "He can't even face me without shaking in his boots." He started to laugh. He found the moment sweetly amusing.

"Baltaseim, let him go," Bartholomew pleaded. "He didn't mean to break any rules."

"Perhaps…" Baltaseim smirked "but he did, and that my dearest brother, is what's important." Baltaseim eyed the frightened child through his slits. "So, you're the fool who wants to extinguish me. Many have tried…and I am still here. What makes you think you could handle such a task?"

Joshua remained silent. Unable to hold Baltaseim's fiery gaze, he stared at the ground feeling shame, fear and a deep-seeded hatred. *I've gotten myself into something that's over my head.*

Bartholomew could feel his captors relaxing their grip. Perhaps out of boredom or maybe even out of over-confidence, he didn't know which. Either way, he planned to take full advantage of the moment. Bartholomew suddenly broke free and leapt for his brother.

"Oh no you don't" Baltaseim bellowed. He moved out of the way. "This child is now mine!"

The animals quickly reestablished their grip on him and this time, they didn't let go. "Let him go! No Eternal belongs to you."

"You mean…no bright Eternals." His voice would have sounded almost pleasant if it weren't for the undertone of sarcasm. "My dear brother can you not feel the hatred coming from this so-called innocent child."

An expression of disappointment covered Bartholomew's face. Probing the child's being revealed his worst fears. Hatred is an emotion that was not allowed amongst the Brights' community. Sadness filled him. Staring at the child, tears of regret and helplessness rolled down his worried face. *Joshua what are you doing? Now my hands are tied and I can't help you.* Bartholomew stared silently, waiting for his brother to show a sign of mercy.

Baltaseim tilted his head slightly. He was enjoying the moment. His stump had all but stopped bleeding. Anger and resentment flowed through him at the sight of his dismembered hand on the ground. "You have nothing to say," he said, squinting his eyes, taunting him. "I didn't think so." A satisfied grin came over his face. "According to your rules, what hates," he spat with fury, "is mine! And I claim my prize joyfully."

Bartholomew stomped on the gargoyle's right foot with all of his strength. Startled, the beast let go momentarily. It was enough time for the soldier of truth to free himself. He turned quickly, facing the beast. "Die!"

he declared, bringing his sword swiftly to the beast's neckline beheading him.

Pulling his bloodstained blade from the body, he turned his head and stared at his evil brother. "Baltaseim let go of this child. He doesn't know what he is doing."

Baltaseim gave his surroundings a quick glance. All of his minions near him were dead or dying, no one could help him now. He clung tighter to the child as fear gripped him.

"Oh but I think he does," Baltaseim snickered nervously. "Joshua, do you hate me?"

Joshua looked at the monstrous face of his captor. An overwhelming urge to spit in the face of the monster washed over him. "YES I DO!" he screamed, his hatred consuming him. "IF I HAD MY WAY YOU WOULD NOT EXIST ANYMORE!"

Baltaseim wiped the spit with the bloodstained sleeve of his handless arm. The deformed face that was once handsome, smiled. "Good. That's real good. Maybe one day you will get you wish, but not today. Today you are invaluable to me. You will keep me safe from exile."

"I won't help you," Josh declared defiantly, struggling to get free. "As far as I am concerned you can stay in exile for eternity."

"You may not know it child, but you, my little friend, are making me stronger already."

"You're lying! Let me go! I won't help you; I would rather die!"

"Well," Baltaseim replied, smiling awkwardly at him, "you will die in a way. Your temporary body—your Cooma—will die. But you are eternal, and Eternals don't die."

"I don't believe you!"

"Suit yourself. Soon you'll find out that I'm speaking the truth."

"I won't help you!" Joshua repeated unbelievingly.

"Oh yes you will. You will protect me from my brother. If you're part of me, he would never dare exile me."

Baltaseim brought the kicking and screaming child to his rotting chest. Crossing his arms over him, like a protective shield, he forced the defenseless child through his chest. The sound of Joshua's screaming voice was suddenly muffled and he disappeared into Baltaseim's cavity. He was surprised by the sudden surge of energy that coursed through him. *His hatred is strong!* he mused. *Rarely have I encountered such dark and powerful emotions from a child.* His curiosity got the better of him. He couldn't help but to listen to the child's thoughts.

I hate you! Let me go! Help! Somebody help me! Joshua shrieked, his pleas went unheard except in Baltaseim's mind. He laughed. A lustful glow washed over him. "Yesssss!" he said, unable to resist the immense pleasure he reaped from the tortured child. "That's it," he said under his breath. "Feed it...let it simmer and grow." Looking at his brother's expression of shock, He broke out into a sinister laugh. "Now," Baltaseim said gloating, "what are you going to do? Your duty tells you to exile me, but your heart doesn't want any harm to come to the child. What will you do?"

Bartholomew's heart sank and the decision weighed heavily upon him. *I'm sorry Joshua,* he thought sadly. *I hope that one day you'll understand.* "My duty always comes first," he declared with as much authority as he could. "You should know that."

"So you would send an innocent child to exile to assure my imprisonment?"

He closed his eyes and took a deep breath. He looked at his brother and answered. "Yes."

"Don't you have a heart?" Baltaseim mocked.

"I don't have a choice. When you imprisoned this child within your being, you sealed his fate. This pains me more than you know."

"I doubt it."

Bartholomew ignored his brother's last comment. Although he was calm, he was making Baltaseim nervous. "Baltaseim, the end of your reign is near. Ask Saavatha for forgiveness before it's too late."

"I will never ask for ANYTHING FROM THAT BASTARD!" Baltaseim spat furiously.

"You send me to exile," he reminded his brother, "and you will also condemn an innocent child along with me. Can you honestly say that you will be able to forgive yourself for that?"

"What I can or cannot live with is irrelevant. I will do what I must to regain the balance of this kingdom," Bartholomew replied.

"Child," Baltaseim told the terrified youth that was listening inside him. "Listen to what that friend of yours is saying. Maybe your loyalty has been misplaced. Your so-called friend is willing to send you in exile as a sacrifice to protect the kingdom from Eternals like you and me." Baltaseim snickered. "Bartholomew, my dear brother do you take me for a fool? I know you, and this will eat at you until you become mad with regret, especially after getting so close to Joshua."

Bartholomew's face went blank. "What do you mean?"

"Oh don't play coy with me. I know who you are. Remember? I used to be one of you."

"And?"

"I know how close the two of you have become over the last few weeks. I can hear your thoughts brother, feel your pain—Saavatha's parting gift if you will."

"One you stole."

"None the less, it has come in handy from time to time. Tell me brother, which persona you go by these days, Bartholomew or Master Gwen?" His face grinned in mockery. "It's all very confusing, don't you agree? Saavatha's ways again…myself I prefer one persona…" his closed fist thumped against his chest, "Me!" He pointed an angry finger towards his brother. "How are you going to live with yourself once your dirty deed is done, humph?"

"I will manage just fine. Saavatha will understand."

"Yes I'm sure he will, but what about you? How will you handle your guilt?"

Bartholomew didn't answer; didn't have to. He knew the answer to that question. No one would keep him from his duty this day...that he knew for sure. He looked at his brother who by now had realized the finality of it all.

"We are not going to go willingly," Baltaseim declared, grabbing his sword from the ground. "I will fight you and all of Saavatha's army for our freedom." Sparks flew as Athraw lunged and the blades danced on one another. Even with broken ribs Bartholomew could easily outmaneuver a one handed swordsman.

"Baltaseim!" he pleaded. "Give it up—you can't win this."

"Never! I will never surrender to you!"

The soldier of truth took a deep breath. It hurt him to put his brother through such pain. A feeling of guilt and regret hit him. He was suddenly reminded that Baltaseim was responsible for his own actions, and he was only an extension of Saavatha's justice. "Have it your way," he said and forced the battle to end abruptly by dismembering his brother.

Baltaseim's shriek deafened his own ears. He saw his arm still holding the blade, fall to the ground. "Remember who fought for your freedom, child!" Baltaseim cried out. He watched helplessly as the menacing blade approached. The blade slipped through his ribs. The coolness of the knife, the pain took his breath away. A gasp escaped his lips and the blade pierced his darkened heart. "You may have won this battle," he spat defiantly. "But you have not won the war. Tell Saavatha to expect my return in a millennium." His rotten and deformed face contorted from pain. "I will take good care of your prodigy," Baltaseim told him breathlessly. Those were the last words that Bartholomew heard before his brother fell to his side and lost consciousness.

Bartholomew fell on his knees, grief-stricken. *It's my fault...*he thought unable to restrain the tears that were about to overflow. *I should have known Joshua would follow me here.* "Why father!" He screamed, beating the mud with his clenched fists, sobbing like an infant. "Why didn't you warn me? You should have warned meeee!"

His strong shoulders shook. He wiped his tears and stood up on weakened knees. Bartholomew took a deep breath as he collected his thoughts. *Saavatha help him. I've just sent Joshua into the depth of this abyss. Alone...with Baltaseim...forgive me.* "Farewell child..." His voice trembled with sadness. "...I pray that Saavatha protects you."

All victories come with a price. He hoped that with time he could live with the horror that his duty forced him to do. As Bartholomew turned to walk away and return to the battlefield he was reminded that even though Baltaseim was gone the war was far from over. Sending the child to exile was a heavy burden for Bartholomew to bear but victory must come to Saavatha, at any cost.

Chapter Eighteen

Baltaseim cringed when he finally awoke. He felt for his hands and was relieved when he touched them. Suddenly he was thankful to be an eternal. Even the temporary loss of his limbs disturbed him. He didn't like feeling helpless, it made him weak. *And weakness,* he thought *must be exploited or destroyed.*

Surrounded by darkness, only the coolness of the floor told him that he was lying down. Baltaseim was familiar with this stifling darkness. He had been here twice before. *That plan worked just fine, look at this Garden of Life! Home sweet home, I hate this place.*

The sound of Joshua's sob reminded him of his weakness and failed attempt at freedom. "Stop your insidious whining!" Baltaseim yelled at the child that sat a few feet away. "You make me sick. You and I are going to be here for a long time, so get over it."

"I hate you," Josh spat back. "Leave me alone!"

"Well now that this imprisonment forced our separation," Baltaseim yelled back, "I just might. After a thousand years in this stifling darkness, you'll learn to appreciate me."

"Never! Leave me alone," Joshua said, with resentment. "I hate you!"

Baltaseim got up and walked toward Joshua's voice. He stopped and looked at the place where the child should be. "That's it!" he said, insulted. "You're on your own. Maybe some time in this place by yourself will teach you some respect! I'm leaving!" With a grunt Baltaseim turned and left the boy behind, alone.

Joshua could feel his heart pound in his chest. He could hear Baltaseim's footsteps fading into nothingness. Realizing that Baltaseim was serious, he panicked. Even his company would be better than to be left alone in this darkness.

"Oh no...don't go! I didn't mean it! Come back!" he sobbed. "I don't want to be left here! Please, it's dark in here! It's so dark." Sitting cross-legged on the cool floor, his small shoulders rose and fell with the rhythm of his sobbing. Looking down, something in his mind snapped and terror took over. "Pleaaase come back...don't leave me here!" he wailed uncontrollably. His pleas fell on deaf ears.

Joshua's thoughts turned inwards while he tried to understand the seriousness of his situation. *I miss my family. I wish they were here.*

Founder, I'm sorry. I should have listened. "I want to go home! Saavatha help me!" Joshua pleaded hopelessly. Even Saavatha could not hear this child.

It had been fourteen days since Qwenthrey had been held captive by this unforgiving labyrinth. He was walking throughout the void, searching for new arrivals. With only his Inner Light to guide him, he paid close attention to his other senses. He was glad for his Inner Light—it protected him from the cloak of darkness. But it was not enough.

Suddenly his attention was captivated by a faint cry, almost a whisper in the darkness. *What was that? It almost sounds like a crying child...it can't be. No children are allowed to take part in any war.* Turning his footsteps towards the whimpering, he walked cautiously. He didn't want to run into another gargoyle—one was enough. *I must be getting closer; the whimpering is definitely louder.* Reaching his destination, he shined his Inner Light around the unidentifiable shadow sitting a few feet away. "Joshua, is that you?" Qwenthrey cried out in shock.

The beaten-looking child sat with his shoulders slumped forward, his head hanging low. He was sobbing uncontrollably. In his grief, it took a few moments to realize that someone was talking to him. The light that chased the darkness away, suddenly registered in his head. Joshua looked up and saw a familiar face. *I'm not alone?* He dared not to hope. *Somebody else is here with me?* "Master James?" he asked, unsure of this vision, standing before him. "Is that you? Master James?"

Qwenthrey stared at the child's face, mesmerized. Joshua's reddened eyes, still wet from tears, looked up at him with a hopeful expression.

"What in the Damned Hall are you doing here?" Qwenthrey asked, baffled. "You're still supposed to be in the kingdom!"

Joshua lowered his head in shame. "I know," he replied under his breath. "I made a big mistake by following Master Gwen through the Jewel and now it's too late to go back and fix it."

As hard as Qwenthrey tried, he couldn't stay mad at the young child. Looking at his tear-stained face, Qwenthrey felt sorry for him. *What a place for a child to be in. Let's hope that you've learned something from this.* "Yes you did." Qwenthrey said sternly. "However you are here now and it's too late to do anything about it. At least, you are not alone in this lightless pit." Qwenthrey concluded and picked up the child.

A faint smile came over the child's relieved face. Still shivering from his latest fright, he hugged Qwenthrey tight, not wanting to let go. "I'm glad you found me," he said, resting his head on the strong shoulder of his rescuer. His eyes took a distant look. "I thought that I was left alone, I couldn't bear it anymore."

Qwenthrey could feel the child shivering in his arms. He hugged him tighter, hoping to reassure him. *He's trembling, poor child,* he thought. *He needs to be in the light...like the rest of us.* "Let's get out of here. What do you say?"

Joshua nodded silently. Staring into the stillness he couldn't shake the uneasiness that overcame him. It reminded him of something. He stiffened suddenly when it came to him. *Baltaseim!* He thought, horrified. *This place is like being in Baltaseim! So dark, empty and full of hatred...so much hatred. He's cold and uncaring and I'm nothing like him. No matter what he says, I'm better than that...am I not?* Joshua tightened his grip around Qwenthrey's neck.

Qwenthrey was in tune with Joshua's reaction. He could feel his pain. *I wish that I could bear your pain child,* he thought with compassion. *You're too young to be going through this. How could Saavatha let this happen?* "It's OK," Qwenthrey said soothingly. "It's all over. Soon you will be amongst friends in the light."

"How many Eternals are here?" he asked numbly.

"Too many as far as I am concerned," Qwenthrey replied. "About five hundred billion I think. The numbers are always changing as more Eternals arrive."

"Does that include Athraw?"

"If he is here, then yes."

"He's here," Joshua replied. "He found me on the battlefield and...and...he absorbed me! I still can feel him. I will never forget what happened. It was horrible being stuck helpless in him. Master Gwen couldn't stop him. Why?"

"I wish I knew," he said. "I'd ask him if he were here. I don't know. He must have had a good reason."

"Anyway," Joshua continued. "After I was absorbed, the Master killed Baltaseim and we ended up here! I don't understand...why am I here? I'm not bad...Baltaseim's bad. Now I'm stuck in this darkness. I want to go home!"

Qwenthrey took a deep breath. He wished that there were an easier way to break the bad news. "I know," he said. "I want to go home too but we can't for a thousand years."

Joshua's eyes opened as wide as saucers. He pushed himself away from his protector, and looked at Qwenthrey's solemn face.

"A thousand years?" Joshua cried in disbelief. "My founder will kill me if he remembers me after all this time."

"Oh he'll remember you," Qwenthrey assured. "They'll all remember us."

A sudden wave of grief took possession of the lost child. Crying uncontrollably in Qwenthrey's arms, Joshua felt himself tire, and with heavy eyelids, he fell asleep.

Qwenthrey felt the child go limp in his arms. He looked at the exhausted child. *I'm not surprised. All of this has been pretty hard on him. What possessed him to follow Gwen through the portal, I wonder? And why did he let Baltaseim take the child? Well, I'm sure that he had a good reason. Gwen is not the one to make irrational decisions. Once Joshua is in the light, he'll feel better.* Qwenthrey's thoughts were interrupted by Joshua's stirring. "You're awake," Qwenthrey said, giving the child a warm smile.

Joshua nodded silently. It was the first time since he entered the battlefield that he felt safe enough to sleep soundly. "How long have you been here?" he asked.

"A few days..." Qwenthrey shrugged his powerful shoulders. "After the first day, every day runs into the next."

"Is this your first time here? It's my first time and I hate this place."

"No...I've been here before. And I don't much care for this place either. It still gives me nightmares."

"You have?"

"Yes I have," he sighed. All the pain and suffering he endured came flooding back. "It seems like yesterday," he recollected. He took a deep breath, trying to hold back the tears that were ready to expose his true pain. "Even after all the millions of years that have passed since, I still remember it vividly."

Joshua looked at his hero perplexed. He was almost sure he saw tears glistening on his cheeks. "I thought that only Athraw was sent here," he replied, staring at him intently.

"I wish that were true." Qwenthrey blinked his most eyes. "So many Eternals could have been spared the agony. Saavatha created this exile for Athraw, but the battle to force him here sometimes takes us with him."

"Like us."

"Yeah like us," he said with a somber chuckle.

Joshua clung to Qwenthrey. The terror he witnessed on the battlefield was still vivid in his mind. He suddenly feared for his safety. "Can he hurt us in here?" he asked out of a need for reassurance more than curiosity.

"Who?"

"Athraw."

"No."

Joshua felt a deep sigh of relief. He looked up and stared into Qwenthrey's vivid blue eyes. "There was an awful lot of blood on the battlefield." Joshua's mind recoiled as the terrifying memories came flooding back.

Qwenthrey lowered his head: he felt shame, as if he were the sole party responsible for the child's predicament. "I'm sorry that you had to see that," he said, his words feeling tight in his throat.

"I saw a lot of good Eternals die," Joshua continued, lost in his own thoughts, almost in a trance. "I thought that we couldn't die."

"We don't," Qwenthrey explained, swallowing hard. "You saw the death of their Cooma."

Joshua looked at him perplexed. "Cooma? What's that?"

He doesn't know what a Cooma is? How am I going to explain that to such a young child? "A Cooma," he began, "is an astral replica of what your physical body would be as a Solid."

"When I was hiding," Joshua said, not really paying attention to Qwenthrey's explanation, "an animal ran into me, she couldn't see me."

"That's because she was Solid," Qwenthrey explained. "You were not. Your Cooma is not a Solid, it inhabits the Solid's body but it's not a part of it."

Joshua nodded silently. He remembered the sickening feeling he felt when the animal passed through him. It was a sensation he did not care to repeat. "How did I get this Cooma? I don't remember."

Qwenthrey smiled, slightly. He could not help but admire Joshua's healthy curiosity. In many ways, Joshua reminded him of himself at his age. "When you entered the Jewel that was in the Hall of Journeys, your Cooma was created."

"That jewel created it?" he asked, more surprised than he let on.

"Yes," Qwenthrey replied. "It's one of the changes you go through before becoming a Solid."

Joshua frowned. He did not like what he heard. *This Cooma is why I'm here. Why do things have to be so complicated? Can't Saavatha see that all he does is making things more confusing? If I ever see him, I will tell him.* "I'm finding out that being an Eternal is a lot more complicated than I thought."

"Yes...more than you realize," the tall man replied. "I wish it were simpler. But the rewards you receive for the good that you do, far outweighs the struggles you must face. Like this place for instance."

"I'm going to be rewarded for being stuck in this place?" Joshua's face twisted with uncertainty.

"No," Qwenthrey explained, "you're going to be rewarded for the sacrifice you made that brought you here."

Joshua closed his eyes. A pang of remorse hit him. He looked up sadly into Qwenthrey's understanding eyes. "I didn't make any sacrifice," he replied, his voice crackling. "I just stuck my nose where it didn't belong and I ended up here."

Qwenthrey looked at the child with compassion. *We all make mistakes.* He reminded himself of his own failings. *He's being too hard on himself. Maybe this will lift his spirits.* "Look!" Qwenthrey said and pointed, hoping to change the subject. "That flicker of light in the distance...do you see it?"

Joshua turned and looked straight ahead. "Yes," he replied. *Light in this dungeon,* he thought surprised. *How can it be?* "Is that where we are going?"

A warm smile claimed Qwenthrey's face. "Yes," he replied enthusiastically. "We'll be there shortly."

Joshua stared at the speck of light in the distance. "Good," he said, relieved. "I've seen enough darkness to last me forever."

Chapter Nineteen

Qwenthrey walked towards the town's perimeter with anticipation in his steps. "Finally! We're here!" He walked past the threshold and entered the light.

Joshua looked around him in disbelief. *It's home,* he thought wide-eyed. *How could this be? The trees and the grass—it's all here. Even the skyline is the same. I don't understand.* "It's beautiful," he said stunned. "How could this be? Are we still in exile?"

"Yes," Qwenthrey replied. "Unfortunately we still are."

Joshua inhaled, taking in the sweet aromas that surrounded him. The tall grass, the blooming fruit trees, even the air smelled familiar.

This was his home. He felt safe here. He smiled despite himself. *On the other side of this creek,* he mused, looking into the distance...*is the place I use to go when I got in trouble. I wonder if it's here.* "It doesn't look like the exile I just saw," he said perplexed. "This is my home. I don't understand...how?"

"This," Qwenthrey said with a wave of his hand, indicating the surroundings, "is a replica of our home. Our real home is still in the kingdom."

"How is that possible?"

"Simple," Qwenthrey replied, transforming into Master James, "there are approximately four billion Eternals here. With our collective thoughts we managed to recreate our surroundings. We may be in exile but we don't have to live in the darkness if we band together."

"Oh I see, how do you keep the darkness out?"

"You see that blue skyline?" James asked, pointing.

Joshua looked at the skyline. He couldn't imagine how anyone could replicate such a perfect hue of blue. *Everything is here-even this never-ending blue sky.* "Yes," he replied.

"Just behind it, is a bubbled dome protecting us from the dark," James explained.

Joshua felt the need to walk. He wanted to take in every aspect of this environment. This was home to him, even if it was fake. "Can you put me down?" he asked. "I would like to walk now."

Master James put the child down on his feet. Joshua was elated. Even the gravel path felt the same. *The warmth of the soil, those tiny rocks that get in between your toes- everything is here. I could stay here forever.*

"Would you like to see my home?" James asked, interrupting the child's reverie.

"Yeah, I would," Joshua replied, giving James a warm smile. "I'm glad that you found me. I like this place. It reminds me of home."

The warmth in the child's face pleased him. For a brief instant, James could almost believe that this war was a bad dream and he was actually home. Even Joshua looked more like himself. "That's the whole point," he answered, being pulled back to reality.

"If we are going to be here for a thousand years, we may as well make it look like home."

Joshua suddenly became very quiet. *Home, I hope I still remember it when I leave this place. A thousand years is a long time.* "But it isn't home," he stated, disappointed. "I miss my home, my family and friends."

"I know…I miss them too," James replied sadly. They walked the rest of the way in silence. Caught up in his own thoughts, James wondered if he could survive in this replicated home. Almost as an afterthought, he decided that he could. It would be hard, but he would manage. *After all, a thousand years is not eternity.* His last thought did little to comfort him. Deep inside he longed to be home just as much as Joshua did. A weak smile came over his face. He could see his lodge in the distance. "Welcome to my humble home," he said, walking to the front stoop. "I know that it is not as big or as luxurious as the place I have in the kingdom but it's all I could come up with on such short notice." He opened the wooden door and waved the child inside.

What the place looked like wasn't really important to Joshua. He was happy to be out of the dark and into a place he could be comfortable in.

A scent of freshly-cut wood filled his nostrils. Taking a deep breath, he closed his eyes for a moment, enjoying the familiar smell. *How I missed it,* he thought, opening his eyes and looking around. *I never realized how much it was a part of me until it was gone.* "I like it," Joshua said. "It looks a lot like my founder's log cabin. It has three bedrooms instead of two and the woodstove is in the center of the place instead of being in the corner."

"I'm glad you like it," James replied, his smile lighting up the room. "I hope that you will feel content here."

"I love it," Joshua said, with an optimistic tone that he hadn't had since before he entered the war.

"Good, this experience must have been exhausting for you. If you wish there's a bedroom with your name on it."

Joshua hadn't realized how tired he was until James mentioned it. On the battlefield he didn't have time to think about rest: survival ruled his every thought.

"Yes, I'm tired," he yawned. "I think that I will go to bed for a while if you don't mind."

James gave Joshua a nod of understanding. *It'll do him some good to rest. Running on fear for this long is really draining.* "No go ahead," he replied. "This ordeal most likely left you exhausted. Get some rest."

Joshua was barely able to keep his eyes open. He dragged himself into one of the bedrooms and collapsed on the day bed near the window. He quickly fell into a deep slumber.

****

Joshua opened his eyes and scanned the room. He knew this room, he was sure of it. If only he could remember. His eyes, not quite in focus, could not make out the outlines around him. The sounds and smells were familiar to him. Frustrated, he felt an annoying tap on his shoulder. "What!" he shouted, turning around, looking at the classmate who tapped his shoulder.

"I heard that you entered the Damned Hall," Peter said, shifting in his seat.

Joshua looked at the dark-haired child who was sitting behind him, smiling cockily. "Yeah," he replied glaring, "so what?"

"Prove it," he snickered. "I don't believe you."

"Not now," he whispered, "the teacher will see us you idiot!"

Peter burst out giggling. "The teacher? He's in on it, you moron!"

"What?" he snapped louder than he realized. "I thought that it was supposed to be our secret!"

"Yeah right," Peter scoffed. "Anyway the story is that any one who enters the Damned Hall becomes the property of Athraw."

Joshua stood up, knocking his desk over. "I don't believe you!" he screamed, petrified at the thought. Suddenly, the room started to spin around him.

He saw his classmates point at him, laughing. One after the other, they pointed, chanted. "You belong to Athraw."

Why are they laughing? I don't belong to Athraw. Their chant was becoming louder. It was so loud that Joshua covered his ears to muffle the noise. *They're in my head! How is that possible?* The noise and the pain, was becoming unbearable for the young child. *I have to get out of here,* he thought. He ran towards the door as his classmates were trying to hold him down. Kicking and screaming, he strove to get free. *The door! I have to make it to the door!*

Suddenly, he was out. Darkness was all around him. He heard something in the distance. He knew who it was. He knew what he wanted. His legs started to run. He had to get away. *I can feel him, he's behind me! I have to run faster! Run Joshua run!* He turned his head momentarily and saw Baltaseim floating with his evil eyes trained on him. The distance between them was narrowing quickly. A surge energized Joshua and Baltaseim slowly fell behind. Joshua sighed with relief.

"You are mine!" Athraw declared, as Joshua ran into his open arms.

"Nooo!" Joshua screamed, struggling to break free. "Let me go!"

"You belong to me!" Athraw cried out, holding him tight.

"Nooo!" Joshua screamed. He felt himself go numb as he sank into the depth of Baltaseim's dark cavity. "I don't belong to you!" Suddenly, he was sitting straight up wide-awake. "Athraw wants me," he said under his breath.

He shivered and was drenched in sweat; he looked for any sign of security he could find. Reaching for his blankets, he pulled them around his small frame.

"Joshua! What's the matter?" James cried out, running into the room.

Joshua silently rocked back and forth. He was barely aware of James' presence. "Where am I?" he asked, his eyes wide with shock. "This is not my home."

James walked to the child and sat on the bedside. "Joshua," he said, taking the child in his comforting arms, "I think you had a bad dream."

"A bad dream?" Joshua replied, his mind still reeling from his nightmare.

"Yes." James caressed the child's damp face. "With everything that you went through, I'm not surprised."

Joshua felt himself being swayed, gently back and forth. Confused, Joshua asked, "With everything that I went through?"

"Yes," James replied. "We are in exile, remember?"

Suddenly, like a dam bursting open, reality came back to him. "Noo!" Joshua wailed, unable to control his grief. "I want to go home!"

"I know, I want to go home too but for now we must make the best of it." James said soothingly. "Why don't you come to the garden with me? It's a lot nicer than this bedroom and I am sure that you would enjoy some light."

Still shaking, Joshua nodded as he dried his tears. He took a deep breath and tried to regain his composure. *Maybe some light will do me some good,* he thought, sniffling. *It couldn't hurt.* He got up and leaned against the old Master, longing for a sense of security. With James' arm wrapped around the child's waist, they left the bedroom behind.

James led the child outside-sure that exposure to light would do him some good. Reaching the center of his yard, he stopped and looked down at child who was still adjusting to the light. "What do you think?" he asked proudly.

"It smells nice," Joshua replied, looking up at his smiling face. "I like how you got all those grapes lined up along the fence line."

"You like that, hey?" James' smile grew to a full-sized grin. "If you like my grapes then you'll love the fruit trees I have by the lake. Want to come and see?"

"I'd love to."

James was relieved to see the anguish in Joshua's face disappear. He led him to his favorite spot by the lake. "This is it!" James said to Joshua as he sat on the shady side of a pear tree. Joshua looked around with a gleaming eye, captivated by all the things around him. "Nice! All of this, I mean, the trees, the grass, was created by using your mind?"

James eyed Joshua over his small circular glasses. The old Master could not refrain from smiling slightly. "Yes Joshua," he admitted. "The mind is a very powerful tool when you know how to use it."

"I can't do it," Joshua replied disappointed. "I tried once to make something happen but it didn't work."

"Well first of all," James explained. "You are too young. You are not powerful enough yet."

"When am I going to be able to do these things?"

"It depends on you," James replied. "The more you learn and progress towards Saavatha the more powerful you become. We Journey to the Solid's realm for only one purpose, to grow closer to our creator. Saavatha is all-powerful. The closer we are to him the more powerful we become."

"Is this place safe from Athraw?" the child asked nervously.

"We are safe now," James replied truthfully. "This place does not however give us the same protection we had in the kingdom. Baltaseim was not allowed near our home but here he comes and goes as he pleases. This is why I have put guards at the perimeter of the dome to keep out the Shadows."

"You mean," Joshua asked, avoiding eye contact, "that Athraw could show up here?"

"If we didn't have the guards than Athraw could barge in unannounced," James explained. "We have to share this place with Baltaseim: that is what exile means. I wouldn't worry too much about that though. Athraw hates the light so he tries to avoid it at all costs."

"I am glad that you are here with me," Joshua told the Master leaning against his chest. "I would be lost without you here." His nightmare having robbed him of much needed rest, Joshua couldn't seem to keep his eyes open.

James felt the child fall asleep. *He's still exhausted. Sleep tight young one.* Leaning against the tree, James closed his eyes. *Maybe I can take this opportunity to rest as well. If Baltaseim is here, the peace we now have won't last. I'm going to need all my wits and being tired is not an option.* A moment later James joined Joshua in a deep sleep, dreaming of home.

Chapter Twenty

Tom became frantic. He gave a passing glance over the situation. His heart felt in his throat. "Get Qwenthrey now!" He cried out to Dale, a large Eternal with broad shoulders and long black hair. A warrior from Equaria, Dale's purple skin would bring a pretty penny to his enemy the Kwans. "We have a situation here!"

What now? Dale thought. *Baltaseim is back to his old self. Can't he leave us alone?* "I'm on my way," he replied, walking into the light. *I have to find the Master fast!* As Dale walked he transformed into Jobb, a mild-mannered librarian. *I will try his home first. If I'm lucky he's there.* He quickened his pace to the Master's domain. He knocked once, and proceeded inside.

"Hello is anybody home?"

Saavatha's despair!! Where could he be? I wonder if he's in the backyard. I hate to enter unannounced but this is an emergency. I'm sure he'll understand. Stepping through the patio door Jobb spotted the Master sleeping by the lake.

"There he is!" He rushed to the lake. "Master!" Jobb shook James, he panicked. "Wake up! Tom has a bad situation at the perimeter."

James' eyes opened suddenly. "What?" he cried out. He could never get used to being roused from his sleep so abruptly. It always put him in a bad mood.

"We need you at the perimeter," Jobb replied, kneeling over James. "The Shadows are here!"

"Who's at the perimeter?" James said still groggy. "The Shadows? Already?"

"Yes!" Jobb replied, exasperated. "A couple of gargoyles are hassling Tom. He needs you there."

Frustration swelled rapidly in James. He rubbed his temple, wishing that his headache would go away.

"Saavatha's honor!" he sighed. "I can always count on my dear brother to start something-so much for peaceful cohabitation." Still fighting the drowsiness that threatened to take over, he rubbed his sore eyes, trying to wake up. "Alright, give me a minute to wake up. How many are there?"

"Two...so far," Jobb explained. "But my guess is that there's probably more on the way."

"Great!" James tried to keep his moodiness under control. "I really needed this. Would you mind staying here with the child until I get back?"

"No I don't mind." Jobb replied, "I will make sure that he is OK."

"I can always count on you Jobb; you're a good friend." Rolling the child to his side gently, he got up and hurried to the perimeter.

James could see a couple of gargoyles from the edge as he transformed into the mighty warrior, Qwenthrey. From what he could see, one of them was in a heated argument with Tom, who was holding his ground. Passing through the threshold, he strode towards them.

"Go back where you came from," Qwenthrey yelled, his eyes cold and determined. "You are not welcome here."

The gargoyle turned his head towards Qwenthrey and tilted it lightly. His black eyes squinted maliciously at him. "We do not care of what you want," the beast spat back. "We are here to prepare the way."

Qwenthrey walked defiantly towards the beast. He looked into those cold and calculating eyes, leaned forward and brought his face close enough to smell the stench of his breath. "Tell your Master that he is not welcome here," Qwenthrey proclaimed. "This place has been claimed by the Brights!"

The gargoyles remained motionless.

Suddenly a booming voice echoed out of the darkness. "Qwenthrey, my dear brother, you disappoint me. I thought that you knew better than to address those lower forms of life."

The beasts retreated slowly into the abyss as their Master came out of the shadows and showed himself.

"Baltaseim!" Qwenthrey cried out with an authoritative tone in his voice.

"What do you want? Are you not satisfied with the grief that you are creating for our father? Leave us in peace."

Baltaseim could not restrain the smirk that was just below the surface.

"Oh, I intend to...brother." He stepped closer so that his sibling could distinguish his features. "I will leave, but not before you return what is mine."

Qwenthrey eyed his brother silently. He had a sneaking suspicion of what Baltaseim was after. "What do you want?" Qwenthrey snapped.

A grotesque smile came over Baltaseim, wrinkling his decaying skin. His exposed cheekbone and nasal cavity shone slightly in the presence of Qwenthrey's Inner Light. "I have lost property recently," he said stepping forward. "The rumor is that you have it. I want it back!"

Qwenthrey could smell his brother's pestilence. He wrinkled his nose involuntarily. The stench was overpowering. "What do I have that you want?"

Baltaseim leaned forward, seething with anger. "The child!" he shouted, his voice booming in Qwenthrey's ears. "I want him back! Give him to me now!"

There was a long moment of silence before Qwenthrey answered. He smiled thinly as he observed his brother. Baltaseim's anger didn't intimidate him. "No," He replied with defiance. "You can't have him! He is not mine to give."

Baltaseim's eyes narrowed to little slits. His anger escalated. He was barely able to keep his savage emotions under control. "You will give me what I want," he spat with fury, "or I will take it myself."

"You can always try," Qwenthrey warned, "I doubt that you will succeed…even in this place you have to abide by Saavatha's rules."

"His rules mean NOTHING TO ME!" He screamed back, his voice resonating like thunder.

"Perhaps," Qwenthrey replied calmly, "however you still have to respect them; it is the way of things. You cannot take a child against his will. Saavatha will not allow it."

"Oh yes," Baltaseim said. He took a step back. "Let us not forget Saavatha. Well look around brother."

He gave an exaggerated wave of his hands, pointing to nowhere in particular. "Saavatha is nowhere in sight." His demeanor hardened. "He cannot come to your rescue this time, brother. I want that child NOW!"

"NO!" Qwenthrey persisted, "Leave this place and go in peace."

****

Meanwhile in Master James' backyard, Jobb sat on the grass and watched Joshua sleep.

Look at this child, he thought. *You wouldn't be able to tell from looking at him that he was caught in the middle of it all. I feel sorry for you child. Your innocence should not have been taken away from you at this tender age. I remember the first time I went to war. I was so naïve. I've never been the same since.*

"Master James!" Joshua screamed, roused out of his sleep suddenly.

Jobb leaned close to the child. "It's OK. He'll be back soon." Joshua looked at the slim Eternal who was staring at him. "Who are you?" he asked, bewildered. "Where is the Master?"

"Well to answer your first question, they call me Jobb. I am a librarian by trade. The Master had to leave momentarily, but he should be back very soon."

"Why are you here?" Joshua asked.

"The Master asked me to keep you company until he returns."

From the look that Jobb gave him, Joshua was almost certain that the old librarian was not totally up front with him. "Where's the Master?" Joshua asked suspiciously.

Jobb's smile faded. "You shouldn't concern yourself with that," he said avoiding eye contact. "He'll be back soon."

Joshua forced Jobb's gaze. "Tell me where he is. I have to know!"

Jobb's insincerity returned. "When he returns," he said, trying to convince him, "I'm sure that he'll tell you anything you want to know."

Joshua could feel his temper reaching the boiling point. "Fine!" he replied curtly. "I will find him myself!"

"Wait!" Jobb said as the child got up to leave. "I will tell you what you want to know. He's at the perimeter."

"At the perimeter? What's going on there?"

"Oh, nothing of importance I assure you," Jobb lied. "He'll be back very soon. Why don't you sit here with me and we'll wait for him together. What do you say?"

Joshua looked over Jobb, trying to get a feel for the man. "I'd say that you're trying too hard to keep me here. I have a feeling that there's more going on than what you're telling me."

Jobb looked at the child and sighed deeply. "Alright, alright, I will tell you!" he finally conceded. "Baltaseim is at the perimeter. He thinks that we have something that belongs to him."

"Do you know what he wants?"

"No," Jobb replied shaking his head. "I don't have a clue. For all I know it could be just another excuse for him to irritate us."

"I'm going to the perimeter," Joshua said, determined.

Jobb's had a bad feeling about this. "Don't," he pleaded. "The Master told me that you should stay put. He does not want you involved."

"I'm going and you can't stop me," he said with a defiant tone.

"You want to bet?" Jobb said grabbing the child's right elbow.

"Let me go!" Joshua cried out. "You can't keep me here!"

"I can and I will," Jobb replied. "The Master told me specifically that he doesn't want you there, period."

"You are not my founder!" Joshua yelled, yanking his elbow free. "You can't tell me what to do. I'm leaving!"

"Joshua! Get back over here! You can't go!" *Just what I need—a kid on the loose,* he thought angrily. *I should have knocked him out when I had the chance.* "Joshua, you idiot!" he said, taking off after him. "You don't know what you're getting yourself into."

****

Baltaseim was losing his patience. He was vibrating with anger. "I want the child now!" he insisted. "He's mine!"

Qwenthrey raised his eyebrows nonchalantly. "Sorry to disappoint you brother," he replied calmly. "The only thing you'll find here is trouble. Move on."

Baltaseim shoved Qwenthrey back.

"Listen here you little cockroach."

With a calm and controlled motion that even surprised him, he wrapped his rotting fingers around Qwenthrey's throat and raised him off his feet.

"You want trouble?" he asked. "If I don't get what I came for, you'll get all kinds of trouble."

"Your kind of trouble is easy to deal with," Qwenthrey replied calmly, staring into his brother's sunken globes.

"Let him go!" Joshua screamed, kicking and punching Baltaseim hysterically. "Let him go! He hasn't done anything to you. Leave him alone!"

"Joshua!" Qwenthrey yelled. "Get back into the light now!" Joshua, suddenly realizing the predicament he was in, ran for the light.

A satisfied grin came over Baltaseim's face. "It seems like I found what I was looking for," he said, violently throwing his brother down. "Not so fast young one!" Baltaseim picked up Joshua by the scruff of the neck. "You are coming with me!"

"No!" he cried. "Let me go! I don't belong to you."

"Sorry kid, but what you feel for me gives me the right to ownership!" Baltaseim declared with a boasting laugh that gave his brother shivers. The Shadows vanished as quickly as they appeared.

Qwenthrey's glare gave Dale shivers. "I thought I told you to keep an eye on him. What were you thinking?"

"He got away from me." Dale felt uneasy. "I didn't think…"

"That's right…you weren't thinking," Qwenthrey interrupted furiously. He glanced back at Zallier who was at his side. Qwenthrey shook his head in disbelief.

"I'm sorry."

"Forget it! It's too late for that," Qwenthrey cried out in frustration. "What I need from you is a way to get this child back! And fast before he gets too far in this cursed darkness. I knew it! I shouldn't have left. It's my fault! By the Garden of Life, what am I going to do?"

Qwenthrey racked his brain trying to think. He couldn't in good conscience leave Joshua to be at the mercy of his brother. "I'm going after him."

"Oh no you don't!" Zallier replied. "You'll only succeed in losing yourself in this darkness if you go. We've lost enough Eternals to this pit today."

"If we went as a group," Qwenthrey suggested, "we could use our Inner Light to illuminate enough of a radius around us to see and keep the dark ones at bay."

Zallier thought it over and chewed his lower lip. "No, too risky."

"What?" he said stunned. "You expect me to leave him with this animal?"

Zallier stared back at him. "We don't have a choice," he sympathized. "Anyway he brought it on himself. You told him to stay put and he didn't listen. I'm not willing to risk losing myself in this hole for someone who should have known better."

"Baltaseim's trick! I can't believe what I'm hearing!" Qwenthrey shouted back. "He's a child. He doesn't know better." Qwenthrey looked at Zallier's unyielding eyes.

"Fine!" he replied in disgust. "You cowards can stay here if you want. As for myself, I have a long walk ahead of me. I had better get going."

Tom looked at his friend, who was getting ready to leave. "Qwenthrey!" He cried out, trying to convince him. "Don't be a fool! Stay here with us."

"Let him go," Zallier said putting a hand on his shoulder.

"Let the fool lose himself in this darkness if he wants. You can't say that we didn't warn him."

"Baltaseim's pride!" Tom cursed under his breath. He looked at Qwenthrey, then Zallier. He shook his head in disbelief and sighed.

"No I can't," he said to Zallier, not believing what he was about to do. He looked ahead at the warrior disappearing into the unknown.

"Qwenthrey!" he cried out with a sense of urgency. "Wait up! I'm coming with you."

Zallier watched the two brave Eternals walk away. "Fools!" he said, shaking his head. "They're going to put all of us in jeopardy."

Chapter Twenty-one

Tom couldn't help but notice Zallier's scowling face. He'd seen more than his fair share of it since his return. *Qwenthrey is still out there, somewhere.* He felt his stomach tighten. *By the Garden of Life! Don't give me that look,* Tom thought. *We've been through this before.* "Prepare another group of one thousand," Tom said to Zallier, who was still giving him a dirty look. "I'm going in again."

Saavatha's mercy! When is he going to learn? They are lost and will stay lost until their time is up. He's wasting his time. "It's been over two hundred years Tom," Zallier replied with an antagonistic tone. "It took you over a hundred and fifty years to return here. What makes you think that you'll find them this time?"

"If I don't find them in this excursion, I will find them in the next."

Zallier's frustration was rising every minute. They had limited supplies and he was forced to consider the possibility of abandoning any other rescue efforts. "How much more time and resources are you going to waste trying to find two Eternals?" he asked with obvious concern.

Tom found Zallier's tone insulting. "What are you saying? Are you implying that we leave them in this stifling labyrinth to rot?" He began to pace around Zallier nervously. From the look on his face, Zallier knew that Tom was about to blow a fuse. "I'm not going to stop looking until they're found!" He pointed a finger angrily at Zallier.

Zallier took a deep breath. "I understand your concerns," he replied calmly. "I share them. But you have to realize that we have more pressing problems right now. You know as well as I do that if the perimeter guards continue to disappear, soon we won't be able to protect what we worked so hard to maintain."

Tom didn't hear one word that Zallier said. His only concern was Qwenthrey's safe return. He lowered his head and waited patiently for Zallier to finish his speech. "Am I going to get my group?" he asked impatiently. "Yes or no?"

Zallier looked at Tom. *I have to give him this,* he thought with a mild sense of admiration. *He's sure dedicated.* He gritted his teeth firmly while making up his mind. *I don't believe I'm doing this. I must be crazy.* "Fine!" Zallier sighed. "I will give you the thousand you want but this is the last time! If you don't find them, we forget about it and focus on the problem at hand."

After what seemed an eternity, Tom finally relinquished. "Alright, alright!" He was none too happy about his choices. "You win. This will be the last time," he lied. "I promise."

Zallier left shaking his head while Tom rounded up his rescue party. Tom knew that the chances of finding them were slim but he had to try. This time he planned to take his team to a remote corner of the abyss. He didn't understand how he could have missed this spot on the last excursion. He had to find them soon. If Zallier is right, he may not have any Eternals left to spare when Tom returned.

****

In a far corner of the abyss, the Prince of Darkness was standing near his throne. Having turned his back on Joshua, he was trying to ignore the insults that were spewing from Joshua's mouth. Reaching his limit, Baltaseim turned abruptly towards the offending Eternal. "That's enough!" He backhanded Joshua, sending him flying down the flight of steps that lead up to the throne. "Prepare him for another feeding!" he commanded his minions with a sense of urgency.

Joshua could still feel the sting of Baltaseim's rotten hand when two gargoyles picked him up. He struggled valiantly against their powerful grips as they tied his hands and feet to chains attached to the ceiling and floor. Left suspended a couple of feet from the ground, he could only wait, forced to endure Baltaseim's cruel whims. The macabre taste that was left on his swollen lips was not one that Joshua would forget.

Baltaseim couldn't help but laugh at Joshua's predicament. "My, oh my," he gloated, approaching him. "How you've grown since I had the pleasure of offering you my hospitality. Look at you, a full grown Eternal. I find myself fortunate. I have in my possession an adult Bright. You have no idea how hard they are to come by these days. How long as it been? Two hundred years?" Baltaseim glowed. "You look about four hundred years of age. That means that you've been with me as long as with your own founder…that makes us almost kin." He grinned maliciously.

Joshua detected an arrogance in Baltaseim's voice. "You're nothing like my founder!" Joshua cried out. "I despise you!"

Baltaseim got a quick glimpse of a beast that was hovering close to his victim. "Get away from him you filthy thing!" He chased the gargoyle away. "I'm the first one to feed! Your disgusting kind can feed on the scraps I leave!"

The beast cowered and left, but not before giving him a glare that would have given anyone else shivers.

Trying to regain his composure, Baltaseim circled Joshua slowly. The tortured Eternal flinched slightly at his slimy touch. "Are you enjoying your stay?" Baltaseim mocked, letting his decomposing fingers linger on Joshua's skin.

"Die you disgusting filth!" Joshua spat.

Baltaseim stopped in front of him. He studied his pray and smiled warmly. "My, my," he said, grabbing Joshua's chin forcefully. "It looks like I'm going to have to teach you some manners."

"Piss off!" Joshua shouted, tearing his head away defiantly.

"You know," Baltaseim said, removing his right leather glove and looking smug, "if you weren't so stubborn, we wouldn't have to do this."

"I will never give in. Do you understand? Never!"

"Have it your way," he replied, not at all surprised. His face turned stone cold and he felt a violent urge to satisfy his worst craving. "Please forgive me," he said between his quick breaths of urgency. "This is going to hurt…a lot." Joshua watched for the thousandth time as Baltaseim's bony fingers entered his abdomen at the center of his black bruise, which covered most of his midsection.

Joshua's agonizing screams echoed throughout the chamber as Baltaseim's hand buried itself to his wrist. Feeling his tormentor's fingers playing with his entrails, Joshua was suddenly overtaken by nausea. Unable to restrain himself, he leaned forward and vomited violently.

"Quite a mess you've made," Baltaseim said, looking at his soiled boots. "Remind me to make you clean this up with your tongue."

"You disgust me!" Joshua replied before spitting the remaining vomit in Baltaseim's face.

He wiped his face and cleared his eyes. "You'll pay for this," he vowed.

Joshua was suddenly struck with an irresistible urge to laugh. "Couldn't be worse than what you're doing to me now," he managed to say, each word taking his breath away.

Baltaseim did not hear Joshua's last comment. He observed Joshua's dark life force travel up his arm with anticipation. Soon the dark energy was over his chest and down to the center of his being, entering at the navel. He whipped his head up, moaning lustfully, enjoying the dark matter that was quenching his thirst.

"Yesss! That's it! So much hatred in your heart…so much darkness." He cried out joyfully, delirious with lust. "Give it to me! Oh…yeah…that's it…oh yeah…feed it to me." An uncontrollable tremble consumed him as the energy absorbed built to a powerful climax. "Oh…. Yessss!" He took a moment to recuperate from the powerful feeling that coursed through him. He closed his eyes and took a deep breath. Slowly, the powerful rush faded to a manageable buzzing sensation. "Oh…that was great!" he said, still feeling the spastic pulses of his legs as he pulled his hand out of Joshua's rippling abdomen. "Was it good for you?" he mocked. He enjoyed seeing his victim hanging there powerless. Feeling his energy drained from his beaten being, Joshua fell unconscious.

****

"The perimeter has collapsed!" Barry heard over the chaotic atmosphere. "Someone must go and find Zallier!" Panic threatened to consume the only semblance of security that everyone had known since entering this dungeon. The flickering skyline had robbed the confidence of the community. With their future uncertain, the community was in desperate need of their leader. Barry raised his hand over the small group that was gathered near the perimeter. "I will get him," he said waving, hoping to get someone's attention. Through the crowd he made eye contact with a perimeter guard. "I know where he is," he said, getting an acknowledging nod from the perimeter guards.

With the whole community on edge, Barry was aware of the importance of finding Zallier quickly. Making his way through the crowd, he rushed to the place where he was sure to find him. Entering the master's library, Barry found him at a desk reading.

"Master!" Barry looked at the small and frail Eternal with albino eyes and transparent skin. "I've been looking all over the place for you. The perimeter has collapsed. We have to get everyone together. It's the only way we can survive the darkness without losing anyone."

"Baltaseim's demise!" Master Stephan cursed then closed his book. He stood and transformed into Zallier, a warrior with white hair. "Where is Tom?" he asked, frowning. "He should have been back by now!"

"I haven't heard anything."

"Alright," he said coming to a decision. "We'll have to proceed without him." He gave Barry a quick glance. "Let's go and find the others, while we still can."

"How bad is it?" Zallier asked Barry as they approached the perimeter.

Barry looked at him, but didn't reply.

This is not good. I hope that we have time to gather everyone together before the lights go out, he thought, worried. "Make sure everyone is huddled together," he said. "The last thing we need is to lose more Eternals to those damn gargoyles." Zallier looked up at the flickering sky and cursed. *Where in the Damned Hall are you Tom? From the look of this sky, we don't have much time left.* A hush fell over the one hundred thousand or so Eternals left as the sky flickered one last time and gave way to the unforgiving darkness. *Baltaseim's demise! Tom, you're on your own.* "Alright everyone!" Zallier cried out. "Don't panic, we have everything under control."

"What are we supposed to do now?" Zallier heard an Eternal ask.

"We should stay here," another Eternal said.

"Staying is not an option," the leader replied. "It's too dangerous. We're going to be moving out shortly. We have over a thousand Eternals in the abyss already. We are going to try to join up with them."

"We should stay here!" yet another Eternal said. "Out there, who knows what's going to happen. At least here we are safe from those monsters."

"No!" Zallier insisted. "We are sitting ducks here. We have to leave. Too many have been lost already. I don't want any more losses. I need you to concentrate on your Inner Light. Keep it strong. It's the only way to keep Baltaseim's minions at bay. With any luck we'll be joining Tom shortly. Remember, keep together. Move out!"

Zallier led the group of a hundred thousand strong into the jaws of darkness. Vaguely remembering Tom's last position, he counted on his strong sense of direction to lead them to where he hoped would be a place out of Baltaseim's reach.

****

A soft giggle escaped Baltaseim's lips when he saw Joshua stir. Amused, Baltaseim sauntered over with an insincere smile plastered on his face. "Oh, you're awake," he said, clamping his bony fingers around Joshua's chin, and raising his slumped head forcefully. "Good, very good."

Unable to focus, Joshua fixed his exhausted gaze on his tormentor. "Why don't you leave me alone," he pleaded with barely enough strength to speak.

Baltaseim released his grip, letting Joshua's head slump back down. "You know I can't do that," he replied flatly. "If we were out of this prison and in my realm, we wouldn't need to feed on you. We'd have the whole realm to feed on."

"You're lying," he said between breaths. "I never felt hungry, ever."

"Of course you haven't," Baltaseim replied resentfully. "You have Saavatha's light to nourish you." He paused for a moment, still feeling the sting of betrayal. "When Saavatha banished me," he went on with his tone turning to anger. "he also made it impossible for me to be nourished. Any contact with light causes sheer agony. So as you can see, there's no Solid in sight. And if I have to choose between feeding on you or my colleagues…well, I choose you."

"Master!" a soldier interrupted.

"Yes" Baltaseim acknowledged his presence without looking at him.

"We have been kidnapping and scattering the Brights throughout the abyss as you asked."

"Good." He took his leather glove off.

"Their perimeter has collapsed and the Brights have lost their sanctuary."

"Excellent!" he said, grinning grotesquely. "Now they'll truly know how it feels to be stuck in this forsaken place"

"But there's a small problem."

He turned his gaze on him. "What problem?" he spat, his eyes burning a hole right through the soldier.

"Um…yes…you see…um…we just spotted a large congregation of Brights coming this way."

"What!"

For a brief moment the soldier was not sure if he should continue. "Yes, you can see their light approaching slowly."

"Double the perimeter guards. They are wandering aimlessly...with any luck they'll pass right by us."

The soldier saluted and returned to his post.

"Now." Baltaseim returned his attention to Joshua. "Sorry about the interruption...where were we? Ah yes...feeding. We need to feed."

"Feed or what?" Joshua interrupted. "Die? Now wouldn't that be a shame."

Baltaseim snickered softly. "Die?" He stared at his victim. "No...we are Eternals like yourself." He explained coldly. "We do not die...but I can tell you from personal experience that the hunger you feel is enough to drive you insane."

"That is sad," Joshua replied with a certain tone of sarcasm in his voice. "I almost feel sorry for you."

"From where I'm standing," Baltaseim said, his tone turning cold, "I'm the one who should feel sorry for you." He took a deep breath and his face turned serious. "That reminds me, are you ready for another feeding? I was certain you wouldn't mind. See how considerate I am!" He smiled. His smile faded and an urgent look flashed across his face. "Now hold still. This is really going to hurt."

On a turret close by, a couple of guards looked at each other fearfully. They understood the reason for the shivers that were crawling up their spines when they heard Joshua's screams from the opposite end of the castle.

Chapter Twenty-two

A few days passed since Zallier was forced to take his followers into the abyss. The surrounding darkness was starting to have an effect on the Eternals; their edginess was apparent, and not likely to get better. *We've been walking for eight days now. Why haven't we reached Tom yet?* Zallier looked back at them and for the first time wondered if leaving was the right choice. *We must be walking in circles...we have to be. If only I could get better bearings. This damned place makes it almost impossible to recognize where you've been.* Suddenly Zallier's thoughts were interrupted when he heard a faint murmur in the distance.

"What in Baltaseim's pride was that?" he asked startled.

"What was what?" Barry said with a bewildered look on his face.

"That noise," Zallier replied, "didn't you hear it?"

"No."

Zallier stopped and strained to hear the unidentified sound. "It's way too noisy," he said, trying to listen. Frustrated, he turned to his peers and cried out over the idle chitchat. "Could you please all be quiet! I'm trying to hear something."

Slowly the sporadic whispers dwindled to give way to complete silence.

A few moments later, the faint unrecognizable whisper returned. *I knew it, I wasn't imagining it. I heard something.* "There!" Zallier said, convinced that he wasn't hearing things. "Did you hear it?"

"Yes," Barry replied. "This time I did. It's so faint that you can hardly make it out. What is it?"

"I don't know. It sounds almost like a scream. What do you think?"

"Whatever it is, it sure seems to be in a lot of pain."

"This may be our salvation," Zallier said full of hope. "I wonder if Tom's group ran into unanticipated problems. I think that we should investigate."

"Yeah if it's Tom, it sounds like he needs our help. Let's follow the noise to its source and see where it leads us."

"Agreed."

****

A nervous lieutenant made his way to his Master. *He's not going to be happy,* he thought. *I hope that he won't take his frustration out on me.* Entering the throne room, he found Baltaseim hovering close to the suspended victim. "Master! We have a problem."

Baltaseim turned and gave him a stare that would freeze Saavatha himself. "What!" He hated being interrupted.

The Shadow felt his heart beat in his ears. With panic, he walked cautiously towards the annoyed Master. "A large number of Brights are congregating close to our perimeter," the soldier said, avoiding eye contact.

Baltaseim's glare burned a hole right through him. "What! Watch them carefully. If it looks like they will cross the perimeter, send a full contingent of gargoyles. I don't want them near this castle...understood?"

"Perfectly!" the soldier replied, saluted and returned to his post.

****

Zallier noticed a faint glimmer in the distance. The light approached until recognizable forms appeared. "Tom!" Zallier cried out surprised. "I'm glad that you're alright. I thought those screams were yours."

"No, as you can see it wasn't me," Tom replied. He looked at Zallier's following with confusion. "What is going on? Why are you all here?"

"Our town has vanished. Baltaseim made sure of that," Zallier said with sadness. "We were looking for you when we heard screaming. We followed it to here."

"Yeah we heard it too. That's why we're here," Tom replied. "Did you run into any gargoyles yet?"

"No. We haven't."

Tom crinkled his nose, and made an unpleasant face. "We ran into a few," he said. "Can you smell the stink?"

Zallier took a deep breath and almost choked. The pungent odor was almost overpowering. "Yeah it's pretty bad actually. We must be close to Baltaseim."

"That's what I thought."

"Did you find Qwenthrey?"

"No. Qwenthrey is who I thought might have been screaming."

"You're right," Zallier replied with a somber look. "It may be Qwenthrey. I was told that Qwenthrey and Baltaseim never got along even before he was banished."

"We need to get inside the castle," Tom said with determination. "It's the only way to find out if Qwenthrey is held captive."

"I doubt if the gargoyles will let us get close."

"Then we need to take over Baltaseim's castle."

Zallier's thoughts raced through his head. Suddenly, an idea came to him. "I think I know how," he said. "We could surround the perimeter and hopefully with our combined energy we could vanquish him from his domain."

"Yeah," Tom said rubbing his beard. "That might work if we have enough Eternals to pull this off."

"I think we do."

"Well it couldn't hurt," he replied. "It's better than sitting here twiddling our thumbs. It's worth a try."

"OK everyone," Zallier cried out to his group. "I want each and every one of you to get as close to Baltaseim's perimeter as the gargoyles will allow. Remember it's vital that everyone holds hands. It's the only way we can unite our energy."

****

Standing over his well, Baltaseim waved his hand over the dark oily liquid. The surface rippled momentarily as images of the current events appeared. *What are they doing?* Suddenly, the answer came to him. "They wouldn't dare!" he bellowed in disbelief. He watched helplessly the bright dots surrounding his castle, his worst fears were confirmed when the dots connected, giving way to a solid line.

"Damn you!" he cursed. "How dare you do this to me? This is not over... I promise you!" He could hear a chant outside of his room. He shook as anger overwhelmed him. Staring helplessly he could see the thin white line expanding towards the center of the circle...his castle.

He joined his lieutenants. As he exited the castle he was hit with the sudden realization that his fate was sealed. He would be driven to the deepest part of this void, where he would no longer be a threat.

"What are we supposed to do Master?" a soldier asked nervously.

"We stand our ground!"

"Are you kidding me?" he asked in shock. "But the light is coming. We should retreat!"

"Look around you," he snapped. "You fool, there's light all around us. Where do you suggest we retreat?"

After analyzing the situation, the soldier realized the futility of his question. "We shouldn't stand here and be destroyed!" he said panicking.

"Don't worry my minion." Baltaseim said trying to sound reassuring. "You're not going to be destroyed. We'll be in agony for a while, that's all."

"Agony?" the soldier replied, his voice shaking slightly. "I hate pain—you know that. I don't want to be in pain."

"Oh my dear coward...you'll get over it," he replied. "Trust me. We don't have a choice in the matter. The Brights have won...." He muttered under his breath, "Remember the pain...the agony...turn it into hatred...let it simmer until we meet their kind again. Then you will be able to take revenge for what they're about to put you through." The soldier nodded uncertainly. Baltaseim felt his fear, he shared it.

"Prepare yourself," he said nervously. "Remember this day! Here it comes!" He screamed covering his eyes from the blinding light.

Screams that would be only recognizable from the depths of hell were heard as light overtook the castle. Baltaseim and his minions vanished suddenly. What was once dark was now light and the Brights were occupying it. Rebuilding is never easy, but there was hope that the remaining time in this void would be peaceful. Scouts were sent into the darkness searching for the missing Eternals. Finding them would not be easy.

Chapter Twenty-three

With Baltaseim vanquished, the Brights were now free to rebuild in peace. The castle was the only remnant left of Baltaseim's mighty legion. It was the first time since its inception that light had illuminated the dark corridors that were infamous for the horrors they witnessed. Tom entered the castle cautiously in the hopes of finding his lost friend, Qwenthrey. The large arched door creaked loudly as it shut, startling him. With his heart in his throat, he looked back at the door that was still faintly swinging on its old and rusted hinges. Taking a deep breath he continued into a large corridor, the main artery that branched to many different rooms.

Weaving from corridor to corridor, room to room, Tom was looking for the most important one, the throne room. *Qwenthrey is in here. I know he is. I can feel a strong presence within these walls. If only I could find that damn room. This place is like a maze. Wait! I think this is it.* He looked at the dark prince's insignia carved on the rock archway. Satisfied, he clicked the latch open and put all of his weight on the large heavy door. With great effort he swung it open. The hinges strained under its weight, creaking loudly before the door stopped inches from the opposing wall.

He entered the room. The hair at the back of his neck stood on end and he stopped in his tracks. The scene displayed before him made him gasp in horror. "Zallier!" he screamed at the top of his lungs. "Get over here, quick!"

Zallier heard Tom's scream. He was not happy. *What does he want now? I've got better things to do than run to him every time he calls. I will tell him that when I see him too!* "I'm coming, I'm coming," he mumbled, taking his time. Zallier followed Tom's voice for what seemed an eternity before he finally found himself at the throne room's entrance. Entering, Zallier's face went white when his eyes rested on the horror. He opened his mouth, but nothing came out.

"They are Brights, like us." Tom said staring at the naked forms hanging spread-eagled from the ceiling.

Zallier felt a pang of regret before pushing the thought aside. "They are still unconscious," he managed to say once he got over the initial shock. "Do you know who they are?"

Tom looked back and shook his head. "No, I don't recognize them," he replied. "Look how bruised the abdomen on that left Eternal is," he said pointing to the man's midsection.

The bruising caught Zallier's eye right away. He had seen bruises of this nature before, but this one was the darkest he had seen yet. "Yeah," he replied. "It's typical of Eternals who let hatred control their being. From the severity of his bruises, I would say that someone has been feeding on him…probably Baltaseim himself."

"Looks like it. We should cut them loose."

"Yeah, give me a hand." Zallier said, reaching for the cuffed hand of the blond Eternal. "Grab his left hand. We'll pull him up a bit."

Joshua stirred and opened his eyes, trying to lift his head.

"He's coming to." Tom said, noticing movement. "What's your name?" he asked, pulling Joshua's long blond hair out of his beaten and sweaty face.

"Josh," he whispered in a tone barely audible. "Joshuaa," his head slumped forward, as unconsciousness wrapped itself tightly around him.

"Joshua?" Tom cried out, stunned. "Could it be after all this time?"

"It's Joshua!" Zallier said with disbelief.

****

It had been three days since Joshua and Gord were found. Missing for more than a millennium, Gord was glad to be back into the light. He still remembered the warning that Master Gwen gave him so long ago. He only wished he had followed it. Joshua on the other hand still hadn't regained consciousness. Katy, a petite red-head, had been caring for him in her two-bedroom cabin. Joshua was in the middle of a king-sized bed, near a large open window. Burning with fever, he'd tossed and turned since his arrival. His sweaty body soaked through the sheets carefully tucked around him. She laid her hand on his forehead to check his temperature. *He's still so hot. I hope he wakes up soon.* Out of the corner of her eye, she noticed the curtains swaying gently from the light breeze coming through. She took a deep breath and smiled to herself. *Wild flowers always did put me in a good mood,* she mused. Grabbing a cloth from the nightstand, she dunked it into lukewarm water, wrung it out thoroughly and wiped the perspiration from his forehead. "You'll be just fine," she whispered to him.

Joshua frowned in his sleep. His breathing quickened suddenly as he started to toss his head from side to side. He arched his back and screamed at the top of his lungs before settling back down on the bed.

Katy jumped out of her skin. She leaned over and wiped his face again. "It's OK," she whispered. "I'm here." She sat at his bedside. *He's getting more restless.* She took his hand. *I don't like his breathing. It's too fast.*

"No!" he shouted in his sleep, almost hyperventilating. "Go away, leave me alone! Why are you doing this to me? No!" His eyes opened wide and he sat up abruptly. Breathing hard, he felt his heart pound. With terror still lingering in his thoughts he scanned the bedroom with confusion. The scent of wild flowers that permeated the room had a calming effect. His eyes stopped and examined the stranger's face. Her look of concern confused him even more. "Where am I?" he asked looking around nervously.

"At my house," she soothed. "Relax, you're safe here."

Joshua fixed her gaze, trying to shake the cobwebs out of his head. "Who are you?" he asked suspicious.

"My name is Katy," she smiled. "I won't hurt you."

He looked around one more time, to make sure that she was the only one in the room with him. "Where's Baltaseim?"

"He's gone," she said. "We took care of him."

Joshua looked at her, not knowing what to think. *Nobody takes care of Baltaseim.* "You destroyed him?" he asked full of disbelief.

"No," she replied. "But we banished him to the furthest side of this void. I doubt if he'll cause any more problems."

"Don't underestimate him."

"Don't worry," she reassured. "We have everything under control."

"For my sake I hope so."

"You really—" Katy began and stopped mid-sentence when she realized that Joshua had slipped into unconsciousness again. She got up and bent down to give him a peck on his forehead. "Sleep Joshua," she caressed his sweaty face with the back of her hand. "Regain your strength. I will be here if you need me." A worried look crossed her face when she looked back at him before leaving the room.

Three more days passed as Joshua drifted in and out of consciousness. Finally on the seventh day he awoke.

She entered the room to check on him as she did every day. To her surprise Joshua was awake and sitting up, resting against some pillows tucked behind him against the headboard. "I see that you're finally awake!" she said, smiling radiantly.

A shadow of suspicion and confusion came over his deep blue eyes as he stared at her. "I'm sorry," he said. "Am I supposed to know you?" Joshua couldn't help but be captivated by the beautiful and vivacious smile of the stranger walking towards him. He frowned suddenly as his headache demanded his attention. "Have we met?" he asked, rubbing his aching temples.

Katy sat down on a chair close to his bed. "We've met," she said taking a deep breath, "long ago."

"I'm sorry," he said staring into her emerald green eyes. "I don't remember you. What's your name?" he asked. A sudden sharp pain got his attention. "Ohhh, my stomach," he complained and held his gut. "I think I'm going to lie down."

"You shouldn't be sitting up quite yet. You've been through a lot," Katy replied with a hint of concern. "Anyway you can call me Katy."

Joshua slid down gingerly, trying to pamper his aching stomach. Finally lying down comfortably, he grimaced as he tucked a pillow behind his head. "OK Katy," he said, managing a sly grin. "Maybe you can tell me how long I've been under your care."

"Seven days," she replied.

His eyebrows shot up as he looked at her with round eyes. "I see," he replied. "And where is my enemy?"

"Baltaseim, I assume?"

"The very one."

"We've banished him to the furthest side of this domain," Katy replied. "You really don't remember a thing do you?"

An embarrassed look came over his face. "Not much of it," he said, avoiding her stare. "I was pretty out of it."

"I told you all of this already. He's gone—hopefully for good."

"Baltaseim is never gone for good," he said under his breath.

For a moment Katy found herself staring at him. His demeanor, his body language, it all told the same story: helplessness and deep-rooted hatred. "You really hate him don't you?"

"I despise him," he muttered under his breath. "Can't you tell?"

"That's what I thought," she replied, taking a deep breath. "I've never seen a bruise that dark before. Your hatred for him must be really strong."

"Yeah it is," he scoffed proudly.

A sudden flash of anger swelled inside her. She wanted to take him and lay him across her knee. "That's nothing to be proud of," she scolded. "Hatred is not an emotion to be harnessed."

"Why not?" he asked. He didn't like to be told what to do. He appreciated everything the woman did for him, but he felt that she had no right to scold him for the hatred he felt towards his aggressor. *She doesn't have a clue. She doesn't know what that monster did to me.* His eyes narrowed with anger. "You may not approve," he spat. "But it works for me!"

She caught his cold stare and it frightened her. She had seen that stare before, in her own eyes, long ago. "First of all," Katy said louder than she expected. "Saavatha does not allow it. And what do you think is responsible for the nasty bruise you have?"

Joshua's guards went up. He didn't like being attacked like that. *Which of Baltaseim's minion does she think she is?* He glared at her. "The bastard," he replied, unable to restrain his hatred from seeping through, "who fed on me, is responsible!"

"Wrong," she said stubbornly. "He fed on you because you had this bruise already. We are white Eternals. If you start harnessing negative emotion like hatred, you produce dark matter which centers in the middle of your being. The darker the emotion, the darker the energy."

Joshua glared at her silently. He knew she was right. He had noticed his bruise long before Baltaseim laid a hand on him. He didn't like to be outdone. It made him feel inferior. "You're wrong," he replied sharply. "You don't know what you're talking about."

"Oh I know I'm right," she said, raising her eyebrows. "And you know it too. You're just too proud to admit it."

"You're wrong!"

"No, I'm right, and you know it," she said. "So don't give me this sob story. I'm not buying it. You're responsible for your own misery. If you hadn't given in to your hatred, he would not have been able to feed off of you."

She had him. He knew it and he didn't like it one bit. He scowled and looked down, evading her eyes. "I'm tired," he said coldly. "I'd like to be alone now."

"Fine," she sighed with disappointment. She got up and held his hand. "I want you to think about what I said." He looked up at her, his eyes still frosted with anger. "You've been through a lot. You still need to rest, but this discussion is not over."

Joshua watched her leave the room silently. He took a deep breath and reflected on her parting words. A wry smile crossed his lips as he thought about her argument. What she said made sense, though he would never admit it. He rolled over on his side and winced. In the middle of all this commotion, he forgot the agonizing ache in his abdomen. He pulled the cover over himself and closed his eyes, trying to get some rest. *She's quite something,* he thought as drowsiness took over. *I could get to like her.*

****

The following morning Joshua woke up to the sound of rustling sheets. He opened his eyes and gasped. He was stunned by the sight greeting his eyes. The curtains on the window by his bed were partially open, letting in a slim stream of sunlight. Katy was in the middle of this stream, folding some linen. The sunlight illuminated her, capturing the highlights in her hair. She looked radiant, full of life. He craned his neck to get a better view when a groan escaped his lips.

"Oh, you're awake," she said putting the basket down. "I was hoping that you would wake soon. I took the liberty of changing the sheets while you were sleeping. I hope you don't mind."

Joshua realized that he was staring. He couldn't help it; she was so beautiful. "No I don't mind." He flustered and lowered his head in embarrassment. He looked down at his bed and for the first time he noticed that he was lying in a fresh bed. *How in Baltaseim's Pride did she do that without waking me? This woman is sure full of surprises.* Joshua watched her come and sit down beside his bed.

"How are you feeling?" she asked, smiling at him.

Joshua truly looked at her for the first time. *Those high cheekbones, that small nose of hers and those eyes—I could lose myself in those eyes. Why didn't I notice her?* The answer came and hit him like a brick wall. He was so involved in his own pride that he let anger blind him. His face darkened to a deep shade of red. "I'm doing alright," he said, looking up at her timidly. "My stomach is still sore, but I got a good night's sleep."

"Good," she said, getting up. She sat on his bed and leaned over. Joshua looked at her quizzically as she ran her slender fingers along the contour of his face, leaving behind a cleaner and more energized appearance.

"What are you doing?" he asked.

Katy straightened up and gave him a quirky smile. "I'm cleaning you up," she said. "Your fever broke and I thought that it would make you feel better."

His grin broke into a full-blown smile. "You sure are full of surprises," he said.

"I am?"

"Yes you are," he replied, suddenly aware of the effect she was having on him. "All those fancy ways of doing things. I can't do that."

She leaned forward and resumed her cleaning caresses. "That's because you're not strong enough," she said smiling. "You haven't Journeyed yet."

The word "Journeyed" sounded familiar to him. He reached into the deepest part of his mind, trying to recall the meaning of this important word. *I should know this,* he thought frustrated. Finally, he conceded defeat. "Journeyed?" he asked.

"Yes, Journeying," she said, looking at him oddly. *He doesn't remember,* she thought. *Baltaseim really screwed with his head. This is not going to be easy.* She took a deep breath before beginning. "In order for us to grow stronger, we need to Journey to the world of the Solids."

Joshua frowned with concentration. The word "Solid" sounded familiar to him as well. *They're people like me, but different. Why can't I remember? I know this; I know I do.* He strained to listen to Katy's explanation.

"There, we test the knowledge we acquired from our studies of Saavatha's doctrine," she said. "If we pass the tests, then our essence becomes stronger."

"Our essence?"

"Yes, our true being," Katy replied. From the look on his face, she knew that she wasn't making any progress. She decided that a demonstration would clear things up. She stood up close to his side. "This is our essence," she said.

Joshua watched her form energize brightly. An overbearing light at the center of her being broke through the energized form, radiating like a thousand suns. The bright nucleus floated a couple feet from the ground.

The complete room was saturated by white light. "This is who we are," he heard her voice booming across the room.

"Baltaseim's tricks!!" he screamed and fell out of his bed. "What in Athraw's domain are you?"

"I am an Eternal, just like you," the essence replied. "When my founder tore off a piece of his essence, I was born, and my life began. At inception, Saavatha gave me my true persona." Suddenly, the essence was gone and replaced by a small child standing near him. "As I grew," the child said, "I learned Saavatha's ways. I studied his doctrine until I was ready to Journey." The child went through the growing stages of his life and stopped at adulthood. "My true persona is Tom," the dark-haired man said, looking at the stunned man on the floor. "As I Journeyed, I took on many different forms." Tom disappeared and was replaced by different people, flipping from a man, to a woman, to a child. He continued to change forms until he reached Katy's and stopped. "This woman is my favorite. This is who I like to be during peacetime."

Joshua stared at her with terror in his eyes. For once in his life, he found something other than Baltaseim to fear.

"I'm sorry Joshua," Katy said to him, smiling. "I didn't mean to scare you… you should get back into bed."

Joshua was transfixed. As hard as he tried, he couldn't move a muscle. After what seemed an eternity, he managed to crawl back into bed, never letting his eyes leave her. "Can you do me a favor?" he asked nervously.

"Sure," she replied "anything."

"When you're around me," he said still shaking. "No shape-shifting. It gives me the creeps."

"Fair enough. Now close your eyes and relax."

"Why do you want me to close my eyes?" he asked suspicious. "What are you going to do?"

"Don't worry!" she said, a little annoyed. "I'm only going to give you some of my energy. It'll help you feel better."

"No, no, no…I'm fine…just fine," he said filled with fear. "No funny business, you promised."

"Don't be so paranoid. One counteracts negative energy with positive energy," she told him, putting her palm in the center of his bruise.

"Careful!" he scolded. "It's tender!"

Ignoring his whining, she closed her eyes and took a deep breath. Joshua's jaw dropped when he saw Katy's hand glow white. He was even more surprised when his body absorbed all the energy that Katy gave him.

He looked at his abdomen with surprise, and then glanced up at Katy. "My bruise is almost gone!" he said, astonished. "How did you do that?"

"You weren't supposed to be looking!" she said, slapping his belly playfully.

"Ouch!" he cried out in mock anger. "That hurts!"

"Big baby," she chuckled, "I didn't feel a thing."

"I'm sure you didn't."

"This fix is only temporary," she warned. "The only one who can remove this bruise permanently is you."

"What do you mean?" he asked dumbfounded. "Won't it go away by itself?"

"No. For that to happen, you need to stop hating."

"I don't think I can do that."

"I know. It's hard not to hold a grudge. But you must for your own good."

"I'm not hating now!" he said, trying to lighten the mood.

"That's because Baltaseim is nowhere in sight," she replied, scooting closer to him.

Despite Katy's demonstration, Joshua couldn't help but feel an attraction to her beauty. *She said she was an Eternal, like me. It's hard to believe, but after seeing her demonstration, I'd believe anything she'd say. If she's right, then there is something wrong with me. And she seems genuine enough. She is striking.* He looked into her green eyes. "Perhaps," he said, captivated by her beauty, "Right now I've got only one Eternal on my mind."

"Yeah," she said with a coy smile, "who?"

"You!" Joshua said tenderly putting his hands around her neck entangling his fingers in her red curls. His gaze riveted into her green eyes as he leaned forward and kissed her.

Katy pulled back surprised and shocked. *Am I that transparent? What have I done? Katy little girl...you have to be more careful. You can't wear your emotions on your sleeve like that.* She stared at the young Eternal's longing eyes with silent anticipation and curiosity as she absentmindedly brought her fingers to her lips. *No, this is not right, he's from another house. I can't get involved.* She lowered her gaze.

"What's wrong?" Joshua asked.

"Nothing."

"Right, from the looks of you, I'd say that you've just lost your best friend. So spill it!"

Katy stared at Joshua with beaten eyes. She really liked him. But Saavatha's rules were explicit: no fraternization between houses. "Whatever you have in mind for us..." she said evading his eyes. "It can't happen!"

"Really? Why?"

"It's complicated."

Joshua studied her. He didn't like what he saw. *She looks like she's about to burst into tears.* "Things are only as complicated as you want them to be. Look," he said holding her gaze. "I like you. You saved me from that bastard! How am I supposed to feel? I know you like me, I can see it in you face. Why can't we be together?"

Katy's eyes started to moisten as she observed his pleading face. She could feel herself tremble as her emotions threatened to take over. She brought her hands to her lips. "It's not that simple."

Joshua cupped her face with both hands and kissed her watching her eyes glisten as tears rolled down her rosy cheeks. "Tell me that you didn't want this," he said, looking deep into her eyes, "and I will never bring it up again."

"I'm not allowed." She sobbed in earnest. "I'm not allowed." Not being able to face him for another moment, she left the room, running and sobbing like an infant.

Not allowed? He thought his eyes following her features out the door. *What do you mean? Not allowed?* He sighed deeply and lowered his head. *This is going to take some work.*

The next morning Joshua woke up to the sound of soft rain beating on his window. It was appeasing. He felt his bruise and for once he realized, it didn't wake him during the night. Fresh linens had been put on his bed; he reasoned that Katy had come during the night to change his sheets. He got up and walked to the window. It had been a long time since he had seen rain. He felt the need to touch it, feel it on his skin. He opened the window and inhaled deeply.

"You're up, it's about time."

He turned and looked at Katy who had just entered the room. "Yeah," he said his eyes fixed on her. "The rain woke me."

"About last night..." Katy said letting the words trail in her voice.

Joshua walked towards her. "It's OK. No need to explain."

Katy took and deep breath. "No," she felt uneasy. "I want to explain, I have to explain. Please." Her face was flush and her timid nature bothered him. He sat on the bed. "Alright," Joshua said wistfully. "Explain away."

Katy sat beside him and took his hands in hers. Suddenly she felt very nervous. She was about to do something that was totally out of character, but she didn't care. She had made up her mind. "Last night," she began looking at her lap, "took me by surprise. I should have seen it coming but I didn't. I was too caught up in taking care of you it didn't occur to me that I could feel the way I do." She looked up and held his gaze. "Until you kissed me...."

"Well that's nice to know," Joshua said brushing a strand of hair off her brow. "Now that I know your feelings, why can't we explore them further, and what's this thing about not being allowed?"

She brought her fingers to his lips, hushing him. "Please, let me explain. This is hard for me."

Joshua watched her pleading face and melted. He nodded silently.

She took a deep breath. "What I feel for you is forbidden. You do not belong to my house. I cannot get involved with you. Those are Saavatha's rules."

"Well that's stupid."

"Please let me finish."

Joshua took a deep breath and waited silently.

"I agree. It's a stupid rule. But it's a rule none the less. I'm sure that Saavatha has good reason to want things this way."

Joshua was about to say something when Katy raised her hand cutting off his train of thought. "I'm about to break a very important rule. I want you to know the difficulties and consequences that this may bring." She took a deep breath and caressed his hand affectionately. She looked up at him. "Not every one will approve." She broke her gaze and stared at the floor. "My founder will be the first one to protest I'm sure. They may try to separate us and convince us of the error of our ways.

"But," she said looking up at him with a smile in her eyes. "I don't care. They can all join Baltaseim's army if they don't like it. "

Joshua didn't know what to say. Suddenly he had an irresistible urge to kiss her. He cupped her chin with one hand and kissed her with a passion that was long forgotten. Katy knew that what she was doing was wrong, but she didn't care. She loved him and that's all that mattered. *I'm in big trouble,* she thought, returning his kiss. *Real big trouble if they don't understand.*

Chapter Twenty-four

Many things had changed since Joshua entered this labyrinth five hundred years ago. Imprisoned for the first two hundred years with his nemesis Baltaseim, Joshua had used the remainder of his time to try to find peace and had worked hard to put his life back together. Katy was one of those rewards. Living together in her cabin for a least a century, they could not imagine their lives being any other way.

Katy was sleeping in her bed alone. The window was open and a light breeze was flowing into the room. The sunlight that streamed through the window caressed the sleeping Eternal. The curtains swayed gingerly, blocking the sun from her face now and then. The scent of flowers permeated the room, pulling her gently out of her sleep.

A lazy smile came to her lips when she realized that a new day had begun. Her eyes still closed, she reached for Joshua, but found only emptiness. Surprised, she opened her eyes and looked at the empty space beside her. *Didn't he come to bed?* she thought, still half asleep. *Maybe he did and got up early. Why didn't he wake me?* Getting up she reached for her housecoat and wrapped it around herself as she walked out of the room. She stumbled into the dining room and spotted him in the library, sleeping on a sofa-chair. *He fell asleep reading again.* She shook her head. *He looks so peaceful. I hate to wake him as he has had very few peaceful moments. Baltaseim still haunts his dreams. I should let him sleep. No, I think I will wake him. He needs some fresh air.*

She leaned over and watched him sleep for a moment. "Josh," she whispered in his ears, "sweetie wake up." She watched him stir a bit and repeated her plea when he turned away from her. "Josh!" she said shaking him, "Wake up, it's time for you to get up." With a low moan, he opened his eyes and stared at her. "Rise and shine."

"How long have I been sleeping?" he asked groggily.

"All night." she replied. "Why don't you join me. I was thinking about riding the unicorns."

"Right this minute?" he said, rubbing the sleep out of his eyes.

"Yeah! Why not, you know how they love it when we ride them."

He sat up and passed a hand in his hair. "OK, just let me wake up a bit."

"You can wake up on the way," she said grabbing both of his hands and pulling him up on his feet. "Come on big boy," she giggled. "Let's go riding."

"I'm not awake yet!" he protested. "Give me a minute to wake up!"

"You'll have lots of time to wake up once we're riding. Now come on," she beckoned, "we'll have fun."

Trailing close behind, Joshua was holding onto Katy's hand. They walked through the front door and Joshua noticed much to his surprise, two unicorns, saddled and ready, tied to the balcony.

"Josh," Katy said turning to introduce the animals. "The one on your left is Triss and this is Buck. They were both in my battlefield complement."

"Nice to meet you two," he said warmly. "I think," he continued, flashing a sly grin in Katy's direction, "that we will have an enjoyable ride." Jumping off the balcony he mounted his ride, taking the reins casually in hand. "Where are we going?" he asked Katy, who was already seated on her mount.

"I thought that we could ride around the lake once," she suggested, "then maybe just amble through this wonderful little forest that you have here."

"Sounds perfect, you heard the lady," he said to Triss patting her mane. "Around the lake we go."

As they rode, Joshua breathed in the wild scent of flowers, ferns and the enormous evergreens that surrounded him. *I love this place. Never would I have ever imagined having such beauty in the middle of this desolate place. And to have found Katy also...*

"The last one around this lake cooks dinner!" Katy challenged, breaking Joshua's reverie. He smiled at her and she stuck her tongue out at him. Caught off guard, Joshua watched helplessly as Katy urged her mount into a full gallop, leaving him behind in her dust.

"Come on Triss!" he said urging her along. "We can't let them beat us!" The unicorn launched forward, trying desperately to narrow the gap between them. Leaning forward Joshua whispered in her ear while stroking her soft neck tenderly. "I don't think that you can beat Buck at this race. Maybe we should give up."

"Not on your life," Triss replied, "he would never let me live this down." Picking up speed Triss slowly caught up. Katy who looked back and suddenly started to squeal joyfully when she realized that Josh was gaining on her. The two animals were neck to neck and Triss was giving her all to break the tie. Josh reached the balcony first with Katy trailing close behind.

"Ha, Ha!" Joshua yelled triumphantly. "I guess dinner is on you!" he taunted.

"You cheated," she protested. "I saw you rile Triss up. You can't use the animal's emotions to win."

"A deal is a deal," he replied with the teasing smile she loved so much. "You wanted to race and I beat you fair and square."

"I will give you this one," Katy told him, not wanting to concede defeat. "But don't think that I will let you win next time. Next time you are cooking dinner."

"You just can't stand to see me win," Josh said chuckling, "I won this one and you just can't stand it!"

"I challenge you to a rematch at the time of my choosing," she said, pointing a finger at him and laughing in spite of herself. "And next time I won't let you win!"

"We will see who will eat crow," he cautioned grabbing her finger, "I accept your challenge. I have a feeling that maybe you should cook the bird tonight so that you get use to the taste. You will be eating a lot of it in the coming weeks."

"Ha, ha, ha, you think you're pretty funny don't you?" Katy replied. "We'll see who will eat the bird. Come on slowpoke." She grabbed his hand and walked into the cabin.

Katy really didn't mind cooking dinner, she enjoyed her afternoon and a nice romantic dinner was the perfect ending to a perfect day. "Would you like a drink," Josh asked cockily, "before I enslave you in the kitchen?"

"Sure why not, a nice glass of white wine would be fine," Katy replied. "You know you're pretty cocky when you win, you'd better be careful because the next time you could be in the kitchen."

"It's wishful thinking on your part," Josh answers playfully. "I never lose. Here is your wine to go with your fantasy."

She took the glass and took a sip. "Where did you get this?" she asked. "It's really good."

"Master Stephan was kind enough to give me a few bottles," Josh answered. "It's supposed to be a very old vintage."

"You're not going to have any?" she asked, noticing that Josh had no glass in hand.

"I hadn't thought about it to tell you the truth," he replied. "But now that you mention it, yeah why not. I'm going to go get a glass in the kitchen." Stopping suddenly he turned around and gave her a knowing glance. "Aren't you supposed to be in the kitchen cooking?"

"Hold on to your horses," she replied, "I am enjoying my wine." Walking past him she took another sip of her wine. She looked back at him with her laughing eyes. "Slave driver!" she giggled. Entering the kitchen she closed her eyes and concentrated. On the counter top appeared potatoes, onions, carrots, some broccoli and a head of lettuce. Near the sink sat a nice size roast waiting to be prepared.

"You're not cooking this dinner from scratch are you?" Josh asked baffled.

"Certainly," she replied, starting to get all of the ingredients ready. "It's the only way to do it. I want to have a nice dinner with you."

"Lucky me," he teased. He took another sip of his wine. "It's not everyday that someone cooks for me."

"One more reason for you to be nice to me," Katy replied. "If you're lucky I might do this more often."

Josh smiled at her silently. Not needing the nutritional value of food, he didn't usually eat. He found it a waste of time. But for a meal cooked in his honor, he appreciated the effort and would make time to reward the hard work put into it. "Is there anything that I can do to help?" he volunteered, feeling a little guilty.

"Well," Katy replied. "If you want to help me you can come over here and peel some potatoes?"

"Sure, why not," he replied. "Give me the potatoes."

"Take off the skin only." She warned teasingly tossing him the potatoes.

"Okey dokey," he replied, goofing around. Grabbing the knife Katy he started to peel the spuds slowly. Peeling away at the potatoes he remembered the day they invited Master James to stay for dinner so long ago. *I remember doing this,* he mused, *at my founder's home...I think. Master James stayed for dinner...Qwenthrey.* They still haven't found him. I wonder if they ever will. All alone in this forsaken darkness—I would've gone mad. At least in the time I was gone...I had Baltaseim. Yeah, to torture me....but at least, I wasn't alone in the dark.

"Whoa, there cowboy." Katy said bringing Joshua back to reality. "I think this is going to be enough potatoes, we are not trying to feed an army."

"Oh, I guess," he said, pulling himself together. "Is there anything else that I can do?"

"Yes," she replied, putting the vegetables into the roaster. "You can keep me company. I hate cooking alone."

"Sure I can do that."

"We are done for now." She put the roast in the oven. "I hope that I didn't forget anything."

"I'm sure that you didn't. You're pretty thorough."

Dinner will be in a couple of hours," she said thoughtfully. "That will give us sometime to take a walk in the forest if you like."

"You're something else," he said, grabbing her by the waist and bringing her close to him. "I have never met an Eternal like you before."

"And," she finished, "you will never meet another one like me again."

Josh smiled. He was certain that there was some truth to that. *There's one thing that I can thank Baltaseim for,* he thought. *If I was never brought here, I would have never met her.*

They walked out of the cottage hand in hand. The mood between the two of them was playful as they made their way towards the center of the forest. *I just love this place,* Katy thought. *The smells and auras around here are magnificent. It reminds me of home. I wonder what my founder is doing. I sure miss him, even if he makes an ass out of himself. Joel, I will be home soon. Dave and Kevin—I didn't see them here. After Saavatha's victory over Baltaseim they are probably back home by now.*

She sighed and observed the scene before her. *It must have been terrible for him,* she thought glancing at Joshua. *Being trapped and having to put up with Baltaseim's torture is not something I think I could tolerate. No wonder he's so full of hatred. Letting go will be one the hardest things he will ever have to do. I'm glad that I met this young one.* She leaned her head on Joshua's shoulder. *He still has so much to learn but I hope that with my help he will grow in the right direction. I find him irresistible and I don't know why. I care for him and I will stay near him as long as he wants me.* "We should be going back," she said dreamily. "The roast should be done by now."

The wonderful smell of the roast cooking in the oven greeted them as they walked into the cottage.

"I will set the table," Josh volunteered, "while you look after the roast."

"You are such a doll," Katy replied walking to the oven. "It still needs a few minutes."

Joshua walked into the dining room and stared at the table. *I hope this will work.* He closed his eyes and concentrated on the place setting. In his mind's eye, he had a clear picture of what he wanted. He opened his eyes and to his surprise, the table was set exactly as he pictured it. "It worked!" he said under his breath. "I can't believe it! Katy's lessons stuck." *Ha!* he thought, *there's hope for me after all.* "Voilà!" he said full of exuberance, to Katy that was coming in his direction with the roast pan in hand. "I did it. I can't believe it!"

"I can," she replied with a pleasant smile on her face. "You've worked hard for that. It's only natural that you'd get it."

"Yeah I guess you're right," he said full of smiles. "I never thought that I could do those things."

"Well you thought wrong," she replied. "Could you refill my glass please?"

"Certainly," he said. "I think that you have outdone yourself. This smells delicious."

"Sucking up won't work," she snickered with a sly grin on her face. "You will cook next time."

Joshua smirked and sat down at the table.

"Josh, would you do me the honor of giving thanks?" she asked.

"Sure," Joshua replied, "I can do that." Bowing their heads in silence, he began, "Saavatha, we thank you for this meal and this wonderful fellowship that we are enjoying. Help us to grow strong together so that we may be closer to you, Saavatha be praised."

"That was beautiful," she said, squeezing his hand affectionately. "I am really enjoying myself."

Smiling, Joshua raised his wineglass. "To new friendships," he toasted happily.

As the wineglasses touched together, Katy smiled at the young man. "Here, here," she replied with a hopeful tone in her voice. She was enjoying his company and hoped that this was the start of a beautiful relationship. She stared into his deep blue eyes, losing herself. *Such a tender soul,* she thought. She took comfort in the thought that when Josh was here with her, it made the stay in this place a lot more palatable. "What I am feeling towards you is a very good thing," she said passionately. "I would like for us to grow together towards Saavatha. I want to share all of those struggles that this quest will bring you, if you will have me."

Joshua looked at her with misty eyes. *I'm truly blessed,* he thought. He smiled. "There are a lot of things that I am not sure about," he replied, his voice crackling. "But one thing I know for sure. I want to be near you always. Since I've met you my existence changed for the better. I know that I still have a lot to learn. And I know that the struggles that I will go through to grow will not be easy. I promise you this; I will never abandon you unless you want me to leave. I love you Katy and I can't imagine a moment without you."

Having finished their romantic dinner, they went to the living room. Sitting close together on the couch, they stared at the flames flickering in the fireplace. A joyous feeling of hope and well-being flowed through the room as the two Eternals looked forward to a bright and happy future together.

Chapter Twenty-five

After spending a thousand years in imprisonment, every Eternal became excited as the end of the penance neared. There was a sense of relief amongst the community and they were all looking forward to finally going home. The atmosphere of hope and closure overwhelmed the inhabitants and the necessary preparations to go home got underway.

"It's just about over," Jobb told Master Stephan, "I won't miss this place one bit!"

"Yes another week and it will be all over."

"Most Eternals have returned," Jobb said. "There are only a few stragglers left."

"Good," Stephan replied, "I can't wait to return to the kingdom myself. I miss it terribly."

"They found him Master," a tall and slim Eternal with dark sunken eyes shouted. "Come quick! They found him!"

Stephan turned and looked at the Eternal running towards him. "Tim!" Stephan asked with a desperate tone in his voice. "Who did they find, Qwenthrey?"

"Yes!" he replied excitedly. "After all this time, they finally found him."

"Saavatha be praised," Stephan cried joyfully. "Come on boy," he said impatiently. "Lead us to him!" Tim took off running to the perimeter with Stephan and Jobb on his tail.

After five hundred years in the absence of light, Qwenthrey was happy to have finally made it back.

"Qwenthrey!" Stephan cried out.

Qwenthrey turned and gazed at Stephan.

"It's good to see you safe and sound," Stephan said, hugging him ecstatically. "For a while there I thought that we wouldn't find you."

"Yeah," Qwenthrey replied. "I had a lot of time to think about that. Joshua…was he ever found?"

"Yes!" Stephan told him. "We found him here in Baltaseim's castle. Actually Tom found him. Baltaseim had been feeding on him for quite some time."

Qwenthrey lowered his head passively and frowned. "Oh no, how is he doing?"

"He still has a lot of emotions to work on but he's doing pretty good for what he went through."

"I bet," Qwenthrey replied sadly. "When can I see him?"

"As soon as you feel up to it," Stephan said. "You should regenerate in the light for a while to regain some of your strength."

"I've got plenty of time for that," he said quickly. "Where is he?"

"He's living with Tom—I mean Katy. They've developed quite a close relationship in the last few hundred years."

"Good!" Qwenthrey replied. "Katy is perfect for him. He can learn a lot from her."

"Come on," Stephan said. "I will show you where he lives."

Qwenthrey transformed into Master James and entered the light. He smiled inwardly. It's been some time since he enjoyed the presence of the light.

Joshua was sitting in the library reading, when he heard someone knock on the door. He looked up and stared at the door, a little annoyed at the interruption. "Come in!" he replied.

"Knock, knock, knock!"

He looked around the corner to see if Katy was near. "Katy!" He cried out. "There's someone at the door. Could you get that?"

"I'm coming!" she said, hurrying to the door. Opening the door she stood there and froze.

"Katy," James said with a wry smile, "aren't you going to invite me in?"

"Oh my—Joshua!" she yelled. Tears were swelling in her green eyes. "You better get over here!"

He took a deep breath and shook his head. *Why she insists on bothering me when I'm reading.* "What's the matter," he said irritated. "Can't you answer the door on your own?" He walked to the door and stopped dead in his tracks. He gasped as his eyes filled with tears. *It can't be, James, it can't be!* "James! Saavatha help us. I didn't think that I would ever see you again! It's been a long time." He trembled; tears of joy were streaming down his face. "Come on in, come on in!"

James looked at him with surprise. He couldn't believe how much he had changed since the last time he saw him.

"Wow..." he said "look at you! You're all grown up."

Joshua smiled timidly. "We all grow up eventually."

James chuckled. "Yeah...I can see that. You look good"

"Thanks" Joshua replied blushing slightly.

Katy went into the kitchen to make some tea while James and Joshua sat at the oval dining room table, playing catch up.

"After Baltaseim kidnapped you," James recalled painfully. He avoided Joshua's eyes while running his fingers absentmindedly along the smooth oak finish. "I felt responsible for what happened, so I decided to go look for you. I'm sorry. I was careless...this should have never happened."

"For a long time I hated you," Joshua said truthfully. "But later I realized that my hate was focused on the wrong one. That's when I turned it on Baltaseim."

"Hatred is never a solution," James said, getting the courage to look his friend in the eye. "No matter how deserving you think it may be."

"I know," Joshua replied shamefully. "It was a hard lesson to learn."

"To learn and grow is the reason for our existence." James reminded him.

"Yeah, that's what Katy has been trying to pound into this thick skull of mine."

"Is it working?"

"I think so," he chuckled. "I still have a long way to go, but I'm learning."

"Good, that is what's important."

"You look exhausted," Joshua said, pointing out the obvious. "You are staying here until you leave this cursed place, I insist."

"Well," James replied, "if you put it that way, how can I refuse?"

"You can't," Joshua answered, "that is why I insisted."

"Master Stephan was telling me that my sentence here is over."

"Really!" Joshua said, surprised. "When are you leaving?"

"Tonight," James replied enthusiastically, "is my last night in this forsaken place. By tomorrow this time I will be in Saavatha's Garden of Life."

"I am happy for you." Josh told him, almost envious. "I don't remember much of the kingdom. I remember certain events but that's about it."

"You'll be pleasantly surprised, trust me." James patted Joshua's hand lightly as a show of affection.

"I hope so," he replied. "I will find out soon enough I guess."

"When are you leaving?"

"In three days."

"That's not very long after me," he said excited. "Once you're back, come and see me at my Hall of Wisdom. I will show you the place personally."

"OK, I will."

Katy walked in the dining room announcing, "Dinner is ready! Josh, could you come and give me a hand please?"

"Sure," he replied, "James would you please excuse me?"

"Certainly."

"I will be right back." Joshua left the room to help set the table.

James, feeling awkward, asked, "Is there anything I can do?"

"No," Katy replied. "You just sit there and be our guest."

The aromas around the kitchen table overwhelmed his senses. "This smells good." James said, his mouth watering.

"Just wait until you've tried some of this turkey," Katy replied smirking. "I think that I've outdone myself."

"I bet. I can't wait!" he said, rubbing his hands together.

"Wine?" Joshua interrupted, handing James a glass.

"Sure. It's been a while since I've had some."

Joshua filled James' glass and sat at the head of the table. Katy joined the group and sat opposite of James.

"James," Joshua asked. "Would you do us the honor of giving thanks?"

"I would be honored," he replied smiling warmly. Bowing their heads, he began, "Saavatha we thank you for the fellowship that we now enjoy. Bless us with your wisdom as we prepare to return home to you, Saavatha be praised."

"Saavatha be praised! I'd like to propose a toast," Katy said, raising her wine glass. "To friendship," she declared, "May we never lose our way."

"Here, here," the trio voiced in unison as the glasses touched each other in harmony.

The dinner conversation went well into the evening. With the third bottle of wine gone, Katy started to clean off the table and Josh and his guest walked to the living room.

"Grab a seat," Josh said to James, motioning to the large wicker sofa.

"This is nice," James remarked. An unsuspecting grin crossed his face as his weight sank into the soft velvety cushions.

"Yeah I like it," Joshua replied. "Katy?" Joshua cried out. "On your way here, could you bring another bottle of wine with you?"

"Yeah, I will be right there."

"Oh, don't bring out the wine on my account," James said. "I'm pretty burnt out. I think I will turn in if you don't mind."

"I'm sorry. How selfish of me, of course you must be exhausted. I will see you in the morning."

"Very well, goodnight then."

"Goodnight."

James got up and was met by Katy. "Are you leaving us?" she asked.

"I'm afraid I must," he replied, "I enjoyed the meal tremendously. I will see you in the morning."

"Goodnight."

"Goodnight."

Katy sat down beside Joshua. "I am really glad that you let James stay the night."

"What else could I do?" he replied. "He's almost family."

"I know. You two seem very close."

"Yeah I guess we are."

"I'm pretty tired myself," she said, yawning. "I think I will turn in as well."

"OK."

"Are you coming?"

"No, I think I will stay up for a while," he said waving a book. "I'd like to read a bit."

"OK, don't stay up too late."

"I won't."

"Goodnight."

"Goodnight."

Katy glanced back at Joshua. *He'll probably fall asleep in that chair again,* she mused. *I better get up extra early to make sure that he's awake when Master James leaves.*

Chapter Twenty-six

The next morning Katy found Josh asleep in his chair with his book on his lap. *He fell asleep reading again,* she thought. *Is he ever going to change?* Shaking her head in disbelief she walked to him and squatted to his level. "Josh, sweetie, it's time for you to wake up," she whispered in his ear, shaking him gently. "Josh, it's time to wake up, the Master will be leaving soon. You should be there when he leaves."

"What?" he said drowsily.

"You should get up," Katy replied. "The Master will be leaving soon."

"Yeah," he said, rubbing his sleepy eyes. "Is he up yet?"

"Yes, he's getting some fresh air on the balcony."

"Some fresh air sounds good right about now," he said, getting up on shaky legs. "I will be outside for a while."

"OK sweetie," Katy replied. "I will bring you some coffee."

"Oh that'll be great. Thank you."

"You're welcome," she replied with a radiant smile.

"Did you have a peaceful rest?" James asked, seeing Josh walk through the door, shielding his eyes from the bright light.

"Somewhat," he replied, "that sofa is comfortable but it was not designed to sleep on."

"No it was not," James chuckled. "I can remember waking many times to find myself on a particular sofa."

"Did you sleep OK?"

"Yes I did," James replied, his good mood evident from the tone of his voice. "Today is my best day yet."

"When are you leaving?" he asked.

"In a few hours," James replied.

Katy walked to Joshua and handed him a hot cup of coffee. "Here you go, nice and hot. Just the way you like it."

"Thanks, sweetheart," he said smiling back at her. "Why don't you join myself and Katy for a ride in the forest?" he suggested, taking a sip of his coffee.

"Yes perhaps," James replied, "but I'd have to have my own mount."

"Not a problem. You can summon whomever you'd like."

"Great," James replied. He closed his eyes and a small funnel of fog appeared a few feet away. The fog grew at a record pace and vanished just as quickly, leaving behind a beautiful white unicorn. "Josh," he said proudly. "This is Alexia."

"Nice to meet you Alexia."

"The pleasure is all mine, Master," she replied, bowing her head respectfully.

"The pleasure is mine, I assure you."

Alexia lifted her head and looked at him with a twinkle. "If there's anything I can do for you…"

"You'll be the first one to know."

"How is my little girl doing today?" James asked, lovingly petting her neck.

"Very good Master," Alexia replied, she adored the attention. "You seem to be in a joyful mood. Today must be a good day?"

"Yes it is," he replied enthused. "Today is a great day. Today I go home."

"I leave tomorrow myself," the animal volunteered. "I can't wait: I've had enough of this place."

"I know what you mean," James said settling on her back. "I've had my fill of this place as well. Time to go home."

"Where would you like to go?" she asked.

"Take me to the middle of this forest," he replied, stroking her mane. "It's so beautiful there."

Alexia moved with an unhurried gait. She felt James' reassuring weight on her back. With the madness around her on the battlefield, she had missed the security and confidence he exuded. With such little time left together, she wanted to make up for it. The sun streamed through the dense evergreen forest reflecting on Alexia's crystal horn, almost making it glow. The animal held her head high with pride. After all, she was the first amongst her peers.

"I love this forest," James said under his breath. "It's almost time. Come on Alexia put a little speed behind it." Alexia looked at her Master momentarily from the corner of her eye and took off at full gallop, easily avoiding any oncoming obstacle in her path.

"This is it," he suddenly told her. "I can feel it, we are in the center of this beautiful creation. Let's wait here for the others. My time is near and I want to leave from here!"

Josh and Katy were catching up to James quickly.

Good, they're just about here! Alexia was prancing nervously. James petted her mane. "It's OK girl," he said soothingly. "You'll be fine." He walked the panting animal in a tight circle, cooling her down. He smiled at the two Eternals who just joined him. "It is my time to go child!" James declared, locking eyes with Joshua who just stopped near him. "Remember what I asked you. Don't forget. I will see you…"

His last words were silenced when his form became suddenly energized and stretched toward the sky. In a blinding flash of light, the Master vanished.

Chapter Twenty-seven

Katy gave Joshua an understanding glance. "This nightmare is just about over," she said.

Joshua was still emotionally distraught. His eyes were focused on Alexia until she vanished, returning to wherever she came from. The lone unicorn looked unnatural without James on her back. *The Master is gone,* he thought misty-eyed. *Soon Katy will leave, then me. I don't know if I want to go back. This is the only home I remember.* He gave her a distraught glance. "Yeah soon we'll all be out of here."

"Come on sweetie," she said, wiping her tears. "Let's go home."

He took a deep breath. Then with a heavy heart he patted Triss' mane. "You heard the lady," he said. "Home it is."

Katy looked at Joshua with worry. Dejected, he kept his head down and his shoulders slumped forward as Triss trotted home. *Oh Joshua, I will be leaving tomorrow. I wonder if I should tell him. He worries me. There's so much negativity still in him.* "Joshua?" Katy asked, feeling a little uneasy.

He turned and looked at her. His eyes betrayed the desperation he felt. "Yes?"

She couldn't look at him. "I thought that I should tell you that I will be leaving next," she said, evading his gaze.

He lowered his head and frowned. "Figures!"

"Don't be like that," she replied, lifting her head up, trying to stifle her tears. "Soon you'll be in the kingdom with me. You'll be fine."

"Yeah, sure," he mumbled under his breath. "When are you leaving?"

Katy bit her lower lip. She had a hard time controlling her emotions. "Tomorrow," she finally said.

"Great!" he said, his voice dripping with sarcasm.

A wave of desperation flooded over her and she felt the warmth of her tears as they streamed down her cheeks. "What is that supposed to mean?" she cried.

Joshua frowned in anger. "Forget it!" he spat. "I will deal with it."

"Joshua!"

Joshua looked at her and his heart melted. "I'm sorry," he said with regret. "It's just that I'm feeling deserted. To tell you the truth I don't know if I want to go back. I hardly remember home."

Katy stifled a laugh as she wiped her tears with the back of her hand. "So that is what this is about?" she said, moving closer to him. "I'm sorry that you feel this way. This place is not home. The kingdom is our home, yours and mine. Think about your family. They're waiting for your return."

His family. That had been on his mind for quite some time now. He wondered about them, what they were like, what they looked like. "Yeah," he sighed. "I've been thinking about them a lot lately."

"A millennium is a long time without a son."

He looked up at her and the beginning of a tender smile appeared on his face. "Yeah," he sighed. "You're right. You know I have three brothers and I can't remember what they look like."

Katy smiled, a tender smile. She reached for him and rubbed his elbow reassuringly. "I'm sure they'll understand," she said.

"I try to picture them in my head," he said glancing back at her. "When I have their images, they vanish without a trace, leaving me blank. It's so frustrating."

"You've been through a lot more than someone else at your level could handle," she replied. "Give yourself a break. Not every Eternal who has the misfortune of crossing Baltaseim's path has come out of it as good as you have."

His eyebrows raised with surprised. "You think so?"

"I know so. You're a lot stronger than you think. Give yourself a chance to grow and learn to apply what you've learned here."

"I wouldn't give two bits for what I learned here," he replied.

Katy could sense the resentment in his voice. She understood it, but she didn't approve of it. He would have to learn to control his negative emotions before they controlled him. "Joshua!" she said, shaking her head. "Your time here wasn't wasted. You've learned something. Your job is to find out the positive that came out of all these struggles." She observed him silently, waiting for a reply. His demeanor didn't display reflection, but frustration and resentment. After what seemed an eternity, he finally looked up at her.

"Nothing comes to mind," he said flatly.

"You need time to reflect and that's only going to happen once you leave this forsaken place."

"I doubt it," he scoffed, "but there's one thing that you're right about."

"What's that?"

"Time will tell."

They continued their stroll back to the cottage in silence. An uncomfortable atmosphere had developed between them and neither of them knew how to appease it. With the cottage finally within sight, Joshua raised his head to look at the familiar surrounding. "What is Jobb doing here?" he asked, surprised. The pale Eternal was leaning on the balcony rails. When he saw them he smiled and spat out the piece of grass he was chewing on.

Katy looked at the Eternal who was approaching them. "I don't have a clue," she replied.

Joshua's mood changed suddenly. He seemed almost happy. Katy noticed and almost smiled when she saw the spark of life that she found so irresistible, return to his eye. "I haven't seen him in ages."

"Oh, he's been around," she said and raised her eyebrows.

He glanced at her and smiled. "Yeah, you would know. I've been pretty much a hermit since you found me."

"Don't remind me," she scoffed. "The little tantrum you pulled at the castle was pretty embarrassing."

"What do you expect," he replied on the defensive. "You would have acted the same way if you had been tortured there."

Katy looked back at him and shrugged. "You have a point."

"Thank you!" Joshua proclaimed triumphantly. Reaching the balcony, they dismounted and tied the unicorns on the rail. Joshua turned and met the visitor with enthusiasm. "Long time no see!" he said to his guest, genuinely glad to see the old librarian.

The thin Eternal smiled. He hadn't seen Joshua since his abduction. *Has he ever changed, there's something different about him. Something darker, anger? Hatred perhaps? I'm not sure, but I know that he's changed and not for the better. I guess I can't blame him. If the stories I've heard are true, I might feel the same way. Baltaseim can be quite sadistic.* "Yes," he said extending his hand, "it's been a long time. I've been very busy."

"I'm sure you have," Joshua replied taking his hand firmly. "What brings you in this neck of the woods anyway?"

"Oh right. It's Katy. I got word that she wanted to talk to me."

"Really?" he asked, surprised. He glanced at her and raised an eyebrow. "Katy, he's here for you."

Katy flushed. "Right," she replied flustered. She suddenly felt self-conscious. She had hoped for a more private meeting. "I almost forgot. Since you're taking Triss to her stall, could you take Buck too?"

He looked up at her suspiciously. From the way she had reacted, he was sure that she was hiding something. But he couldn't figure out what. It nagged at him. "Sure," he replied. He took Buck's lead rope and went to the stalls.

Katy waited until Joshua was out of earshot before she spoke to the old librarian. "Jobb!" she whispered when she was certain that Joshua couldn't hear her. "I never thought he would leave. I have a favor to ask of you."

"I will help if I can," he replied with curiosity.

She took in a deep breath. She didn't like doing things behind his back but this was for his own good. "If he knew I was asking this, he would kill me," she told him nervously. "Could you stay with him until he leaves? I'm worried about him. I would feel much better if you did."

The old Eternal gave her a radiant smile. "Certainly," he said. "I would love to."

She let out a sigh of relief. "Don't say anything to Josh," she cautioned. "It would complicate things."

He stared at her for a moment. "Don't worry," he finally said. "I understand."

She smiled. "Great. I'm glad that this is settled."

"What's settled?" Joshua asked.

She froze. She could feel her heart pounding. *He's not supposed to be back so soon! I hope that he didn't hear anything.* "Oh! You're back!" she replied, looking at him with this odd expression on her flustered face. "Don't do that!" she said putting her hand on her chest, checking her heartbeat. "You scared me!"

He eyed her with suspicion. "Sorry," he said staring. "I didn't mean to scare you. But what's settled?"

"Oh nothing special," she replied nervously. "I was just telling Jobb that if making tea was going to convince him to stay then it was settled."

"OK."

"I will make the tea," she said excusing herself quickly.

What's she feeling guilty about? I saw her chewing her bottom lip. What's going on? "Sure, we'll be right in." He observed her entering the kitchen. "Let's go in," he said to his guest. "The tea should be ready soon."

Joshua closed the door behind himself. He could hear Katy rummaging through the kitchen cupboards. "What do you take in your tea?" Katy said to Jobb from the kitchen.

"Just tea, nothing else."

"OK," she replied, poking her head through the doorway to glance at him. "It'll be ready in a moment."

Joshua put his hand on Jobb's shoulder affectionately. "Let's go and sit down," he said motioning to the dining room.

They walked in and sat down at the table. Jobb couldn't help but notice the fine craftsmanship sitting before him. The tabletop was a three-inch solid slab of knotty pine. The four-by-six foot surface was finished to a fine gloss. This masterpiece sat on two legs at each end, held together by two four-by-fours that crisscrossed in the center. Everything was held together by one-inch dowels that blended perfectly in the décor. Six matching chairs completed the set. Jobb looked up and saw the hostess coming towards him cup in hand, smiling at him warmly.

"Here you go," she said, putting down a cup of hot tea in front of Jobb.

"Thank you."

"You're welcome," she said, sitting down.

The small group stayed up well into the morning and caught up with various discussions. Jobb could feel his eyes burn from exhaustion. He looked up at the clock on the wall. " I didn't realize it was that late!" *We've been up all night,* he thought, noticing the light through the cottage windows. "If you'll excuse me," he said, rubbing his eyes. "It's time for me to get some shut eye."

"Sure," Katy replied. "You can use the bedroom on the left."

"Thanks."

"I will see you when you get up," Joshua said to Jobb, who was exiting the room.

"Sure thing," he said looking back. "Goodnight."

"Goodnight."

Katy waited until she heard Jobb close the bedroom door before saying anything. "Listen," she said, putting her hand in Josh's. "I will be leaving very soon," she looked at him with misty eyes. *It all seemed to happen so fast, too fast,* she thought. "Why don't we take a walk in this beautiful forest of ours one last time."

Joshua felt like someone ripped his heart. He wanted to scream to make the injustice that he felt known. But he just smiled meekly, and stared into those green eyes, losing himself in her eternal essence. "Sure," he said, squeezing her hand. He put his arm around her neck like a newfound lover. They exited the cottage and walked into the dense forest that surrounded them.

I have a big surprise for you when you join me in the kingdom, she mused. She eyed him from head to toe. The attraction she felt towards him was incomprehensible. She snuggled closer to him. "Why don't you take me around the lake before I have to go?" She asked, smiling at him tenderly.

Joshua looked at the adoring face that was gazing back at him. A wave of sadness threatened to engulf him, as tears swelled in his deep blue eyes. *She'll be gone soon, I can feel it. How am I going to handle being here without her for so long?* "Certainly," he replied, showing her his best convincing smile.

The corner of Katy's lip curled up teasingly. *I can feel your worries, my love,* she thought. "Everything will be fine," she said, caressing his cheek with her fingertips. "Don't worry."

He could feel the tears flowing down his cheek. Embarrassed he quickly looked away. "I know," he replied. He already felt alone.

She brought his face to hers. "You make me very happy," she said, lightening up the mood. A joyful twinkle filled her eyes. "I am looking forward to our first Journey together."

"So am I," he replied his voice trembling.

"I love you very much," she said and gave him a quick peck on the lips.

"I love you to sweetheart," he said fighting back more tears. "I just wish that we had more time before you returned to the kingdom."

"I know." Her disappointment showed through despite her best efforts. "Soon you will be home. Once we are together I have many plans for us."

"Plans?" Josh asked, his confusion coming loud and clear.

"I will tell you," she replied with a touch of amusement in her voice, "when you are home."

"OK," Josh conceded with disappointment, "if you must."

"Look at that spot Josh," she said pointing to a trail that was close to the water. "It's beautiful, let's go there." He smiled. Joshua led the way and stopped when their feet touched the water.

"My love," Katy said, "it's time. Kiss me before I go." He leaned down and kissed her passionately, "I love you," he whispered in her ear. "I will see you soon." Holding her tight, never wanting to let go, he suddenly felt Katy's form energize and vanished.

Chapter Twenty-eight

It took a few moments for Joshua to register what had occurred. He looked across the lake with an empty heart. Not being able to hold himself together any longer, he fell to his knees and weeped. His strong shoulders heaved in rhythm with his uncontrollable sobs. After what seemed an eternity, he felt a hand on his shoulder. He looked up and saw Jobb standing before him.

"Come on Joshua," the old librarian said in a soothing and compassionate voice. "Let me take you home."

"Jobb!" he replied, "she's gone! What am I going to do?"

"You'll do just fine," he said with a reassuring smile. "Anyway I'm here, remember?"

"Yeah," he replied managing a chuckle, "you're here."

"Come on," he pleaded, offering his hand. "Let me take you home."

Joshua looked at it momentarily, took it and got on his feet. "Let's go home," he said, beaten and devastated.

"It's only for a short while Joshua," Jobb said, trying to cheer him up. "Soon you'll be in the kingdom with her."

Joshua felt a flash of anger course through him. "Don't patronize me!" he shouted. "Soon is not good enough!"

"I'm sorry. I didn't mean it like that."

"Forget it," Joshua apologized. "I shouldn't take it out on you. It's not your fault and I know that you're trying to help."

"It's OK," Jobb said. "I understand."

Joshua looked up at him questionably. "Do you really?"

"Yeah actually I do," he replied. "I've been through three wars and was exiled twice. Leaving someone behind is never easy, no matter who you are."

"Yeah," Joshua sighed. "I keep forgetting. You are a lot older than you look."

"That's the fun part of being an Eternal," Jobb replied amused. "You can make yourself look as young or as old as you like."

"Yeah that's what Katy was telling me. I just can't do that yet."

"Oh you will soon enough. Once you've had a few Journeys under your belt come and talk to me. I will show you how it's done. Deal?"

"I don't know about that. Shape shifting freaks me out."

"It's always frightening the first time, but you'll get used to it," Jobb patted his back. "Come on, let me make you something to eat."

Joshua looked at him with a bewildered look on his face. *What, eat? I don't want to eat.* He made a sour face which didn't go unnoticed. "Alright," Joshua conceded, he knew that objecting would do no good. "You win." He shook his head while a sly grin crossed his lips. "I don't know how you can eat at a moment like this."

"A habit that I picked up on one of my Journeys," Jobb said. "It used to help me think."

"I bet. I'm sure that it was not the only thing it did for you."

"Don't remind me," Jobb scoffed. "You should have seen how big I was."

"I can just imagine."

The next three days were very hard on Joshua. Despite Jobb's best effort to cheer him up Joshua couldn't seem to shake the gloomy cloud that hung over his head. The only solace he found was in sleeping the days away, which irritated Jobb to no end.

A pang of anger shot through Jobb as he entered Joshua's bedroom. *He's still sleeping,* he thought, gritting his teeth. *That's it. I've had enough.* He walked over to the bed and leaned over the sleeping form. "Joshua wake up!" Jobb said, shaking him harder than he expected.

"What!" Joshua screamed. He shot him a look that would have burned a hole through Baltaseim himself.

Jobb stared back with narrowed eyes. "Don't you think it's time that you got this lazy ass of yours out of bed?" he asked sharply.

"No!"

He took a deep breath to calm his nerves. "So you're going to waste the remainder of your stay sleeping?"

"Yes!" Joshua shouted. "Now leave me alone!" He pulled the blankets over his head and turned away from Jobb.

"Oh no, you don't!" Jobb said with a sharp, determined tone. "You my friend are getting out of this bed whether you like it or not!" He grabbed the blankets and pulled them off the bed.

Joshua glared at him and went for the blankets. "Piss off!"

"By the Garden of Life! "Jobb shouted, "I've had enough of this!" He grabbed Joshua by the top of his long mop and dragged his sorry behind out of bed.

Joshua yelled out in anger as he hit the floor hard. Losing control, he started to thrash about violently. "Leave me alone!" he screamed while being pulled out of his room.

"No. That's not going to happen," Jobb replied and dragged the kicking and hollering Joshua outside. "No more moping about. This has gone on long enough." With one final shove, he heaved Joshua over the rails and watched him fall into a deep horse trough. "You are going to wake up boy!" Jobb said and leaned over the rail. "And then you and I will have a chat."

A loud splash was heard as Joshua dove headfirst into icy waters. "Ahhhh! Baltaseim's dismay! This water's cold!" he sputtered through chattering teeth. "What was that for?"

"To wake you up!" Jobb observed him from the balcony. "No more sulking. I won't allow it!"

"OK I get your point," Joshua sighed. "Now help me get out of this thing!"

"Alright," Jobb snapped his fingers. "Done!" As quickly as it appeared the trough vanished, leaving Joshua momentarily suspended until gravity took over and brought him back to reality.

"Ouch!" Joshua cried out, hitting the ground hard.

"Sorry," Jobb said unable to resist a hysterical laugh.

"That wasn't funny!"

"Oh yes it was," Jobb replied, still laughing. "You should have seen your face when you hit that water." He wiped away his tears and held his gut from laughing so hard. "I didn't know you could be so animated."

"Very funny," Josh said, his pride still bruised. "Now help me up."

Jobb stumbled down the stairs still giggling. "Here! Take my hand."

Joshua took his hand and Jobb pulled him to his feet. "I'm soaked!" Joshua said angrily. "Look at me. I look like a drowned rat!"

"Oh stop your whining," Jobb replied. "Here," he said and dried him with a wave of his hand as if nothing happened. "Now is that better?"

"Ahhh!" Joshua screamed. "Don't do that! I hate it. It gives me the creeps."

"You'll get used to it," Jobb said with a smirk on his pale face.

"I doubt it."

"You're an Eternal like me. One day you'll be able to do the same."

"Don't remind me."

"Alright," Jobb said, "I will be nice. Come on up and I will make you some tea."

"Yeah," Joshua scoffed. "After what I've been through I need a big cup."

"You only got what you deserved," he replied, looking back at him from the top of the stairs.

"That's your opinion," Joshua said flatly.

"Here's your tea," Jobb said, handing him a large steaming cup.

"Thank you," Joshua replied sharply. He took it delicately, trying not to burn himself. "Humm," he said inhaling the sweet aroma. "I love this stuff. Katy got me hooked on this you know. I still have so much to learn. I don't know if I will be able to keep up."

"You'll do just fine," Jobb reassured him. "Don't worry so much. That's your problem you know. You worry about things way too much."

"You think so?"

"Yeah," Jobb replied. "It takes time and you have plenty of it. We all do."

"Maybe you're right," Joshua sighed, taking a sip of his tea. "Being caught in this war put me so far behind sometimes I don't think that I will ever be able to catch up."

"Oh you will. Talking about catching up, that reminds me. I've got a perfect book for you to read."

"What are you talking about?"

"Well," Jobb replied. "You've said many times that you don't remember much of the kingdom."

"Yeah…and?"

"Well let me finish." Jobb said annoyed. "Anyway I found a book in my library that you might want to read…it might help you remember some stuff."

"Ok…what is it?"

"It's called *The Historical Structure of the Kingdom of Saavatha*," he replied. "I've got it here…I put it in your library when I first came in, let me get it." Jobb got up and walked to the library. "It's very good…you'll see."

"Well, hold on then." Joshua grabbed his cup and got up. "If I'm going to read, then I will sit in the library. It's a lot more comfortable."

"Here you go." Jobb handed the book to Joshua as he sat in his favorite sofa chair.

"Thank you. Nice book." He examined the leather-bound binder. Setting it on his lap he opened the book and started to read. A few hours went by before Joshua finally reached the middle of the book. Suddenly a peculiar feeling came over him. "Jobb!" Joshua cried out. "Something is happening to me!"

Startled, Jobb spilled his tea on his lap. "What's the matter?"

"I'm getting pins and needles all over my body!" Joshua eyes flashed with terror. "Make it stop! Please make it stop!"

Jobb couldn't help but smile. Joshua was going home. "Don't be afraid. This won't hurt you. You are about to go home. What you are experiencing is part of the transportation process."

"I'm going home?" Joshua could see nothing but white fog around him.

"Yes!" Jobb replied. "I will see you soon."

Joshua wasn't able to make out Jobb's last words as the former child's form energized and vanished right before Jobb's eyes.

"It's just about over." Jobb looked at the empty seat in front of him. "Soon it'll be my turn."

When the chasm released the last victim, all traces of its existence vanished, leaving a bitter taste that many Eternals will not forget. It sits, taunting silently once more, waiting patiently for its next prisoner—holding its location in a tight grip of secrecy. Only one Supreme Being could pinpoint its existence but he is not talking. No Eternal knows when this place would be needed again, except Saavatha himself.

Chapter Twenty-nine

After being in the Hall of Journeys for a couple of days, Joshua was losing whatever patience he had left. *All this runaround, what's going on?* He noticed Shawn in the crowd. *There's that bastard!* Joshua's anger swelled as he hurried towards him. Shawn hadn't noticed Joshua coming from behind until his elbow was held in a tight grip. "Where's Katy?" Joshua demanded, spinning Shawn to face him.

Shawn startled, looked up and stared at him briefly, then looked away. "I don't know which Katy you're talking about," Shawn lied. "In this kingdom there has to be millions of them. Be more specific."

"For the umpteenth time," Joshua spat, his patience coming to an end, "she's from the house of Thaabar. Her founder's name is Joel, she's got two brothers..."

Shawn was sure that if he didn't give Joshua what he wanted soon, things might come to blows. He was so entranced with Joshua's demeanor that he failed to notice a short and round Eternal who suddenly appeared behind him. "Shawn," he said with a hint of urgency in his raspy voice, "may I have a word with you?"

It took a moment for the words to register. Shawn turned his head to look at him. "Yeah, sure," he replied. Shawn pulled his elbow free from Joshua's insistent grip. "Excuse me," he said staring Joshua down. "I will be right back."

Joshua watched them move out of earshot. *What was that all about?* he thought. His anger was still simmering just below the surface. One wrong word from either of them and it would explode in their faces. He watched suspiciously, keeping himself on guard.

Teal glanced in Joshua's direction. He suddenly became very nervous. *There's something not quite right with that one,* he thought. *I can't put my finger on it. I better steer clear of him. He's bad news.* Teal looked back at an annoyed Shawn. "I don't think that I can hold her much longer," he whispered, trying not to attract attention. "She's been here every single day looking for him."

"You have to," Shawn insisted. "Saavatha doesn't allow fraternization between the houses—you know that!"

"I know," he replied, "but she won't give up. This time she brought some Master with her to plead her case."

Shawn closed his eyes and rubbed his temple. "Stall them," he said. He failed to notice James, who was approaching them. From the look on his face, James wasn't happy. "I will try to get rid of—" Shawn began.

James had been standing there, unnoticed for a few moments. He didn't like what he was hearing. "Get rid of whom?" James asked angrily.

Shawn looked up with round eyes. "Master James!" he said, startled and embarrassed to be caught. "Why hasn't anyone told me you were here?"

"I did," he motioned towards Teal. "And from what I can see, your efforts to get rid of me haven't worked.

"I would never do that!" replied a red-faced Shawn.

"Spare me your rhetoric," James said flatly. "I know what you two are up to. Saavatha's rules are not written in stone. They are a guideline."

"I thought…" Shawn began.

James was a quiet Eternal, but even he had his limits. "You thought of nothing!" he shouted at an embarrassed Shawn. "I've spoken with Saavatha myself. He has approved their fraternization personally. Now unless you wish to challenge his ruling, I would suggest that you stay out of the way!"

Shawn lowered his head in shame. "As you wish Master."

James broke his stare and moved Katy in front of him. "There's Joshua," he pointed him out of the crowd. "Go to him—he needs you."

Katy felt her pulse rush when she set her eyes on him. With determination, she rushed over to him. "Joshua!" she screamed over the crowd. *He saw me!* she thought. She ran to him and jumped in his strong arms. She squealed joyfully, wrapped her arms around his neck and kissed him passionately. "I didn't think I'd see you again," she said, staring into his blue eyes. "It's so good to see you."

Joshua took a deep breath, and finally let himself relax. "I've been here for a couple of days," he said with exasperation. "This Shawn guy has been giving me the runaround. I don't get it. What's with this guy?"

Katy let out a grumble. "I could just kill him! He's an elder. They think that they are here to enforce Saavatha's rules."

Joshua frowned. "I wish that they would mind their own business!"

"I know," Katy replied. "I wish they'd stay out of it. I'm so sorry."

"It's OK," Joshua said, hugging her tightly. "What counts is that you're here now. I'm so glad to see you." He took her face in his hands. "I thought I was going crazy without you."

"I see that you kids found each other," Joshua heard over his shoulder.

Joshua turned around and his grin broke into a wide-open smile. "Master James!" he cried out. "Oh, am I ever glad to see you." He turned and hugged James tightly. "I didn't think that I would ever get out of that place."

"Yeah I know how you feel." James replied with tears rolling down his cheeks. "You look great!" He held Joshua at arm's length. "Did you tell him?" James asked, looking at Katy.

"No," she replied. "I was waiting for you to tell him."

"Tell me what?" Joshua asked confused.

"You can tell him," James looked at Katy and smiled.

"I didn't want to say anything before I was sure," she said to Joshua.

"Spill it!" Joshua replied. He couldn't stand the anticipation any longer.

"Well," she continued looking into his blue eyes. "I asked Master James if it was possible for Eternals of different houses to join."

"And?"

"We can!" she squealed joyfully jumping up and down. "Master James got special permission from Saavatha."

"And?"

She bit her lower lip nervously. "Well I know that we haven't talked about it but I was hoping that you and…I…I mean we do make a nice couple…don't you think?"

Joshua found himself lost in her green eyes. *You are so beautiful,* he mused. *How could I be so lucky?* A tender smile came over his face. "Yes," he replied.

The anticipation was killing her. She wondered if he really wanted her. "Yes what? Yes we make a nice couple or yes you'll join with me?"

He remained silent for a long moment. He looked down at her pleading eyes, enjoying the sudden power he felt he had over her. "I will join with you," he finally said.

For a moment, she thought her heart stopped. She wasn't sure she heard him right. "You will?"

For the first time in a long time, he was happy. "Yes," he replied with misty eyes. "I will join with you."

Her emotions were more than she could take. She began to sob in his arms. Not knowing what to say, she looked up at him, tears of joy were streaming down her face. She craned her neck and kissed him passionately.

"Come on kids," James said, interrupting their embrace. "There'll be plenty of time for that. Your public awaits you."

Joshua looked at him perplexed. "Public?"

"Yes, you are a hero Joshua," James replied. "We are all heroes, all of us who spent time in exile."

"Why?"

"Because we sacrificed our freedom to ensure the defeat of Baltaseim."

Joshua lowered and shook his head in disbelief. "OK," he said. "This will take some getting used to."

James put his hand on Joshua's shoulder. "You will," he said in a reassuring tone. "Just don't let it go to your head." He gave Joshua a stern look.

Joshua chuckled. "Not while you're around I won't."

James beamed. "You better believe it."

The trio walked outside to be greeted with cheers, applauses and whistles from Eternals as far as the eye could see.

Joshua stopped at the hall's first step. A feeling of awe washed over him. A sea of Eternals stood before him, cheering. For the first time in his life, he felt small. "Look at them all," Joshua said, flabbergasted. "There's got to be millions of them, maybe more."

"Billions of them," James replied, correcting him. "They're all here to praise what we've done."

Joshua couldn't help but stare at the mass who had gathered together in his honor. His eyes swelled with tears. It touched him in a way he had never known before. "I didn't think that the kingdom was that big," he said, fighting to hold the tears back. "I don't know what to say."

"Don't say anything," James replied. "Just be grateful. It's a big family you've got here. Don't ever forget them."

"I won't," Joshua said, wiping the continuous flow of tears from his eyes.

James squeezed Joshua's shoulder in a show of affection. "Where to now?" he asked.

"My Founder's," Joshua said emotionally. "I think it's time I see him."

"Alright," James replied. "I will take you both to him."

The trio made their way through the crowd towards Gabriel's home. A knot of anticipation tightened in Joshua's gut. *It's been so long,* he thought hesitantly. *Will I recognize him? Will he recognize me? Will he still be angry?* The burning feeling in his stomach was at its peak. He couldn't help but fear rejection.

Katy put her hand on Joshua's shoulder. With the gentleness of which she was renowned for, she caressed the small of his back. "You'll do just fine," she said, reading his mind. "They love you. They'll be happy to see you. Trust me!" she looked in his blue eyes and gave him a reassuring smile. "Anyway, you have to give them the good news!"

He looked down at her. "Yeah," he replied. "I think you're right. After all this time I owe them that much."

Chapter Thirty

As they approached Gabriel's home, Joshua's pain intensified. It was almost unbearable. Katy grabbed his arm and held him tight. She was sure that he would bolt any minute now. She had seen this look of panic in his eyes before. She gazed up and gave him her best encouraging smile. He smiled back nervously. His steps were unsteady, dragging behind. He dreaded this moment. Finally, himself he found himself at Gabriel's front door. "This is it!" James said, stopping in front of the gigantic arches. "Well," he said, turning to Joshua, "aren't you going to knock?"

Joshua could feel his heartbeat. Sweat accumulated on his brow. With shifty eyes, he looked up at James. "Maybe you should," he replied, turning pale.

James glanced at him. "Alright if you're too chicken."

Joshua thought he was going to pass out. For a brief moment he wished that he were back under Baltaseim's grip. At least there, he knew what to expect. Baltaseim didn't frighten him as much. Joshua looked at James and lowered his head in shame. "I am."

Katy's frustration was bursting at the seams. She couldn't understand why Joshua was making such a big deal out of it. *Of course they'll be happy to see him,* she thought. *They're his family!* "For crying out loud," she cried out. "Would somebody, anybody knock."

James looked at her and sighed. "Fine," he looked back at Joshua. "I will do it." He knocked on the wooden door three times and waited for a response. After what seemed an eternity, he knocked three more times and waited. Finally he heard some shuffling and someone coming towards the door. "Just a moment, I'm coming!"

Slowly the doors swung open and Gabriel stuck his head out. "Master James!" His face lit up like a Christmas tree. He turned his head to address his boy. "It's Master James, Carl." Gabriel looked up at James who was still waiting for an invitation. "How rude of me," he said with a smile. "Please come on in."

They entered the home and Gabriel closed the doors behind them. James turned to Gabriel and put a gentle hand on Katy's shoulder. "Gabriel," he said smiling at the woman, "This is Katy. She's a very close friend of mine." Gabriel nodded with a soft acknowledging smile. James then turned to Joshua who by this time looked like he was going to faint.

"And this guy," James said looking straight at Gabriel, "is the best surprise yet." James smiled at Gabriel tenderly. "You know this guy; you haven't seen him for a long time."

Gabriel stared at Joshua. His facial features, the long blond hair. It reminded him of someone he'd forgotten many years ago. Suddenly, out of the darkest corner of his mind, a spark of hope ignited. *Could it be? After all this time? Has my son been returned to me?* Gabriel's mind was reeling, too afraid to hope. He couldn't take another devastating blow; it would kill his sanity. His pulse raced. He felt an uncontrollable trembling come forth from deep within his being. With shaking hands he reached for the face of a son he knew so long ago. "Joshua?" Gabriel asked, hardly able to form the words, "is it you?"

Joshua placed his hands on his founder's. He looked down at the fragile-looking Eternal with pleading eyes. Suddenly Joshua knew. He was finally home! In that instant, all of his fears disappeared. They were replaced by a warmth of acceptance. His heart filled with a confusing orchestra of emotions. He felt happiness and also sadness for the years that were lost. It was too much for him and he broke into an uncontrollable sob. "Yes founder," he managed to reply. "I am Joshua, son of Gabriel of the House of Qwenthrey. Please forgive me!"

Gabriel jumped into his son's arms and hugged him tight. The sounds of their weeping was comforting to him. It was over. His son had returned. He clung to him, making sure that he wasn't dreaming. He pushed his son away from him gently. "Have you ever changed," he said, his voice still trembling. "You're all grown up. I thought that I lost you forever." Another fresh flow of tears overcame him. "I missed you so much," he said drying his tears. "Now you are home…it seems so unreal to me."

Joshua took a deep breath to calm himself. He understood that feeling. It still didn't feel real to him. He was afraid that he would wake up at any moment to find himself back into that dark and miserable place that he had called home not so long ago. "I am real, Founder. I've missed you so much. I spent a lot of time thinking about you and what I put you through. I am so sorry," Joshua replied, drying his tears.

Gabriel looked at the guilt-ridden face of his son. The past didn't matter any more. It was over and all this pain was behind them now. Now they had a chance at a new beginning. He was not going to let the past taint the second chance he had been given. "Pay no mind to that," Gabriel said soothingly. "I never held any of this against you. It was my fault, really. If I had been a better parent I would have seen this coming."

Gabriel's last words shook Joshua deeply. He raised his hands and took his founder's face tenderly. "You have been everything to me," Joshua said, his voice still crackling from the pain. "There is nothing that you could have done differently to save me from the fate that I chose."

Feeling shame, Gabriel tried to look away. Joshua, sensing his founder's feelings, forced his gaze on him. "It was my choice to do what I did," he reminded him sternly. "My choice! And I paid for it; it's that simple. You cannot hold yourself responsible for what I did. I won't allow you!"

Gabriel gave him a nod and a weak smile crossed his lips. He took his hands. "I'm just glad to see you home."

An overwhelming feeling of happiness flowed through the small group. Katy took Joshua's arm and James soon became deeply involved in an intellectual conversation with Gabriel. Joshua looked around. The library on the left matched the living room motif. The dining room on the right connected to the kitchen through an archway. It all gave him a vague feeling of déjà vu. He knew this place, at least he used to. *I wish I could remember more of this place,* he thought. *I grew up here with my brothers: why can't I remember?* The sound of Katy's voice broke his reverie.

"This place is unbelievable," she said, "and to think that you grew up here. I can't believe it."

Joshua looked at her with lost eyes. "Yeah, miracles never cease," he replied.

Gabriel took his arm. "Let me reintroduce you to one of your brothers." His eyes were still plagued with disbelief. "Carl!" he cried out. "Could you please come over here? There's someone I'd like you to meet."

A tall and broad-shouldered Eternal walked into the foyer. "Who's here?" Carl said curiously.

Gabriel walked over to Carl and led him to his lost son. "Carl," he began. "I don't know if you remember him, but this is your long lost brother Joshua."

For the first time in Carl's existence, the words that usually came easily now evaded him. He looked up a Joshua and not at word came out of his open mouth. After an embarrassing moment, his voice started trickling in. "Joshua?" he finally said. "I don't believe it…it's you." He hugged his brother. "I remember when you got lost so long ago. I'd never thought that I'd see you walk into this house again."

Joshua looked at his brother. His red hair and beard suited him well. He smiled. "Well, dearest brother, I'm here," Joshua said.

Gabriel couldn't help but interrupt. "Where are your brothers?" he asked.

Carl turned and looked at his founder. "They should be back for the celebration," he replied, rubbing his red stubby beard.

Gabriel broke into a radiant smile. "Perfect! You're staying a while, right?"

"No I can't," Carl replied. "Shawn is expecting me. I should be going. It's sure nice to see you again dear brother." He patted Joshua's shoulder affectionately. "I will see you at the celebration." Carl waved goodbye to everyone and exited the home.

Gabriel surveyed his guest. "Let's go into the living room," he suggested. "It'll be a little more comfortable.

James smiled at the old Eternal and placed a hand on his shoulder. "I should be going," he said. "I have a lot of things to do if I want the celebration to go off without a hitch."

"Are you sure you can't stay?" Gabriel asked.

"I'd love to," he said smiling, "but I really can't. I'm buried enough as it is."

Gabriel nodded. "Fair enough. Thanks for bringing my son home…thank you." He hugged the old Master. "I will see you at the celebration?"

"I wouldn't miss it. Take care." James gave everyone a knowing nod and exited the home. Gabriel closed the door behind him and turned to his remaining guests. "OK, let's all go to the living room," he said, leading the way. "Would any one of you like something to drink?" he asked, waiting for everyone to settle into their seats.

"Lemonade would be nice, if you have any," Katy replied.

"Sure I have some. Anybody else?" Gabriel asked, looking around the room. "OK, one lemonade coming right up." Returning to the living room with a tall glass he handed it to Katy and sat down beside her. He looked at Katy with interest. She seemed to glow.

"Joshua and I have some important news to share with you," Katy said, not able to contain her smile.

"Oh?" Gabriel asked. "What kind of news?"

She turned to Joshua. "You better tell him honey—after all he is your founder."

"Katy and I have decided to join," Joshua said a little red-faced. "We were hoping for your blessing."

"I'm proud of you son and you have my blessing." Gabriel replied. "Baltaseim be cursed!" he voiced. "Not only have I found my son but I also have gained a daughter-in-law. This day could not get any better. Congratulations and my best wishes."

"Thank you so much. It means a lot to us," Katy replied, barely able to contain herself.

"What house do you belong to?" Gabriel asked curiously.

"The house of Thaabar," she replied, smiling at him.

His brow frowned with concern. "Oh no, this might be a problem," Gabriel said, not able to hide his disappointment.

Joshua looked at his founder with surprise. "Problem?"

"We are not usually allowed to join outside of our own house," Gabriel explained.

"That problem has already been taken care of," Katy replied proudly.

Gabriel's eyebrows rose in disbelief. "Really?"

"Yes," She replied with a small amount of smugness in her voice. "Master James came to my rescue. He asked Saavatha himself."

"And?" Gabriel asked barely able to contain himself.

"I don't know what he did or said, but Saavatha agreed."

Gabriel leaned back in his seat and smiled. "I'm impressed!" he said. "Saavatha is not easily swayed."

"I know," Katy replied. "I owe a lot to Master James. He's been so wonderful to us."

"Yes he is like that," Gabriel said. "So if you're from the House of Thaabar then you must be familiar with Master Todd?"

"Yes I know him very well," Katy replied distantly. "We were in fact very close before the war and I haven't seen him since."

"Well now that you're home, you can remedy that situation. I'm sure that he won't mind seeing you after all that has happened."

"I'm sure that he'll be happy to see me," she replied smiling. "In fact I hope to see him at the celebration."

"Oh he'll be there—I'm sure of it. You're staying the night?"

Joshua looked at her. "What do you think?" he asked. "Would you like to stay for a bit before we go and visit your family?"

She thought about it for a moment. She really enjoyed Joshua's family. "I'd like that." Katy really didn't mind staying. She found Joshua's family very warm. This was the perfect opportunity for her to get to know the Eternals that Joshua grew up with. She would not miss this for the world.

"Is there anything you prefer to have for dinner?" Gabriel grinned from ear to ear.

"No," she replied not wanting to feel intrusive, "I am not fussy. Anything you make will be just fine. Just eating with you guys makes me feel like I am a part of the family."

"OK," Gabriel said. "In that case why don't you come and help me decide what to do for dinner." Gabriel told Katy, hoping to make her feel at home. "I have never cooked for any Eternals from the house of Thaabar. I want to make sure that everything is satisfactory." Smiling at her he continued after a short pause. "I was told that Eternals from that house are pretty fussy and I wouldn't want to leave a bad impression on our guests. I thought that if I asked for help, I would be sure to not offend any one."

"Show me the kitchen," she declared smiling, "and I will show you a satisfied customer."

"Come with me young lady," Gabriel said, walking her into the kitchen. "I will show you where everything is."

After a wonderful meal, Gabriel, Joshua and Katy stayed up late into the evening getting reacquainted. After they retired to their bedrooms, thoughts stirred randomly in Katy's mind as she was lying in bed trying to get some rest. *I'm so glad that I met Gabriel. He's like Joshua in so many ways. Joshua really seems happy since he has reunited with his founder. Gabriel was really receptive on our joining—if only my founder could be this way. It would make things so much easier. Tomorrow will be a busy day—better get to sleep. Worrying about it won't do any good. Hopefully I will catch him in a good mood.* She closed her eyes and after a deep sigh she slipped into a tranquil slumber.

Chapter Thirty-one

Joshua and Katy were standing at the front door ready to leave. Gabriel was grateful for his son's return and he wished Joshua could stay a little longer. Gabriel felt a pang of regret—he still had so much to say. *Don't be stupid!* He scolded himself. *He's home now, we'll have lots time to play catch-up.*

Katy smiled at Gabriel and gave him a hug. "That was a wonderful breakfast, thank you." She grabbed Joshua's hand and waited for Gabriel to open the door. "We'll see you tonight at the Congregation Hall," she said, waving goodbye. She heard the door close behind her as she walked down the steps to join Joshua who was waiting patiently. "Your founder is nice," she said. Her warm smile brightened her face as they started strolling towards her founder's home.

All that has happened in the last few days still seemed unreal to him. "Yeah," he replied. "He tries hard."

She wrapped her arm around his. "He really loves you, you know," she said, looking at him with a romantic eye. "It shows."

He glanced at her and quickly looked down. "I know he does," his eyes took on a distant look. "I just wish that I remembered more of him."

"It'll come back," she reassured, rubbing his arm lightly, "in time."

"I hope so." Joshua was still feeling the void from his memory lost. "How much further to your founder's house?" he asked, hoping to change the subject.

"Actually," she said pointing to a completely fenced mansion on a hilltop. "There it is."

Joshua looked up in the direction she was pointing to. He raised his eyebrows. Joshua had never thought that Katy belonged to a family of such a high status. Standing on that hilltop was a glorious castle. Four gigantic turrets stood there, completing the corners of a solid stone fence perimeter. In the center of the stone barrier stood a large dwelling. The individual turrets and stone walls rose far above the protective wall of stone. It was breathtaking. "Wow!" he said, feeling a little overwhelmed. "Is it ever huge!"

"Yeah everything has to be big with my founder," Katy replied, frowning lightly.

"There's no mistaking that," Joshua said as they walked through the arch opening that was cut through the stone. Once past the moat, he stopped and stared. Large willow trees adorned the property. The perfectly manicured lawn added the perfect touch to give this land a park-like appearance. "This is just beautiful," he remarked, looking at her.

"Don't let all this beauty fool you," Katy warned. "My founder can be quite the snob at times."

Joshua was a bit surprised by that statement. He had assumed that she might have had a good relationship with her founder. He thought that they might have been a lot a like. "Oh...really?"

"Yes he is," Katy said matter-of-factly. "Ever since I passed him in evolution, I get the feeling that he resents me a bit."

He glanced at her. "I thought that every Eternal in this kingdom had to be perfect to be here."

"No," Katy replied. "We all have freedom of choice. We can evolve at whatever pace we want."

Joshua noticed a peppered-haired Eternal playing with a dog. "I think that's your founder," Joshua said, pointing to him. "He seems to be preoccupied."

She looked in the direction he was pointing to and smiled. "Yeah," she replied. The sight brought back fond memories. "That's Kiky, his favorite poodle," she said with a hint of pleasure. They strolled towards the Eternal who hadn't seemed to notice them yet.

"I see that you finally decided to come home Tom," Joel said, not bothering to look back at her. He had seen Katy approach from the corner of his eye.

Katy clenched her teeth. How she hated what he was doing. When she had decided to be known under another persona, she knew that she had hurt him. She had hoped that with time he would get used to it. However, as time wore on, he grew bitter. It became even more apparent when she had surpassed him in evolution. "Founder," she said to the tall and slim Eternal before her. "I'm known as Katy now."

Joel looked up at his child. His eyes betrayed his facial expression—he really enjoyed patronizing her. "You're always going to be Tom to me," he replied, his eyes burrowing through her. "And which cat have you dragged in this time?" he scowled, turning his burning glare in Joshua's direction.

"His name is Joshua, Founder!" Katy quickly snapped, insulted by his rudeness.

He chuckled. His sarcasm was evident. He wasn't going to make this easy. "I see," he replied bitterly. He walked to Joshua and put a threatening hand on his shoulder. "So tell me Joshua," he said, his tone sending chills down Katy's back. "What misfortune led you to meet my disillusioned child?" He chuckled again. "Tell me. I need a little entertainment."

Joshua stared at him, unaffected by Joel's glare, he had endured much worse. "We met in exile," Joshua replied without batting an eye.

A vicious smile came to Joel's lips. "I see," he said curtly. "Did Tom ask you to join yet?"

"Yes," Joshua replied, stone-faced. He hated this Eternal. He hated what he was doing to his Katy. She may have been Tom at one point in her life, but now she was Katy and he didn't like what he was insinuating. "Katy has."

"I'm not at all surprised," he said with an arrogant tone. "You have no idea how many strays he brings here to introduce to me. None of them made the cut though. Which House do you belong to?"

Katy looked away. Her anger was taking the best of her. "Founder!" Katy shouted with tears of anger in her eyes. "That's not your business."

Joshua raised his hand in defense and turned to face her. "It's OK Katy," he replied. "I don't mind telling him." He turned to Joel and glared at him defiantly. "I'm from the House of Qwenthrey," he replied.

Joel smiled. He had them and he knew it. "I won't allow this Joining," he said to Katy, his authoritative tone coming loud and clear. "He's not from this House."

Katy glared back at him. "That's not your call," she replied. Her anger was swelling and she didn't know how much longer she would be able to keep it under wraps. "This Joining was approved by Saavatha himself. Stay out of it!"

Joel was taken aback. He never thought that Saavatha would be that stupid. "I see," he said flatly. "So you're going to waste your existence on a peon like him?" He pointed a finger at Joshua.

"He's not a peon!" She screamed back at him. "Saavatha wouldn't have approved this Joining if he thought that it was a waste of time."

"Saavatha doesn't know my Tom like I do," he replied stubbornly.

"So what do you want me to do?" she spat, glaring at him. "Do you really expect me to wait until you find a me partner that meets all of your criteria?"

"Of course," Joel replied his smugness getting on Katy's nerve. "I'm your founder. I know what's best for you. And this...thing," he said pointing to Joshua. "Is not it!"

"That's it!" she screamed back. "I've had it with you! Who I associate with is none of your business."

"Of course it is," Joel replied, putting his hands behind his back. "You are my business. I'm your founder."

"Forget it!" she yelled, frustrated. "I will not let you run my existence!" She shook a finger at him. "When are you going to learn to accept me for who I am?"

Joel approached her silently. She could tell from the look on his face that she had struck a sensitive nerve. "Don't you ever!" he screamed, backhanding her suddenly. "Ever! Speak to me like that again!" Knocked off her feet, she landed flat on her back. She could feel Joel's glare burn through her. "Understand?" he bellowed, affirming his power while towering over her.

Something in Joshua snapped. It was one thing to watch Joel verbally abuse his child, but quite another to sit there and watch him beat on her. With one swift movement, Joshua was off his feet and onto Joel's back with the prowess and fury of a gargoyle. Taken by surprise, Joel was knocked off his feet as Joshua straddled and immobilized him in a blink of an eye. "Don't you ever!" Joshua spat, his face only inches from Joel's. "Touch her again!" He growled, a low and sinister growl, and spit drool onto Joel's graying goatee.

Joel stared at Joshua. There was something sinister about him. He shuddered and could not look away from those icy cold eyes. "I'm sorry," he replied feeling Joshua's hatred. "I won't touch her again, please...don't hurt me," Joel pleaded, his terror having taken root.

"Understand?"

Words could not come to Joel. Paralyzed he could only manage few nods of his head.

Joshua smiled. His darker side was taking over. He loved the terror that he was creating in this Eternal. He enjoyed it tremendously. "Good," he replied. "Just to make sure that we understand each other, I'm going to show you what will happen the next time you decide to be a jerk." He look at Joel sadistically before he violently shoved his right hand into his abdomen.

A scream of agony echoed throughout the castle. Joel's back arched involuntarily. The pain was intolerable. Never in Joel's life had he known so much pain. His body shook uncontrollably and his screams were never-ending.

Katy looked at the scene before her, stunned. Memories came flooding back to her. Once she had witnessed the horror of a feeding. It took her many centuries to get over it. She couldn't believe that the Eternal that she was about to Join was performing a feeding and actually enjoying it. She would have to think about this. If he was going to be part of her life, he would never feed again! "Joshua!" she screamed. "Stop!"

Joshua was too caught up in his own pleasure. He didn't hear her. "Now," he said, getting an almost orgasmic enjoyment from the incoming energy that he was feeding on. "The next time I will drain you until you are comatose,"

Joshua felt a strong hand on his shoulder. He looked up to see who it was, but it was too late. "Get off of him!" Tom screamed. He pulled Joshua off of the terrified founder. "That's enough!"

Falling backward Joshua looked at Tom with fury still burning in his eyes. "Tom? What are you doing?" Joshua said almost screaming. "What was that for?"

"I don't know how it is done in Baltaseim's realm," Tom snapped, moments before returning to his favorite persona. "Here in the kingdom we do not feed on Eternals! Ever!" Katy shot him a frosted glare.

"I told you!" Joel screamed, shaking uncontrollably. "He's an animal! Get out! And take the beast with you!"

"Shut up founder," she snapped back at him. "For once in your existence keep that mouth of yours shut."

Joel recoiled back when Joshua let a low animalistic growl rumble through his lips.

"Joshua!" Katy yelled, backhanding his stomach. "That's enough!"

"I'm sorry!" Joshua replied, almost bent in half from the blow. "I shouldn't have done that…I'm sorry."

"What in Baltaseim's domain has got into you?" She asked completely taken aback.

"When he hit you," Joshua replied sheepishly, "something in me snapped and I lost it."

"I appreciate what you were trying to do," Katy said still angry. "But I can take care of myself."

"I'm sorry. I was just trying to help."

"That kind of help I don't need. You'd better learn to control your temper. I won't stand for another outburst like that understand?"

"Yes I'm sorry. It won't happen again. I promise."

"It better not. I'm not kidding. This kind of behavior will get you into more trouble than you can handle, trust me."

"I won't."

"I'm sorry about all of this," she said, turning to Joel who was sitting on the grass still weak from his encounter with Joshua. "But you did deserve that."

"Get out!" Joel screamed furiously. "Don't come back until you're rid of this Shadow!"

"Fine! I won't," she sighed. "Don't tell me that I didn't try to reconcile with you."

"Get out! And take Baltaseim's minion with you!"

Katy could not hide the hurtful gleam in her eyes. "If that's what you want. Come on Joshua," she told him sharply. "We're out of here."

He looked back at Joel who was still on the grass, terrified. "Where are we going?"

"Anywhere but here," she stormed out of the courtyard, pulling Joshua behind her. *That didn't go over too well. I should have come alone. I don't know what I'm going to do with you, Joshua. Joel sure sounded pissed. Oh well…he'll get over it…in a few eons…I hope.* "I need to think," she said out loud. "Let's go see Master James."

Chapter Thirty-two

James was sitting at his desk near the throne and going over some paperwork. The large emerald desk followed the circumference of the throne's first crystal step. The forty-eight square foot desk seemed hardly enough room for the multitude of papers that covered it, some stacked up two feet high. He peered up over the paperwork and noticed Katy and Joshua coming up the crystal stairs. *Katy, Joshua,* he thought, *here already?* He stood and pushed his glasses back in place. "Nice of you both to come and see me," he said walking towards them. "Actually I'm glad you've come. I'm just about ready to leave for the Congregation Hall. I thought that you might want to leave with me."

Katy smiled. She had come to like James, they had developed a special bond during their exile. "Yeah that would be great," she replied. "We have just come from my founder's place."

James's eyebrows raised. "Oh yeah? How's Joel doing?"

She glanced at him for a moment, then looked down at her shoes. She couldn't hide her disappointment. "Oh him and I got into it again."

"Really?"

"Yeah," she said, then looked at Joshua. "You might say that things kind of got out of hand."

James followed Katy's gaze. When it landed on Joshua, he knew that somehow Joshua had done something that he shouldn't have. Joshua's demeanor told him that right away. "How's that?"

She returned her gaze to the old Master. "Well," she began, chewing on her bottom lip. "I went there to introduce him to Joshua and of course he was rude as usual." A wave a grief came over her. Her eyes filled with tears, but she was determined not to cry. She looked down and put her hand over her brow, trying to control the flow of tears. "That's when all of Baltaseim's minions were set loose." Her voice started to tremble at this point. She didn't know if she could continue, but somehow the words came out. "He hit me and Joshua lost his temper."

"Oh no," James said, concerned. "Is Joel alright?"

"Oh he'll get over it," she said. "Joshua scared Baltaseim right out of him though."

James turned to Joshua and gave him a stern look. "What did you do?" James asked, frowning.

Despite his shame, Joshua looked up. He recognized the look on the old Master's face immediately. James was not happy. Joshua swallowed hard and reluctantly answered. "I fed on him," he said and lowered his head, staring at the floor.

James' eyes opened. *No, that can't be right. Only Shadows feed on one another, not Brights, Saavatha doesn't allow it!* "You what?" he asked, flabbergasted.

"He pissed me off," Joshua said shrugging his shoulders. He knew that what he did wasn't right, but he was still trying to justify his action. "I wanted to teach him a lesson. So I fed on him."

"Joshua!" James said, his anger coming through his soft-spoken voice. "That's not allowed! Saavatha forbids it. His light is the only thing we need to nourish us."

"That's what Katy told me," Joshua replied. "I didn't know. I won't do that again."

"Alright," James sighed. "Remember you are not with Baltaseim any more. We play by different rules here. Don't forget that."

"I will try my best."

"I'm sure you will," James told him with more emphasis on his promise than his trust to do the right thing. "We should be going," he said impatiently. "I wouldn't want to be the last one there."

"Alright," Katy said. "Joshua, give me your hand and take James'. We'll form a circle."

Lowering their heads once they formed a loose circle, James began. "Saavatha take us to the place of celebration." The sunken ball glowed momentarily before shooting a ray of light that touched each Eternal present. Their forms energized quickly, vanishing in the blink of an eye. The trio materialized in the Congregation Hall, a larger version of the Hall of Wisdom. It was filled to capacity with Eternals waiting anxiously for the arrival of their creator, their master, Saavatha himself. With so many Eternals talking and whispering at once Joshua couldn't discern any one voice. His face betrayed the overwhelming effect that it had on him.

"What's the matter?" James asked, looking at the pained expression on Joshua's face.

"How many Eternals are here?" Joshua asked, looking at the sea of Eternals all around him. "This noise is deafening."

"I've stopped counting many years ago," James replied trying to speak over the crowd. "But from the looks of it trillions I would assume."

"What are they all doing in this place?" Joshua asked, covering his ears.

"There here to celebrate your return," James shouted, "and those like you who came back from exile."

"Really?" Joshua asked.

"I don't see Saavatha anywhere," Katy cried out to James. "Can you see him?"

"I don't think he is here yet." James shouted back. "He usually waits until everyone is present before he arrives."

"Everyone?" Joshua asked.

"Every Eternal in this kingdom," Katy replied near his ear.

"The whole kingdom?" Joshua asked, a little taken aback.

"Yes, everyone," Katy affirmed with a nod of her head.

A hush came over the crowd as they noticed the energized ball starting to glow. "Children of my kingdom," Saavatha began, "Welcome. We are gathered here today to celebrate the return of our heroes from exile." In that instant the ball pulsated and flashed momentarily. After the brilliant flash dissipated, a tall and slim Eternal with white hair dressed in a white frock stood in the center of the circular platform.

"Come on!" James said to the two standing beside him. "Let's find our seats. It's just about to begin."

"Do you know where we are supposed to sit?" Katy asked.

"Yes," James replied. "At the table of honors."

"Where is that?" Josh asked.

"The circular tables that surrounds Saavatha's platform."

"All the way over there?"

"Yep," James replied. "We'd better get moving."

The trio shuffled through the crowd, managed to find their places and sat down as Saavatha began to speak. "Eternals of my kingdom," he announced proudly. "Look and admire those who are at my table of honor. They have sacrificed everything to assure the continuing growth that you now possess. Praise them in my honor!"

The cheers and applause overwhelmed the dome as Saavatha turned his attention to his honored guests.

"Children of Exile please forgive the transgressions done by me against you." Walking towards Katy and Josh, he leaned forward and put his large hands on the smooth surface of the table. "Joshua son of Gabriel of the House of Qwenthrey," he told him. "You have suffered considerably at my hand. What you wish for, you have deserved." Turning to Katy he resumed. "Katy daughter of Joel of the House of Thaabar, you have suffered as well. Your wish is granted. You are now entitled to take part in the activities and privileges of an Eternal of the tenth level."

"Thank you!" Katy replied. An odd feeling overcame her as she stared into Saavatha's eyes. His stare seemed blank, like the stare of a statue. The white of his eyes roamed freely, covering every inch of it. Only his facial expression revealed his sense of sight. "I won't disappoint you."

"Do not thank me yet," Saavatha replied, his warm smile looking oddly out of place on his pasty face. "I know of your plans to join with Joshua of the House of Qwenthrey. It is not customary for Eternals of different Houses to join, but I will grant it, on one condition. You must help and guide him to your level of understanding. Give me your word that this will be done and I will grant it. Do you give me your word Katy of the House of Thaabar?"

"Yes," she replied, her voice still trembling. "I give you my word!"

"Joshua," Saavatha said, turning his attention to him. "Your suffering gives me the right to propel you to the eighth level of evolution. You are now entitled to all the rights and privileges of that level. I am aware of the love that you share for Katy. I will grant your wish to join her if you give me your word. You must to the best of your ability follow her advice and strive to reach her level. Joshua of the House of Qwenthrey, do you give me your word?"

"Yes Saavatha," Josh replied, looking at the bearded Eternal. "I give you my word."

"My children," Saavatha said turning to the crowd his hands rose towards the sky. "You are my witnesses to the words that were spoken by these two Eternals."

"Would the head of the houses represented here, come forward." Saavatha asked looking at his sons.

Thaabar and Qwenthrey came forward and stood at the side of the children of their hierarchy. "Qwenthrey," Saavatha asked. "Do you allow this child, Joshua to join outside of your house?"

"Yes I do," Qwenthrey replied.

"Qwenthrey," Saavatha continued, "do you take full responsibility for the growth of this child?"

"Yes I do," Qwenthrey replied.

Turning to Thaabar he repeated the questions, "Thaabar, do you allow this child, Katy to join outside of your house?"

"Yes I do," Thaabar replied.

"Thaabar," he continued, "do you take full responsibility for the growth of this child?"

"Yes I do," Thaabar replied and smiled at Katy.

"Joshua son of Gabriel," Saavatha asked placing his right hand on the top of Joshua's head. "Do you accept this joining willingly, without pressure?"

"Yes!" Joshua replied.

"Joshua the purpose of this joining is to accelerate your growth towards me. The road to me is never easy. Do you accept willingly and without pressure, the responsibility and the difficulties that this goal represents?"

"Yes I do."

"Katy," Saavatha asked, placing his left hand on the top of her head. "Do you accept this joining willingly, without pressure?"

"Yes!"

"Katy the purpose of this joining is to accelerate your growth towards me. The road to me is never easy. Do you accept willingly and without pressure, the responsibility and the difficulties that this goal represents?"

"Yes I do."

"Should you decide in the future to separate, I will annul this joining only if your collective vows are interfering with your growth towards me. Do both of you accept willingly and without pressure the precedence before you?"

"Yes we do," they replied together.

"By the power that I possess," Saavatha said, raising his right hand towards the sky. "I pronounce you joined."

In that instant a golden filament tied together the two Eternals at the center of their being. The couple stood up, taking each other's hands and bowed to Saavatha, glorifying him.

Joshua looked at his navel with bewilderment in his eyes. He quickly glanced towards Katy who was captivated by Saavatha's presence.

"Thank you Saavatha," he heard her say, "Creator of All Things for this joining today." He looked around for guidance and notice Qwenthrey whispering for him to follow Katy's lead. He turned and looked Saavatha in the eye. He tried his best to follow…he didn't know the words.

"In our combined effort we will honor and glorify your presence. Together we will strive for the perfection of our beings so that one day we may be graced by your presence once more. It is our vow; it is our promise to you."

"Saavatha," Qwenthrey and Thaabar vowed, "we have witnessed their promise to you. We will guide them and hold them accountable in their vows to you."

"Katy of the House of Thaabar and Joshua of the House of Qwenthrey you are now joined," Saavatha announced joyfully. "You must prepare for the difficult Journey ahead."

The festive mood could be felt throughout the hall as Saavatha gave every deserving Eternal his turn of glory. Turning to her love, Katy put her arms around his neck and looked deeply into his troubled eyes. "I guess we are finally joined," she told him, still glowing. "Are you up to the challenge?"

"I don't know," he replied, his smile lighting up the twinkle in his eyes. "I guess you'll find out."

Katy grabbed him by the collar pulling him close to her. "Don't you dare change your mind," she said teasingly. "Saavatha may be all forgiving…. but I am not."

"Temper, temper," he replied. "You better learn to control that temper of yours. It might get you into a whole lot of trouble."

"Very funny," she said to him with mock anger. "Using my words against me, that's just not allowed."

Joshua smiled. He couldn't help but lose himself into her twinkling green eyes. Leaning forward he gently touched his lips to hers, kissing her passionately. In the tender embrace he knew that his destiny had changed for the better.

Chapter Thirty-three

Katy smiled as she woke up. *Last night was the best night of my existence,* she thought stretching her arms over her head. *It sure was nice of Gabriel to invite us back to his place. Joshua is lucky to have him. I wish my founder were more like him. Look at this beautiful being sleeping by my side. I still can't believe we're joined. I should wake him. We have so much to do today.*

Cuddling up to his back, she caressed the side of his face down to his cheekbone. "Josh, sweetie," she whispered, a faint smile appearing on her face as Joshua began to stir. "It's time to get up." Turning on his stomach, Katy began to play with the curls of hair near his neckline. "Josh, wake up," she said, pleasantly frustrated. "It's late and we have a ton of things to accomplish today."

"It's not time to get up already, is it?" Joshua said, waking up suddenly, raising his head from the pillow.

"Rise and shine," she said, tapping him on the back on her way off the bed.

Josh turned on his right side and observed Katy while she was getting ready for the day ahead. *I'm a lucky guy,* he thought. *I can't believe how beautiful she is. What a night. I won't ever forget it.* An overwhelming feeling of giddiness came to him as those thoughts crossed his mind. *"The filament is the tie that never breaks," that's what James said if I remember correctly. 'It joins your beings together at the center of your essence. It can never be removed, except by Saavatha himself.' This thing is just amazing.* He played with the golden filament, never able to truly hold it as it flowed through his fingertips: it was weak yet strong. "You look beautiful this morning." He propped himself up on his elbow.

"Not a bad start first thing this morning," she said, giving him a sly grin as she looked back. "But you are going to have to do better than that if you want to convince me to let you sleep any longer."

"You think you're pretty smart this morning," he said, throwing his pillow at her. "Wait until I get up, you'll truly be amazed by my magnificence."

"Ah!" she smirked throwing the pillow back at him. "Magnificence you say, at the rate that you are going, I won't see any of that maybe until the next thousand years."

Katy squealed joyfully as Joshua leaped out of bed and tackled her to the ground. Giggling out of control she finally conceded defeat while Joshua caressed the side of her face. Wrapping her arms around his neck she kissed him passionately. "We have a lot to do," she said after breaking the embrace. "We should get started."

"Alright," Joshua replied reluctantly, getting up to start his day.

"Look at me!" Katy said a little frazzled. "I'm a mess."

"You look just fine," Josh reassured. "It's not like we're going anywhere."

"Ah yes we are!" she reminded him. "Don't you remember?"

"Remember what?"

"We're suppose to meet Master James early today," she said exasperated.

"Oh…yeah," Josh replied, suddenly feeling like an idiot.

"Now that we're on the same page," she said, raising an eyebrow. "would you mind getting your ass in gear, or we'll never make it there in time."

"Good morning," Gabriel said as they walked into the dining room.

"Good morning," Katy replied, grabbing a cup of coffee before sitting down beside Gabriel.

"You guys are sure up bright and early this morning," Gabriel said, taking a sip of his tea.

"Yeah," Katy replied. "James wants us to meet him this morning to go over a few things before we Journey."

"Isn't that a little soon?" Gabriel asked, troubled with the rush.

"Not after a millennium," Katy replied. "He's a little behind."

"I can see your point," Gabriel smirked.

"See whose point?" Joshua asked, sitting down beside him.

"Katy's," Gabriel answered. "She said that you were a little behind. That you should Journey as soon as possible."

"That's an understatement," Joshua exclaimed with a short laugh. "After being stuck in exile for so long I didn't think that I would ever have the chance to Journey."

"Have you decided where you want to Journey?" Gabriel asked.

"No," Josh reached over the table and grabbed Katy's hand. "We still have to talk to the Master and get the stamp of approval from the elders."

"Which elder are you going to deal with?"

"Shawn," Katy replied.

"You'll have fun," Gabriel said, his sarcasm coming out loud and clear.

"I don't think so," Katy replied, a little taken aback by Gabriel's attitude. "I know that he is a bit stuffy, but with him it has to be by the book."

"That's the problem with him," Gabriel began. "He follows rules like they were written in stone."

"Yeah he does," Katy admitted.

"Rules are supposed to be guidelines," Gabriel replied, "not absolutes."

"Well," Katy said with a carefree attitude. "I'm sure that Master James will make sure that he doesn't get out of hand."

"Yeah," Gabriel replied, "you're lucky to have him on your side."

"May Saavatha praise that thought!" Joshua exclaimed, raising his coffee mimicking a toast.

"We should get going," Katy said to Joshua, taking the last sip of her coffee. "We're already late."

"I'm done," Joshua replied, getting up and putting his cup away. "We'll see you later, Pops."

"Alright son," Gabriel said, a faint smile appearing on his face. "Give James my best."

"We will," Katy replied giving Gabriel a peck on the cheek. "We'll see you later."

"Come back soon," Gabriel said as he observed Katy and his son exit his home.

Chapter Thirty-four

Katy could see James sitting at his desk, buried in paperwork as she ascended the last crystal step. She looked back at Joshua who was close on her heels. Katy pulled back an annoying stray curl of red hair from her face. "Sorry we're late," she said, a little annoyed with herself. She liked to be punctual. She knew James' time was valuable. Her shoes clacked loudly against the marble floor as she walked up to him. "We got a late start this morning. I hope you don't mind."

James stopped writing and looked over his small circular glasses. "No it's OK," he replied. "I'm a little behind myself."

She walked around the desk and stood a few feet from him. "So what's on the agenda?" she asked casually, putting her right hand on her hip.

James shifted his chair towards her. He pushed his glasses up his nose. "I've made arrangements with Shawn to go over the Journey's preliminaries with us. I'm hoping that he'll have everything ready when we get there."

"When can we get started?" Joshua asked, casually rubbing his short blond beard.

James shifted his eyes to Joshua. "As soon as I'm finished this paperwork," James replied, feeling a little flustered under the pressure. He looked back at the mound of work he had hoped to finish before seeing the elder. *This is going to take forever. I can't let these kids wait that long. I will have to come back to this mess later.* He took a deep breath. "This can wait," he said to them getting up. "I can finish up later. If you two are ready, we can get going."

They walked on the other side of the desk and formed a tight circle. Taking each other's hands, Joshua and Katy waited patiently for James to begin. "Saavatha," he finally said. "We thank you for the light that you provide and we are grateful for the opportunities that you give us to grow towards you. Please take us to the place where Eternals begin their Journey." The sunken ball in the center of the dome pulsed brightly, triggering an energy surge that enveloped the small group. Their forms glowed with an eye-straining brilliance and, in a flick of an eye, they vanished.

An instant later, they found themselves in the Hall of Journeys. Joshua looked around. An uneasy feeling came over him. Suddenly a vague memory crept towards the forefront of his mind. *I remember this place. If my memory serves me right, the last time I was here this place was packed with soldiers ready to fight. It looks so empty now even with all these Eternals here. Where's the jewel? There, I see it. This is where my nightmare began. It's ironic that I should return here to begin my Journey.* Joshua was so caught up in his past that he didn't notice Shawn walking up to them.

James looked at the approaching Eternal and extended a hand. "Shawn," he said. I'm glad that we caught you. He turned to Joshua. "This is Joshua."

Hearing his name, Joshua was suddenly brought back to reality. He looked at James, then turned his gaze on Shawn and frowned. "Yeah, I remember you!" he said. They could clearly hear the resentment in his voice. "You're the one who tried to keep Katy and I apart."

Shawn looked uncomfortable. "Sorry about that," he replied a little red-faced. "I was just doing my job."

"I bet you were."

Shawn felt the hair at the back of his neck stand on end. Something about Joshua made him uneasy. He quickly looked away and turned his attention on James. "Anyway," he said, rubbing his neck trying to appease the sudden tenderness. "I've got everything ready."

James smiled. "Great! Let's get started."

"The first thing we're going to do," Shawn began, "is introduce you folks to the other Eternals that are taking part in this Journey." He looked at each and every person. "If you'll all follow me," he said, taking the lead towards a small room close to the Journey's platform.

Joshua followed Shawn's lead and entered the room. His eyes opened when he saw the number of Eternals cramped into that small room. *By Saavatha's garden! How many Eternals do we need for this Journey? There's has to be at least thirty of them in this room alone!* He gave Katy a quick questioning glance.

Shawn saw Joshua's apprehension and walked over to him. "Joshua," he said, putting a reassuring hand on his shoulder. "These are some of the Eternals who you will be working with."

Joshua looked at him with disbelief. "You mean there's more?" he asked.

"Yes," Shawn replied, giving Joshua a teasing smile. "A few more. You would be surprised how much time and effort is put into a Journey like yours."

"I can see that," Joshua replied, a little taken aback. He never thought Journeying would be so complicated. He started to have some serious doubts about all of this.

"Usually an Eternal of your age plans their own Journeys. Master James explained to me the unusual circumstances that have surrounded you. It was decided that this Journey would be planned for you."

Joshua shot a confused look in James' direction. "I see," he replied. "So, what am I doing?"

"I will get to that," Shawn said, smiling at an impatient Joshua. "First things first, I want you to meet the Eternals that you are going to be closest to amongst the Solids. This is Tina." He pointed to a dark-haired woman. "She's going to be your birth mother."

Joshua looked at the tall woman who was well over six feet tall. Joshua was surprised how well her form was proportioned for her height. She was as tall as Master James. Her shoulder-length hair gave the woman an aesthetic quality. Her dark eyes held a profound mystery. He knew that there was more to this woman than she was willing to let on. When their eyes locked, she smiled, blushed and quickly looked away. Despite her efforts, he could see her holding back a smile.

"The man beside her is Allen," Shawn continued. "He's going to Journey as a woman called Berenib. She will raise you."

Joshua turned and greeted Allen. Unlike Tina, Allen was short and scrawny. His graying hair had enough curl to make it look messy. His slim face had the worn look of time, betraying the vitality of his icy blue eyes. When he smiled, his face came to life.

"Beside Allen," Shawn went on, "is Greg, he is going to be your father."

Joshua smiled at Greg. Out of the three, he looked like James the most. Much shorter than James but stockier, Greg had dark long hair that spanned to the middle of his back. Unlike James, his hair was braided up into corn rows and tied back in a high ponytail. His light green eyes drew many curious stares. Joshua looked back at Shawn. "A man Journeying as a woman?" he asked. "How's that possible?"

"We are Eternals," Shawn reminded him. "We are neither man or woman, but we can be both. The purpose of our Journey determines who we become."

Joshua looked at Shawn with a disbelieving eye. Then he remembered Katy's uncanny ability to change from one sex to another. *I hate it when she does that.* He felt a shiver run through him as he remembered what Katy told him. *All Eternals can do this. As soon as you have a few Journeys behind you, you'll be able to do that as well.* The sense of fear was taking over. *I will never do that.* He rubbed the goose bumps on his arm.

"As a Solid," Shawn went on, "it takes both sexes to produce children, to become parents."

Joshua gave Shawn a questioning look. "Parents?" he asked.

"Yes parents, they play a similar role as your founder does," Shawn explained. "They'll help you grow and become the Solid that your are supposed to become. He then turned to Katy. "Now Katy," he said. "As a Solid, you will be his first cousin, whom later on you will marry."

"So what's my role in this big and happy family?" Joshua asked.

Shawn looked up at him and smiled. "I'm coming to that," he said. "Be patient. You are going to Journey to the land of Khem. There, once you reach adulthood you will learn leadership skills and rein over the future land of Egypt." Suddenly there was a knock at the door. Shawn turned his attention towards the noise. "Yes?" he replied.

The door swung open and a tall, stocky Eternal with a long white beard entered. "I hope that I'm not intruding," he said hopefully.

"Oh no," Shawn replied. "Come on in, we're just about done here."

"Great," he said giving Shawn a radiant smile. "I heard that Joshua was back from exile so I wanted to stop by and see him before he Journeyed. Is he here?"

"Yes. Actually, he is standing right beside me." He motioned towards Joshua.

The old man's eyes came to rest on Joshua. He couldn't believe the change. He wouldn't have recognized him if he tried. "Oh my," the visitor said a little red-faced. "Have you ever changed? I'm sorry. You probably don't remember me. My name is Master Gwen," he said extending his hand.

"Nice to meet you," Joshua replied, taking Gwen's hand and shaking it amicably. "You look very familiar; I have a feeling that we met before?"

Gwen looked up at Joshua's gaze and held it for a brief moment. Then he looked away. The guilt that he had all but forgotten, enveloped him. "Yes," he said. "Long ago I'm afraid."

A spark of recognition flew in Joshua's mind. He jerked his hand away suddenly as if burnt by fire. "I know you!" he snapped, his eyes narrowing into a malicious glare. "You're also known as Bartholomew, are you not?"

Gwen looked down for a brief moment. He knew that Joshua had recognized him. He knew that whatever judgment Joshua was about to pass on him, it was nothing compared to the judgment he had passed on himself. *I'm sorry. I wish that it could have been any other way.* He looked up and faced his accuser. "Yes, I am," he replied. "Master Gwen is the persona I like to be known under when we are not at war." Gwen saw Joshua's face go cold. He knew that the verdict was in.

"I remember you," Joshua said, his voice reaching a new level of hostility. "You're that bastard that sent me into exile!"

Katy's eyes shot up. "Joshua!" she yelled in Gwen's defense. "Watch your mouth!" From the look in her eyes, Joshua knew that he had hit a sensitive nerve. "The Master had no other choice. He did what he had to do."

Joshua felt his anger build. He felt hurt and belittled. *How dare she take his side?* His anger was ready to burst. *If that's the way she wants it, fine, I will show her!* He turned and glared at her. "Stay out of this!" he shouted, taking her by surprise. "You're not the one who was stuck in Baltaseim waiting to be rescued. He could have saved me but instead this coward," he said, pointing an accusing finger at Gwen. "left me to be at

Baltaseim's mercy. How could you?" he asked, turning to Gwen with hurt in his eyes. "I trusted you. How could you leave me there to suffer?"

James walked in between the two of them and put a reassuring hand on Joshua's shoulder. "Joshua...there was a lot more to it than what you remember."

Gwen felt hurt and humiliated, but in a strange sense, he felt that he had it coming to him. He looked at his brother. "James," he interrupted, "it's OK. There's no need to take my defense. Joshua's right. I did let him down. And I will have to live with that for the rest of my existence." Slowly he turned and looked at Joshua with guilt-ridden eyes. "For what it's worth," he said, his voice crackled despite himself. "I wish that I could have done more to save you from the horrifying ordeal that you went through. I let you down. I'm sorry. Now if you'll all excuse me I have work that needs to be done." On his way out the door, Gwen gave Joshua an apologetic glance as he walked past him.

Katy was fuming. She couldn't believe what Joshua just did. *How can he judge this sweet man,* she thought, enraged. *He doesn't even have all the facts. He's in for a wakeup call that one.* She stomped towards him. "Are you happy now!" she shouted, giving Joshua a shove. "In one fell swoop, you managed not only to humiliate probably the kindest Eternal here, but you also chased him away. Shame on you!"

"The kindest Eternal here you say?" Joshua shouted back. "You obviously don't know what that bastard is capable of. If you've forgotten, I had first hand experience on what he is able to do."

"I know what happened," she cried out in frustration. "I was there!"

Joshua's face went blank and looked at her stunned. In all the dealings he had with her, she had never mentioned this. For a brief moment he wondered why. "You were?" He finally replied, still overwhelmed by the recent revelation. "Why didn't you ever tell me?"

Katy looked at him, raised her arms up in frustration and shrugged. "Because it wouldn't have changed anything," she replied, her defensive tone still noticeable regardless of her calm demeanor. "What's done is done. You have to understand," she said, softening her tone. "You were very young. You were in a war that you really weren't supposed to be in."

"But I remember him sending Baltaseim into exile while I was still stuck inside him," he replied in his own defense.

"You remember bits and pieces," she explained. "You cannot in good conscience judge an Eternal of his stature based on the little bit that you remember. It's not fair and it's not right!"

Joshua lowered his head in shame. *I've done it again. Opening my big mouth before I've got all the facts.* The expression on Gwen's face was etched into his mind. As guilt started to build, he wondered if Gwen would ever forgive him. He looked up at Katy. "You're probably right." He mumbled, embarrassed by the fact that he had made an ass out of himself.

"There's no 'probably' about it." Katy chastised. "You had no right talking to Master Gwen this way. Not only was it rude but it showed disrespect towards all of us who had to stand here and listen to Baltaseim's song!"

He looked around the room nervously. "I'm sorry," he said, feeling two inches tall. "I flew off the handle and made a fool out of myself."

"Alright!" Shawn said, rubbing his hands together, hoping to change the mood. He gave Joshua a calming smile. "Now that this is settled, maybe we can finally focus our attention on the matters at hand."

Chapter Thirty-five

After a grueling hour with Shawn, Joshua was almost asleep with boredom. Shawn went into the very mechanics of Journeying. Joshua, understanding very little of it, dismissed it in its entirety. He still hadn't gotten over the little stunt that the Elder had pulled on him. Joshua resented the fact that he had to sit there and listen to someone who probably had it in for him. *He doesn't know what he is talking about,* he thought, the contempt more than visible on his face. *The only thing that I'm getting from this guy is lip service. I will have to talk to Master James; this is stupid.* Suddenly his eyes flew open when he caught the last few words that came out of Shawn's mouth. "What do you mean?" he asked, "We lose our memory?" The hostility in his voice was clear.

Shawn paused. He didn't like to be interrupted. *But under the circumstances it's only natural.* He turned to Joshua. "That's exactly what I said," he replied. "Before your Journey begins, you go through the Eye of Amnesia. When you fall through the storm, you forget everything about who you are and where you come from."

"Well that's stupid!" Joshua scoffed, his hostility mounted with every word. "What's the purpose of that? I'm just starting get some of my childhood memories back. I don't like the idea of losing what little I managed to keep."

Shawn smiled. "Don't worry," he said. "It's temporary. Once you return to this kingdom you'll remember everything. I promise."

"What's the purpose?" Joshua asked still not pleased. "I don't get it."

"When you're amongst the Solids, life is a lot different," Shawn began. "We wouldn't want you to come home early when things get too tough. You must finish the Journey you start at all costs. Only in extreme circumstances are you allowed to abort your Journey and come home."

Katy, who was sitting by his side, put a reassuring hand on his thigh. He looked at her and his eyes told her everything. "Don't worry," she said, she reached and gently let her fingertips caress his cheekbone. "I've done this at least a thousand times. You'll be fine—trust me."

Looking at her tender face Joshua could not help but to give her his complete and unconditional trust. Taking a deep breath he returned her caress and cupped the soft skin of her chin. "I trust you," he replied with a soft smile. "If you say it's OK I believe you." He turned and looked at Shawn. "Are there more surprises I should know about?"

"Yeah, on your way down to the Solid's plane your Cooma will be created and a silver filament tying it to the physical body will appear."

"What's the line for?"

"It provides nourishment from your essence, so it can survive," Shawn replied. "All physical matter, no matter how small needs this energy. Without it they perish."

Joshua's brow furrowed. He vividly remembered what happened when your essence was drained on a continual basis. Baltaseim made sure of that. "Won't this drain me?" he asked.

Shawn gave him a cock-eyed smile. "Yes it will," he replied. "That's why all Solids require a sleep cycle; their Cooma leaves the physical realm and goes to a specified dimension where they will stay and replenish their energy from Saavatha's light."

Joshua mulled over what Shawn had told him. He didn't like everything that he heard, but he trusted Katy's judgment. If he was going to Journey, he would have to make up his mind soon. He looked at Katy for reassurance and came to a decision. "Alright," he said with determination. "I've heard enough, we should do this before I lose my nerve."

Shawn looked at him for a moment, trying to anticipate his mood and nodded. "OK then let's get to it."

Suddenly Joshua became painfully aware of the dwindling attendance in the small room. Besides Shawn and James, Katy and he were the only ones left. It made him nervous. "Where are all the others?" he asked, feeling a knot forming in his stomach.

"They started their Journey already," Shawn replied. "Everything has to be in place so that your Journey can begin."

Getting up, the four Eternals exited the room and made their way to the Journeying platform. As he approached the jewel, Joshua couldn't help but be fascinated by its almost hypnotic greenish glow. He turned to Shawn. "Everything is ready, right?" The knot he felt before had become an inferno in his stomach. His nervousness was evident to everyone, especially Katy.

"Yes," Shawn replied, "everyone is where they're supposed to be."

"OK," Joshua said, building up the nerve to walk to the translucent jewel. "I can do this." In a moment of weakness he looked down at the bottomless pit that awaited. A wave of nausea came over him. The strength in his knees left him. Losing balance, he almost fell in. His pulse raced to a feverish pitch. His face lost all color and instinct took over. "I can't do this!" he screamed, panic written all over his face. He stared with terror at the greenish eye of the hurricane; that waited patiently for his arrival. "I'm not ready!" Joshua felt someone take his shaking hand.

"Yes you are," Katy said, coming to his side. "Don't worry, I'm right behind you."

"I will go down through the storm with you, if you'd like." James volunteered. Joshua couldn't hear anything; his fear had taken over. It was only a matter of time before he would lose consciousness.

"Joshua!" Katy yelled, snapping Joshua out of it. "James will go down with you. It will be all right honey. I love you. You can do this; I know you can."

He nodded as she took a step back and James came forward. He looked up at him, petrified. *How in Baltaseim's love did I get myself into this?* Joshua thought. *Now it's too late to back out, I have no choice; I've got to do this.* Taking James' hand he dared to take one last look into the emptiness awaiting him.

James gave him an understanding glance. "Are you ready?" he asked. He felt sorry for Joshua. Because of his ordeal, he was extremely behind. *If he was younger,* James thought, *it would be easier on him. The young ones are more trusting and have an underdeveloped sense of danger, so it works in their favor. He'll have to muddle through it. Soon he won't remember a thing.*

Nodding, Joshua summoned the last bit of courage that he possessed and gave James the go ahead. The two Eternals stared at one another for what seemed an eternity. Finally in unison, they jumped into the eye of the storm. Falling at an incredible speed, they were pulled helplessly towards the bottom of the pit. Joshua was starting to hyperventilate; he was almost hysterical. James felt his fear. *Soon the effect of the storm will take its toll and Joshua will lose this fear.*

Suddenly out of nowhere a green lightning bolt struck Joshua, enveloping his whole being. A translucent substance was left behind as the light dwindled away. Then suddenly another bolt savagely attacked him. His whole body shook as the predator ravaged him. When it was over, the light left behind a silver filament that was firmly attached to his navel.

James could feel Joshua's hand trembling with terror as the final lightning bolt struck him.

Screaming in agony, he let go of James' hand and covered his temples with both hands. "My head! My head, it's on fire!" The pins and needles he felt elevated to a climax. Feeling his heart beat behind his eyes, he let out one last gurgling scream as the needles crested and faded until they were but a bad memory.

Joshua felt dazed. His head was in a fog. He shook his head trying to shake out the cobwebs. *Where am I?* He thought looking around. His eyes came upon James. "Who are you?" he asked.

James smiled. "A friend."

"Hi, I'm..." Joshua started, but stopped momentarily stumped at the memory loss. "I can't remember who I am," he said with disbelief.

"It's OK," James replied. "Don't worry, everything will be fine."

He looked up and stared at him. The stranger felt familiar somehow. *If only I could remember,* he thought with frustration. Finally he spoke. "I don't know you," he said, puzzled. "But somehow I know that I can trust you. Weird don't you think?"

A chuckle escaped James lips. "Yes there are some things that just can't be explained."

Joshua nodded in approval. "You're right." A wave of drowsiness took hold. He felt completely drained. His eyes closed. If you'll excuse me," he said and yawned. I'm really tired for some reason. I need to sleep."

James observed Joshua in silence. *He's done it. After all this time.* "Sleep tight," he whispered, as if he was afraid to wake him. Nothing could wake Joshua before he was ready. James knew that. "I will see you soon." He admired Joshua's courage. James watched Joshua grow in the womb of his mother and was reminded of all the trials that he went through to attain the level he now enjoyed. "I'm proud of you," he said knowing that Joshua couldn't hear him. He planned to keep a watchful eye on this child to make sure that all that was supposed to happen came to pass.

Chapter Thirty-six

3066 BC. After twenty years of strained relations, the land of Khem was in chaos. The country's two factions, North and South, had been at each other's throats for years. The rich and educated people of North Khem believed that they should rule over their neighbors in the south, the poor and the farmers. King Menes who ruled the poorest part of the land found the ideals of the north preposterous and he was ready to defend his kingdom's honor at any cost.

It was the middle of the night and King Menes was ready to turn in. The pressures of the day had finally made it to his head, giving him an eye straining migraine. His eyes felt like they were about to burst out of his head. He wandered into the Royal Sleeping Room, up a few flights of stairs and down a long hallway. He couldn't silence the invading thoughts that had plagued him since the spy he'd planted in North Khem had returned with the dreadful news. King Pheret wanted his land. War was imminent.

He took a deep breath as he climbed the last flight of stairs. His mind was restless. *What a legacy I will have,* he thought sadly. *I've only been in power for two years and King Pheret as already declared war on us. What am I going to do? My people are poor and they are poor soldiers. War is not what I had in mind. If only the negotiation for unification didn't fall through. Maybe we could have found a peaceful resolution. Now I'm stuck with a predicament that could lead to all our deaths.*

Those thoughts preoccupied Menes as he entered his bedroom on the second floor of the royal palace and laid his eyes on the two ladies who slept peacefully on the bed they all shared. *Look at those two lovely flowers sleeping side by side,* he thought. *I knew that Berenib would warm up to Neithotepe. I shouldn't have waited eleven years to marry for the second time. I might have avoided all the resentment Berenib has for my new wife. What is this war going to do to them? To my son that is on his way? Neithotepe is four months pregnant. I could very well lose them to the enemy. I have to win this war...somehow, there's just no other choice.*

He was lured onto his balcony by the moonlight reflecting on the Nile's surface, Menes stared at the full moon that lay ahead just above the horizon. He was so caught up in his thoughts that he failed to notice Berenib, a petite woman with long jet-black hair sauntering towards him silently. *Neithotepe,* he thought as he felt her warm body snuggling to his back. *Your sweet body is so warm...your charms so inviting. I don't know how I lived without you all these years.* "Neithotepe," he said not taking his eyes off the magical scene that was unfolding on the horizon. "I'm sorry if I woke you."

Berenib froze and her mind recoiled in anger. *Neithotepe!* She still felt the sting when her lover married for the second time. *He thought that I was that conniving little wench! Grrrr! I hate her: she's not even from this land. He only married this little twit because I cannot bear him a son. I can't believe how she managed to take my place already. I won't let that happen. I've got something special planned for you...my little friend.* She took a deep breath. "My King," she whispered. Her tone was soft and alluring; she had learned long ago how to hide her true feelings from her king. She leaned forward and extended her tongue and flickered the dark haired Khemian's right earlobe teasingly. She wrapped her arms around his slender waist and told him seductively. "It is late. Come and keep me company in our bed."

Menes flinched. Berenib's relationship with Neithotepe was strained at its best. With one swift move, he had unknowingly added fuel to an already volatile situation. *Women!* He thought with exasperation. *They should just learn to get along.* He turned in her arms facing her. "Berenib!" He replied surprised. "I'm sorry. I thought it was…"

She reached up and put a finger on his lips, silencing him. "It's almost impossible to tell who's who in this darkness."

Menes could see the outline of a faint smile on her lips. He knew that her smile was for his benefit. He had hurt her, but she was hiding it well. He dared to admire her in the glowing moonlight: she was beautiful. She wore a see-through garment that revealed all of her secrets to him. His hardness surprised him. He held her close. "Even after all these years," he said, his lustful eyes caressing her exposed body lit by the moonlight. "You still hold a special place in my heart."

He reached and caressed her right breast and felt her nipple stiffen under his touch. Berenib moaned softly as she backed away slowly leading her king by the hands to their bed. Climbing under the covers, he laid beside Neithotepe, who was awoken by the shifting weight. Berenib lay beside her King and wrapped her arms around his neck. He kissed her with a hunger he hadn't felt in many years. She kissed him back, tasting him, enjoying the feel of her tongue on his palate, outlining the smoothness of every tooth.

Menes' passion built and stayed most of the night as he made love to his two wives. When it was over, their bodies glowed with perspiration. They lay peacefully, enjoying the moment. They embraced passionately one final time and Menes snuggled up between his two wives and fell into a deep slumber.

He awoke suddenly. It was still dark. He sat up and realized that there was a stranger in the room with him. *King Pheret doesn't waste time,* he thought, anger rising within him. *He sent an assassin already.* "If you are here to kill me," Menes cried out into the darkness. "You have failed. Show yourself and I may take pity on you and not kill you where you stand."

The silhouette walked into the stream of moonlight that was entering through the balcony. Menes recognized the stranger immediately. "Father," he cried out perplexed. "Why are you here? Did you not make it to the afterlife?"

The rugged-looking man smiled. His short beard accentuated the wisdom he exuded. "Yes my son," Narmer replied, his familiar smile comforting Menes somehow. "I am part of the afterlife and you will be as well when it is your time." He paused for a moment. Menes could feel the tension in the room. "I come for a much more important reason than to validate your beliefs about the afterlife. I am here to warn you of an oncoming danger. Pharaoh Pheret is planning a surprise attack on your land. Come, we have much to discuss if you are to be ready for him."

He pulled the covers up and swung his feet on the floor. He looked at his father who took his hand. Once standing, he wrapped a robe around his naked body and followed his father out of the bedroom. As they crossed the bedroom's threshold, everything turned bright white. Menes closed his eyes from the blinding light. When he opened them again, he suddenly found himself in a large rectangular room with his father in the company of the gods.

Sitting in the middle of the room at a large wood plank table was Amun, the creator God. His pasty face gave the illusion of a living statue. Larger than life he sat quietly stroking his long white beard. Thoth the god of writing and knowledge was seated to his right. Smaller than Amun but stockier, Thoth wore his jet black hair in a braid intertwined with gold and silver filaments. The royal blue garment covering his body was wrapped loosely around his frame. A silver silk belt was wrapped around his waist accentuating his slim hips. The royal protector god, Horus, was there as well. A mountain of a man, this god looked formidable. His dark complexion went well with his dark, riveting eyes. He wore a red silk wrap around his waist that hung to mid-thigh. Adorned with gold and silver jewelry he sat quietly staring at Menes with a sour expression.

Osiris, the god of death and rebirth was sitting at Amun's left. His small stature made him look minuscule in comparison to Amun's enormous size. Wrinkled and bald, Osiris' eyes were sunken into his skull. His stare was cold and infinite, death itself. He sat stone-faced, his eyes shifting from one god to the other. Menes recognized Seker. He was the god of light and the protector of the spirits of the dead as they passed through the underworld en route to the afterlife. Dressed in white, this thin god wore his white hair loosely over his shoulders. His high cheekbones and smooth skin gave him feminine qualities.

The god of war, Montu, was also present. The golden form fitting chest plate looked odd against this god's pale skin. Painted in war colors, the black and red hieroglyphics over his body depicted war and victory over the enemy. Sekhmet, his counterpart, was seated beside him. This goddess wore a high headdress covering most of her jet-black hair. The silver chest plate she wore did very little to conceal the voluptuous quality this goddess possessed.

There also was Ma'at, the goddess of justice and truth. Her light blue dress was loosely fitted around her small frame, which was snug around her waist by a black satin belt. The bluish hue of her black-tipped feathers went well with her dress. Attached from her wrist to her waist, the plumage mimicked the wings of an eagle when her arms were stretched over her head. Showing a healthy cleavage this backless dress actuated this goddess' beauty and allure. Her long dark hair complemented her sultry eyes which demanded respect.

Anubis was seated beside Ma'at. This jackal-headed god looked odd amongst his peers. Towering a foot over everyone, his athletic build attracted attention easily. The green wrap he wore around his waist was tied to his left hip. This god is the gatekeeper. Only those who are lighted-hearted are let into the afterlife. At death, Anubis' duties are to weigh the heart of the deceased against a feather of Ma'at's plumage. If the scales are balanced, the newly departed is allowed to enter the afterlife.

"Welcome Menes, sit. We have much to discuss." Menes looked up and realized that it was Amun who spoke. Once Menes and his father were seated at the only two empty seats at the table, Amun continued. "The land of Khem is in chaos and we are troubled by the events that are about to occur. King Pheret's intent is to take your land and plunder it until all of its resources are gone. He has no love for the people and in his hands the land of Khem would perish."

"I am honored to be here in your presence," the tall Khemian said as he stood up. "I am aware of the trouble in my land but I am only one man. What can I do other than try to defend my people to the best of my ability? If you are so concerned about the recent developments, then I suggest that you do something to help stop Pheret. You are the gods of this land."

Amun listened to Menes' words, and chose to ignore Mene's arrogant tone. "Yes we are the gods of this land." Amun stood and looked into Menes' dark eyes. "We have made a decision that will impact your life. We have designated you to carry out the events that will change this land forever. The war is brooding at your feet. You will welcome it and we will help you defeat Pheret."

"How?" Menes asked. "King Pheret's army is well skilled in the art of war. I am unprepared and my soldiers are inexperienced. I am not willing to sacrifice my men at your choosing."

"I understand your concerns," Amun replied. "But do not worry about simple trivialities. We are at your disposal. You are destined to unify this land once more. You will call this new land Egypt and this great nation will be known throughout the world for generations to come. It has been written, so it shall be done. Remember Menes, we are counting on you."

Chapter Thirty-seven

Menes awoke to the gentle rays of the sun streaming through his window. His second wife Neithotepe was snuggled up to his right, still sleeping peacefully. To his left, his first wife Berenib was awake and eyeing him tenderly.

"I had a night vision," he said staring into her loving eyes. "My father took me to see the gods of this land." A surge of confidence swelled within. He smiled, his giddy mood became apparent. "We will win this war," he said, full of enthusiasm. "The gods are on our side. When my victory is assured they want me to call this land Egypt."

Berenib let her fingers run through her silky hair. "Egypt," she replied dreamily. "The name sounds powerful like our Gods."

"Amun told me that this new nation will become great one day," he said with excitement. "It will be known around the world for many generations to come. I must prepare." His brows knotted with determination. "The north is mounting a surprise attack and I must be ready for them. Call my generals, I want an audience with them."

That afternoon Menes spoke with them and prepared to depart. He hated the idea of leaving his wives behind but he knew that soon he would return victorious. Once all of the preparations were ready, Menes and his army of ten thousand soldiers marched away from the city of Necropolis. He gave his island home one last look from a distance before departing. He vowed under his breath to return as soon as the north was defeated and the land unified. The gods had given him a sacred duty to perform and he planned to complete his assignment.

****

After five months of intense warfare King Pheret was dead and the war had ended. The unification was complete. The King was anxious to return home. On his return, his thoughts were on his second wife. *Neithotepe,* he mused. *How I long for your sweet treasures: your long silky golden hair, the sweet tastes of your lips, the soft touch of your breasts. The sweet scent of your womanhood calls to me.* Menes's thoughts were interrupted when his single horse chariot hit a pothole. He whipped his horse to gain speed when he saw in the distance the port that would bring him home. To his dismay he noticed a sandstorm brewing close to the shore. He cursed Seth the demon god under his breath as he realized that the chance of missing the storm was slim. Halting his escort in an effort to assess the situation, Menes turned to his advisor Jurbs who was on his right. "I need to be on this raft now!" he cried out in frustration. "Seth is blocking my only way home."

Jurbs squinted. He put he hand on his brow, scanning the chaos in the distance. "Pharaoh," he replied with hesitation. "I think it would be wise for us to wait out Seth's anger. If we appease him, then maybe he will grant us safe passage."

The King whipped his head towards Jurbs with disbelief. His hesitation angered him. His face scowled and his eyes narrowed to tiny slits. "You can wait here like a coward," he scoffed, venom dripping from his voice, "or you can face Seth like a man worthy of his King." He sat there giving his army a disbelieving stare. *They're afraid of him!* He thought. Anger flared within. *Most of them fought at my side, defying death itself. Now, they cower to a spirit.* He gave one last disgusted glance at his army. Enraged, he whipped his horse and departed, galloping toward the storm.

Horus, Menes prayed to the royal protector God of Pharaohs, *Don't fail me now! If I'm to make it through this forsaken storm, I'm going to need your protection.* He cursed the storm as his horse entered the perimeter of this devastation. Menes bundled up as tightly as he could, trying to protect himself from the unforgiving sand. Feeling his flesh being sandblasted from his bones, he covered his face, trying to shield the blinding winds that were assaulting him. In agony he looked forward to be relaxing in a hot bath with his two wives pleasing his every whim.

The raft came into view through his stinging eyes. It waited for him patiently. He thanked Horus as his horse stepped on the familiar planks that would lead him home. The overweight raft's man gave the King a knowing glance. And he untied the rope before returning to the slaves bound on either side of the raft.

The stench of sweat hovered in the air. Menes winced as the smell overpowered his senses. The tempo of the drums assured a synchronized effort from the men who were rowing mercilessly towards Memphis Island. The taskmasters pacing on each side of the raft whipped the exhausted slaves who could no longer keep up. Menes could hear them moaning and screaming as they labored mercilessly to maintain the raft's slow-moving pace.

Menes was listening to their whining with indifference. His only concern was his return home. Seeing the island in the distance he was anxious to get off this sweatbox. As the raft approached the dock, Menes patted the mane of his favorite horse Montu on his way up the chariot. Picking up the reins, he felt the raft's gentle jar as it docked and was anchored to shore. Once the barrier lifted, King Menes galloped off the raft. His thoughts were brought back to Neithotepe and the seriousness of her condition. *Isis,* he thought, his eyes taking on a distant look. *Protect my childbearing wife. Horus! My royal protector I command you to watch over her. I cannot lose her and my son. He is Egypt's future King.*

Finally after what seemed an eternity, he entered the courtyard. He barely missed a frantic slave that was racing towards him. "My King! My King!" He pulled on the reins hard bringing the chariot to a stop. He didn't have time to get off when his slave met him in a panic. "My king come quick!" she shouted, her features paler than usual. "Your wife Neithotepe is ready!"

His pulse quickened. He dropped the few parchments he had with him and tossed his scepter aside. He ran up the grand entrance's marble stairs and up to the second floor. Racing down the hallway, heart thumping, he stopped at the open doorway. A feeling of excitement and fear overwhelmed him as he entered the room and ran to his wife's bedside.

"Is it time?" he asked, taking Neithotepe's sweaty hand.

"Yes," she whispered, sweat pouring from her exhausted body.

"It's going to be fine, you'll see," he said to her, not quite believing it himself.

"Unghh!" Neithotepe cried out getting another contraction. The intense agony bent her in half. "Something is wrong!" she screamed terrified. "Unghh!"

A cold sweat washed through his body as he was forced to watch helplessly. "Slave!" he screamed in shock, petrified that his wife may die. "Come quick!"

"Yes, Master?" she called out from the bedroom's door.

"Get me some towels and some hot water—hurry!" Getting up he walked to the statue of Isis, goddess of women, bowing his head in prayer. "Isis mistress of women, please, I implore you save my wife and child." Feeling a hand on his left shoulder he turned angrily to chastise the person who dared interrupt his sacred plea. Instead of a stranger, he found his first wife Berenib.

"I have been praying for her since you left," she said with a somber look on her face. "I think that Osiris wants her."

A flash of anger and desperation coursed through his eyes. "The god of death cannot have her yet!" he screamed.

Berenib bowed her head in submission. She felt the sting of his words. *He blames me.*

"I won't allow it! I will pray to Horus, he will protect her. She is carrying my child! He doesn't have a choice but to protect her!" His riveting stare was broken when Neithotepe's cries distracted him.

"Unghh! Menes, please," Neithotepe cried out, interrupting the argument. "I fear that I may die. The pain is so intense that I can't stand it."

Walking to his wife, he saw the look of despair on Neithotepe's face. For a moment he felt it too. He took her hand and sat at her bedside.

"Neithotepe," he said with his best reassuring smile. "You won't die. I will pray to Horus, and he will protect you."

"Unghh! Please Amun," she winced as another contraction hit her. "Have mercy on me!"

The slave finally arrived with the hot water and towels. Menes sponged off the sweat from Neithotepe's face as he tried to make her more comfortable.

"Menes," Neithotepe pleaded, delirious with fever. "When I deliver this child and die, you must promise me that you will love this child regardless of what happens to me."

His heart skipped a beat and he lost all the color in his face. He couldn't bear the thought of losing her. "Neithotepe don't be foolish!" he cried, trying to reassure himself more then her. "You are not going to die. You will be just fine."

Anger and hurt flashed into her crying eyes. "I am not being foolish!" she shouted back with the last bit of her remaining strength. "Unghh! Promise me!"

He looked at her. His heart sank. He feared that she may be right. "I promise," he conceded.

Neithotepe relaxed. She let herself sink back into the soft mattress. She turned her head and looked at her king. "Thank you," she said, smiling weakly, satisfied that if she died, her child would be well taken care of. "Menes," she said squeezing his hand. "If the child is a girl please call her Cleopatra. But if it turns out to be a boy he must be called Djer and I would like his middle name to be Menes after the love of my life." She reached with her hand and caressed her husband's burning cheek. A soft glow exuded from her smiling face. "I've loved you ever since I met you Menes," she whispered. "I've had a good life. You are a good man."

His eyes filled with tears and suddenly he knew. He would lose his loving wife. "Neithotepe don't talk like that," he chastised softly. "You will have a good and long life by my side."

"If Amun wishes it," she replied with a faint smile on her pale face.

Chapter Thirty-eight

In the eternal realm, James was on his way down to check on Joshua's progress when he noticed a demon near Neithotepe. The corpse was hunched over her belly, sucking energy out of her and her child. "This Shadow is acting under my explicit orders—the child must die!" Baltaseim told him.

James rushed to Joshua's aid. "Get away from him!" He waved his arms at the demon who was threatening to end Joshua's Journey prematurely. "Saavatha forbids you to interfere!"

A grotesque face turned and sunken eyes glared at him. "This is not Saavatha's domain!" he spat, his eyes rolling in green puss. He growled, showing his rotten teeth, putrid saliva dripping off his chin. "You are not welcome here!"

As the demon made his stand, James walked confidently towards him. His anger rose within him. "All is Saavatha's domain!" he shouted back with authority. "Leave this child be" he warned, pointing an angry finger. "Or I will be forced to remove you."

A taunting laugh escaped the demon's lips. "You cannot touch me here!" The minion heckled. "This is my Master's territory," His sadistic grin widened on his deformed face. "I would leave if I were you—before I destroy you!"

James cocked his head and sighed. "I'm sorry. Saavatha," he said, looking up towards the kingdom. "Forgive me for what I'm about to do."

A flash of panic entered the minion's eyes. A mixture of anger and self-righteousness filled his rotten heart as he voiced his protest. "Wait a minute!" he screamed. "You can't do that! It's not fair!"

"You leave me no other choice," James replied walking calmly towards Baltaseim's servant. "Saavatha," James began, lifting his right hand and pointing his palm at his opponent. "Send this vile and disgusting being back to where he came from." A small circle of eternal light formed on the Master's open palm. Light from within struck the minion square on his chest. Agonizing screams filled James' ears as he forced the beast back to the darkness. His shrieks could still be heard long after he vanished.

James rushed to the mother and put his right palm on her stomach. "Saavatha please help this precious child in crisis," he said, praying to the all-powerful. "Your son Baltaseim has sent one of his minions to kill him. May your wish be done as I attempt to save him and his mother." White energy emanated from James' palms and enveloped Neithotepe's body completely. "May this protection be enough," he said...his tone hopeful that he had done his best. "Keep a close eye on them Saavatha. They will need your help."

Neithotepe's pain suddenly subsided and she started to feel warmth coming from deep within her. "Menes," she cried out in disbelief. "My pain is gone! I don't know why or how, but suddenly I feel awake and strong, full of energy, like I have slept for days."

"The gods have heard our prayers and saved you," Menes replied. He couldn't hold back the tears of joy from streaming down his face.

The slave who was at Neithotepe's side fell to her knees, sure of the god's mercy. "Glory to Amun," she praised. "He has seen your pain and has mercy on you."

Menes walked to her and put a soft hand on her shoulder. "Yes it would seem so," he said with an expression of relief. "The gods are smiling on us." He turned and gave Neithotepe a lover's gaze. The corner of his lips curled up slightly, giving her a quirky smile. "Thank you," he whispered to the gods, relieved that his ordeal was just about over.

The rest of the evening was pretty quiet while Neithotepe finally got some much-needed rest. Menes was drawn to the window. The storm, like his wife, was finally resting. The moon at its fullest gave the Nile an exotic glow. Walking to the balcony to calm his nerves, he was plagued with thoughts of the recent events. His reverie was suddenly broken by a familiar voice.

"It's beautiful isn't it?" Neithotepe said, looking over Menes' shoulder, admiring the beauty of the Nile for herself.

"What are you doing up?" he replied startled. "A woman in your condition should not be up and about. You should be resting and regaining your strength. The baby will be here soon and you'll need all the strength you can get."

Smiling at him she knew that he was concerned, with good reason. A while ago she did not think that she would survive the night. But with the grace of the gods at her side she knew that she would be fine. "I am feeling just fine my king," she said soothingly. "I want to spend the time and enjoy what we have. This experience really frightened me. I don't want to take things for granted. Our time here on this land is very short and I don't want to miss anything while I am here."

Taking her in his arms, he kissed her passionately. "I am the most fortunate man for finding you." He was losing himself in her sparkling blue eyes. "And now you are about to give me an heir, what else could a King want?"

Smiling to herself, Neithotepe leaned on her husband's shoulder and enjoyed the security that she felt when she was near him. She knew that a son would please him and hoped that the gods would be good to him and answer his wish.

"You need to get some rest," Menes said, walking her back to bed. "The child is not born yet. You are still weak and as much as I hate to bring this up, you are not out of trouble yet."

Neithotepe walked quietly with him. She knew he was right. The worst was still to come and she must be prepared and be well rested. Conceding to her husband's wishes she laid down and slipped under the covers.

At three in the morning, Menes was still pacing the hall when he heard his wife calling. "Menes, get over here quick. I think that it's time; the water flowed and I can feel the child moving."

He rushed to her side. "Are you OK?" he asked, his face pale from worry. "Do you feel any pain like the last time?"

She smiled and took her husband's hand. "I feel some pain but it is not like the last time," she replied. "I don't know how to explain it but this time I know that I will be alright. Get some fresh water, I feel the baby coming."

Menes turned to the door and was annoyed when he noticed that he was the only one in the room with his wife. *She should be in here!* he thought angrily. *This rivalry is going to stop, I will make sure of that.* "Berenib!" he called out from the bedside. "Get some more water. Come quickly the baby is almost here!" He turned to his pregnant wife. "Is there anything that I can do?"

A couple of slave girls ran into the room. One carried water and the other hovered close to Neithotepe, getting her ready to deliver the coming child.

"I will deliver this child," Menes curtly said to the slave. "But I want you here...in case I need you."

The older woman nodded silently yielding to her king's wishes.

Neithotepe looked up at her husband with docile eyes. *He's worried,* she thought. *I can see it in his face.* "Stay close," she replied, getting out of the covers, "and keep me company." She laid on her back, grabbed her legs at the knees and pulled them up as much as they could go. Berenib was in the room by now and placed a damp towel under Neithotepe's rump to absorb the coming mess. Menes moved to the foot of the bed, and he was ready to assist as best he could. He prayed to Isis, the goddess of women to guide his hands and help deliver this child without a hitch. Neithotepe's breaths were coming short and shallow.

Her husband urged her on. "That's it," he said with excitement. "Keep pushing I can see the top of the child's head."

Neithotepe shrieked in agony as she felt the sharp, searing pain that was threatening to rip her apart. As she released, she felt the child move down. Exhausted, she couldn't go on. But something deep within her pushed her against her will, forcing her to go on. "I curse the gods for giving me this pain!" she pleaded. Her body was covered with sweat. Her back hurt and she felt like someone had ripped her innards out. She began to sob uncontrollably. "Please Menes make it stop! I can't take much more of this."

He looked up at her with sweat dripping from his brow. "Hold on tight," he told her. He looked at his first wife to make sure that she was still there, sponging Neithotepe's face. "It's just about over. One more push should do it; give me one more push!"

Neithotepe gave her husband what he wanted. A low rumbling grunt rolled off her tongue a moment before she screamed. As the excruciating pain became unbearable, she pushed one more time.

"One more push, and it will be over," he said. "Give me one more push and his shoulders will pass."

Neithotepe grunted as she gave a final push. The child was shot out into his father's arms as the shoulders finally passed. Menes grabbed the slippery child by the left leg and he proceeded to spank the child's behind to make him breathe. Neithotepe sobbed, exhausted and relieved that this ordeal was finally over.

Menes' eyes grew as he shook the limp child in his arms. His stomach tightened as fear grabbed him. "No!" He smacked his son one more time. "Isis!" he pleaded. "Help us!"

A cold sweat washed over Neithotepe as she watched her husband. "Menes?" she asked, her voice becoming panicky. "What's the matter? What's wrong?"

Menes couldn't hear her. He was overwhelmed by grief. "No!" he cried out with tears of rage. "This can't be happening!"

Neithotepe sat up. Panic took over her being. "What's wrong? Tell me!"

He turned and looked at her with blank eyes. The tears that had just flowed moments ago were still visible on his face. "Our child is dead!" he sobbed, bringing the limp body of his son to her. "Osiris took our son!"

The blood drained from Neithotepe's face. She cradled her head in her hands. "No!" she cried out. Menes laid their son at her side. "My baby, he took my baby." A cold and hardened look came over her face. "How dare you! How dare you take my precious baby!" Her cries softened to a quiet sob as she tenderly caressed the child's bloody face.

Chapter Thirty-nine

Neithotepe cried quietly, cradling her stillborn son. Sagging in her arms, the bloody child's stare chilled her soul. "Why?" she asked, caressing his hanging jaw. "I don't understand."

Menes felt nothing—the anger, despair and grief he felt numbed him. The whole scene felt unreal; he was going to wake up any moment now and realize that it was just another nightmare. But deep inside himself, he felt, he knew that this was no nightmare. It was real. "Neithotepe," he whispered to her softly. "Our child is dead. We need to prepare him for the burial ceremony." He leaned down to take the child from her.

Neithotepe looked at him with hardened eyes. "No!" She turned away from him. "You can't have him!"

"Neithotepe," he said. "I am your husband and your king. We need to prepare the child. Give me the child, please."

Looking into his eyes, she saw the pain that Menes was fighting off. Reluctantly she handed him the child. An overpowering wave of grief washed over her as Menes took the child from her trembling arms. Weeping uncontrollably, she curled up into the fetal position. Rocking herself gently back and forth, Neithotepe tried to soothe her aching soul.

Menes turned and handed the child to his first wife Berenib. "Take him," he said. "We need to prepare him."

With tears of grief streaming down her face, she took the child and exited the room.

An odd sensation coursed through Neithotepe's body as another contraction hit her. "Menes!" she cried out in shock. "I don't understand, I think that there is another child coming. Could we be that blessed?"

He looked into those grieving eyes and saw a glimmer of hope. Maybe not all was lost after all. "What?" he replied. "Are you sure?"

"I'm sure!" Neithotepe said short of breath. "The Gods have blessed us, another child is coming! I've got more contractions coming!"

He rushed to see for himself and prepared to deliver this second child. Neithotepe let out a sigh of relief when she heard her child's first cry.

"We have a son," she heard as Menes put the small child in her arms.

"He's beautiful!" she said, almost forgetting the earlier tragedy. "Djer will be his name."

Berenib felt a twinge of envy while she watched from a distance. *He's mine!* she thought, her anger simmering just below the surface. *He was my husband before he was yours. I will make sure that you never forget it!* She stormed out of the room unnoticed.

"Look!" Menes said overjoyed. "He has your eyes."

She smiled. "Look at the size of his hands. He's going to have big strong hands like his father."

Menes was proud; Neithotepe had given him a son. He thanked the gods silently for the gift that was given to them.

"He's hungry!" The wet nurse came forward and attempted to take the child.

"Get away from him!" Neithotepe screamed pulling the child away from the servant. She hugged him tightly, like a precious jewel. "I've lost one child today. You will not lay your filthy hands on him! I command you to leave!"

The wet nurse gave Menes a questioning glance. He nodded sympathetically and the slave left. "It's alright," he said with reassurance, "no one will harm this child."

Neithotepe took a deep breath. She knew he was right. "I know, I need to take care of him myself! I will not lose another child!"

Menes sighed. There was no way to reason with her. "That's fine, I will let you take care of our son if that's what you really want."

Neithotepe nodded silently. No one would take this child away from her. She felt the intense suckling of Djer's mouth on her breast and smiled. "That's it… eat as much as you want. When you're done I will clean you up and put you to bed."

Menes observed the infant suckling on his wife's breast. The miracle of childbirth always had an awe-inspiring effect on him. *The miracles of life,* he thought. *Only the Gods are powerful enough to understand it.* The child started fussing and pushed the nipple away. "Is he done?" he asked.

She looked up at him. The glow of motherhood was unmistakable. "Yes, I think so," she replied. "He's done. I don't think he could swallow another mouthful even if he tried."

A content smile came over him. "Good," he said. "You need some rest." He reached for the child and saw panic in her eyes. "Don't worry. I will take him now. Come here little one," he said, smiling at his son as he took him out of his mother's arms. "Time to clean you up and put you to bed." He turned and gave his son to one of the slaves and saw his wife's protest in her face. "Don't worry, it's only temporary. She'll take good care of him. You need your rest. Once you're back on your feet he is all yours. I will see you in the morning." He gave her a tender peck on the lips. "Get some rest."

"I will," she replied, hating to give in to his wish, but he was king…her king. She waved at the two loves of her life as they left the room. Exhaustion finally taking over, she fell into a deep slumber.

Neithotepe was sleeping soundly when an uninvited guest sneaked into her room in the middle of the night. The moonlight trickled through the open patio doors, betraying the intruder's presence by casting a shadow on the opposing wall. A warm summer breeze was flowing through the curtains, flapping them lazily against the open doorway. The intruder stopped momentarily and stared at the sleeping infant in his crib. The door latch clicked faintly as the doors were closed quietly. Hoping to avoid detection, the curtains were drawn closed, giving the intruder the cover of darkness. Standing near her bed, murderous eyes was cast towards the sleeping mother.

Waking up suddenly, Neithotepe was startled when she saw a shadowy figure at her bedside. "Berenib! My goodness," she cried out. "You scared me!"

"How are you feeling?" Berenib asked, trying to mask her intent.

"Fine," she replied a little uncertain how to take this changed attitude from a woman who never hid the fact that she didn't like her. "What are you doing here so late?" she asked suspiciously. "Why is it so dark in here? Who closed the doors?"

"I did." Berenib coyly replied walking close to her. "I wanted to make sure that we were not interrupted."

"Interrupted?" Neithotepe asked. "Interrupted for what? What do you want to talk about?"

"Oh nothing much. I just wanted to come and see how you're doing. She picked up a pillow beside her. "Let me make you more comfortable." With a speed that even Berenib didn't think she possessed, she quickly covered Neithotepe's face with the satin pillow.

Neithotepe's eyes bulged as she gasped for air. Tossing her head from side to side, fighting for a breath, she tried to scream. The satin pillow smothered her cries for help as she tried to free herself from the death grip that Berenib had on her.

"Shhhh!" Berenib whispered. Her face contorted into an expression of sadistic pleasure as she held the pillow firmly over Neithotepe's face. "You have to be very quiet. We wouldn't want anybody to walk in on us would we?"

Neithotepe's pulse raced as she struggled to get free. *Osiris, have mercy on me,* she thought. *It is not my time.* As her brain starved for oxygen, her struggles became sluggish until they stopped entirely. *I'm sorry Menes,* she thought before losing consciousness. *Please forgive me.*

The bedroom door was pushed ajar slightly as the unsuspecting eyes of a slave peered into the room. Unbeknownst to her, she had just witnessed Neithotepe's last moment of life.

"Here," Berenib said with a sadistic smile pulling the pillow away. "Isn't that better? It's your fault you know," she said, pointing a finger. "If you wouldn't have taken my king away from me, this would have never happened." Berenib was suddenly hit with a fit of laughter. "It works better this way…I have a son…and my king. I told you I would win, and you thought I couldn't."

Fear gripped the girl's spying eyes. She felt her heart beating, and gasped when she noticed Berenib's cold glare cast her way. She took off like an arrow, hoping that she hadn't seen.

"Thoria!" Berenib screamed, running after the tiny girl. "Stop!" Catching up to her outside Neithotepe's room, Berenib grabbed her by the elbow and stopped her in her tracks. "What are you doing here?" she spat viciously.

A shadow of fear veiled Thoria's ebony eyes as she looked up at her mistress. Berenib reveled in Thoria's terror. "I heard some voices," the girl replied terrified. "I thought that Mistress Neithotepe was awake, I was going to ask her if she needed anything. That's when I saw you standing there…over her…"

Berenib's nostrils flared in anger and her eyes narrowed. The scowl on her face was purely demonic. "You breathe one word to anybody!" she warned, "and I will make sure that it's your last breath, understand?"

"Yes Mistress!" Thoria replied lowering her head. "I understand."

Berenib grabbed a fistful of Thoria's jet-black hair and pulled her head backwards. "Remember," she whispered venomously, "I own you, your brother, your sister, I even own your mother. You speak and…" Berenib ran her thumb across her throat.

"I understand."

She released her grip and straightened the girl's hair. Her eyes softened and a warm smile hid the seething anger within. "Now be gone!" she said calmly. "Forget this ever happened."

The next morning Menes was greeted with a shriek from another slave girl. "Master! Come quick, I think there's something wrong with the mistress."

Rushing to Neithotepe's bedside, the lifeless body of his favorite wife sent him into shock. "Oh no! Neithotepe, why? Osiris, why did you take her as well, wasn't one son enough for you? I hate you, you selfish god." He wept over Neithotepe's lifeless body.

"Come," Berenib said, putting a hand on his shoulder and trying to hide the smug look on her face. "There's been enough mourning in this house. We have a son to take care of, the future king of this land."

Menes lifted his head and composed himself.

"You're right," he said, wiping his tears. "We have to look towards the future. I'm going to miss you," he said, kissing his finger then placing his hand on Neithotepe's lips. "I will always be grateful for the son that you've given me. You were my favorite."

"I know she was." Berenib looked back at Neithotepe's body as they left the room and smiled.

Chapter Forty

It was now year 46 under the Majesty Menes of Lower Khem and the fifth year of the new united nation called Egypt. Djer was now five years old and had pretty much the run of the palace. Being the only child, he spent a lot of time playing with the assortment of toys that his father spoiled him with. No matter how much Berenib voiced her concern, Menes somehow always managed to convince her that Djer absolutely needed the newest toys available. Djer was playing quietly when he felt a presence in the room. The child looked up and gave the stranger an uncomfortable smile.

"Hello," he said.

"Hello," the stranger replied. "My name is Master Gwen." He gave the child a warm smile. "Looks like you're having fun Djer. You sure have lots of toys!"

Djer smiled. "Thanks, my daddy gave them to me. Do you want to play with me?"

"What are you playing?" Gwen replied amused.

"I am playing with my brand new toy," he said enthusiastically.

"See," he picked up the toy and showed it to him. "It's a chariot, and my horses make it go very fast. It can go all over the world. My daddy tells me that one day I will own a real one."

Gwen kneeled down and eyed the toy. "That's a nice toy you have there. I hope that you will take good care of it."

"Yes I do," he replied. "My daddy says that I have to take good care of it, if I want to have a real one."

"Your daddy is very wise," he replied. "One day you will do great things that will benefit all human kind." He caressed Djer's black head. "I have to go now but I will be back later."

Djer looked at Gwen momentarily. "Will you play with me when you come back?"

He stood up and straightened his tunic. "When I get back we can play whatever game you want," he promised. "But for now I have to go, I will see you when I come back."

Djer waved at the Master as the old Eternal left the room. Having returned to his toy, Djer was suddenly overjoyed when he heard the Master return to play with him. He ran to meet him, only to stop suddenly. A tall, handsome stranger dressed in black leather was standing before him holding a black sword in his hand.

He looked up at the intimidating form. "Hi," Djer said with a timid smile. "Who are you?"

"My name is Baltaseim my prince," the stranger replied. His voice was soothing and had a hint of playfulness buried within it.

Djer looked up at the stranger. He wondered how he knew him. "Mr. Baltaseim," Djer said confused. "How do you know that I am a prince?"

Baltaseim kneeled and smiled at the young child. "You are the prince of Egypt as well as my prince," he replied, bowing respectfully. "The prince of all living things, everyone knows that. I am at your disposal. Ask me anything and I will do it."

A glimmer of disbelief flashed across Djer's eyes. "Make this toy roll across the floor," he asked. "If you are who you say you are then you can do this."

Baltaseim smiled and waved his hand over the toy. The chariot took off and rammed into the opposing wall at the other end of the room.

Running after the toy, Djer picked up the broken pieces and turned glaring angrily at the stranger. "You broke my favorite toy!" he spat furiously.

"My prince forgive me," Baltaseim replied, amused by the child's temper. "I can give you more than just a toy," he reassured. "I can give you the world at your disposal, all you have to do is ask."

Berenib could hear her son talk to someone in the room. *Curious, no one should be in there with him. I better go check.* "With whom are you talking, sweetie?" Berenib asked popping her head in the doorway.

"I am talking to my new friend, Baltaseim," he replied turning towards his mother's voice. "He told me that I am the prince of all living things. I want you to meet him."

"There is no one here but you, sweetie." Berenib looked into the room. "Come down and eat your dinner." She took his hand and led him out of the room. Dragged out faster than he wished, Djer excitedly looked back, hoping to see a trace of his new friend. Maybe if he asked him really nicely the stranger might teach him the trick he did with his toy.

Baltaseim was excited as well, but for different reasons. He was pleased with the result of his first contact with the boy. His façade worked perfectly. Soon the boy will believe in the fairytale he has fabricated and this, he was certain, will lead Djer right into his arms.

****

Tina jumped out of her skin when the knock at the door interrupted her concentration. The child on Joshua's lap was completely immersed in the words spoken. The old Eternal looked at the child who was about to burst in tears. He smiled at her and put his reassuring hand in hers. "It's OK sweetie," he glanced at the door. "Come in!" The door of his library swung open slowly to reveal Shawn who was astounded by the children's conduct.

"Looks like you have a way with children," he chuckled. "Maybe I should bring them here more often."

Joshua eyed him. He didn't like the implication he was making.

"They were good," he replied.

"Ya," Tina piped up, feeling a bit more like herself. "We were real good. Master Joshua told us a really good story."

Joshua smiled at the small child.

"Did he?" Shawn replied with a warm smile. "I hope you enjoyed yourself."

"Yes I did, this Master is cool. Baltaseim is trying to trick Joshua...who is Journeying as Djer," Tim exclaimed. "Baltaseim is bad."

"Yes," Joshua sighed. "He can be quite a handful."

"Well children," Shawn began, "we should be going. Your founders are probably worried sick by now. You should have been back home two hours ago."

"Do we have to?" Tina asked. "The Master is not finished telling us his story."

Joshua picked up Tina and stood her on her feet. "Well that's enough for tonight." He stretched his legs. "We'll have to finish this story some other time."

Shawn couldn't believe his ears. *It's an invitation to come back if I ever heard one. Master James was right. Joshua is finally starting to soften up a little. Maybe one day he'll have children of his own.* He smirked at the thought. He had known Joshua too long to believe that. *Who knows? He sure came a long way. I never thought he would ever rejoin the kingdom.*

"Come on kids, we have to go."

"I don't want to go yet," Tim protested. "I want to find out if Djer finds out that Baltaseim is bad and...and..."

"You can come back another day," Joshua said smirking slightly at the fidgeting child, "and I promise to tell you more."

"Really?" Tim asked excitingly. "Does he beat Baltaseim?"

A smile came to the old Eternal's face. "That's another story."

Joshua watched in anticipation as the children gathered around Shawn who was ready to leave. Shawn smiled at Joshua, "I appreciate all that you did tonight, thank you."

Joshua smirked. "Give Master James my salutations, remind him that my house is his house."

"I will, thanks again."

The children waved and said their goodbyes and Joshua watched them leave in silence. The sound of the door latch clicking shut reassured the old Eternal that the evening was finally over. Alone in his library once more, his mind drifted to the refreshed memories of his past. *So many years have passed, it seems a lifetime ago. So much has happened. Katy, my dearest. I haven't thought of you in many years.* He sighed deeply and reached for the golden filament that no longer existed. *Gone, the tie that bound us together is gone. How I've missed it over the years. I've lost you and it was all my fault.* He sauntered towards the door. Exhausted, he looked forward towards a decent nights sleep. Joshua opened the door slowly, turned and scanned the room with a euphoric eye before blowing out the candle illuminating the room. *Maybe one day,* he thought, *she'll forgive me.* He took a deep breath and closed the door behind him. *Tomorrow...is another day.*

ISBN 1-41203711-5